DEAD SILENCE

A TRUTH SEEKERS NOVEL - BOOK TWO

SUSAN SLEEMAN

Published by Edge of Your Seat Books, Inc.

Contact the publisher at contact@edgeofyourseatbooks.com

Copyright © 2019 by Susan Sleeman

Cover design by Kelly A. Martin of KAM Design

1

Kelsey didn't like this. Didn't like it one bit. Since her husband Todd had been fatally shot outside his hotel on a business trip, she'd been on guard and tried to avoid being outside after dark. But she'd planned poorly today, and her unease was now the price she paid.

"Let's hurry, Jace." She gripped her stepson's hand tightly as she exited the grocery store with cupcake supplies for his school party tomorrow.

She took off as fast as she could in her mile-high wedge sandals, and the five-year-old had to run to keep up. Her ankles were quickly swallowed up by the soupy fog swirling around the large parking lot, and unease skittered down her spine.

Sure, the dark had nothing to do with Todd's death. He was just in the wrong place at the wrong time. Mugged on his way to his hotel room after dinner, but she couldn't stem her fears. They scratched at her like a cat with claws bared, ripping down her back.

Stop it. Just stop it. There's nothing to be afraid of.

"Can I lick the frosting bowl?" Jace asked, his innocent little voice helping to settle her nerves a bit.

She shifted her grocery bag and smiled down at the dark-headed boy with chubby cheeks dotted with freckles and humor shining in his brown eyes. "I'm afraid you'll be in bed asleep by then."

He shook his head hard and jerked his hand free to cross his chubby little arms. He planted his feet and gone was the sparkle in his eyes. "Nu-uh. It's my birthday tomorrow. I'm not sleeping tonight."

She didn't like how he was taking such a stance, but he'd been through so much losing Todd that she ignored it. "But you'll have to try to sleep."

His arms dropped to his sides. "Okay, but can I get up if I don't fall asleep?"

She started to nod, but footsteps quickly approached them from behind, catching her attention. She shot a worried look over her shoulder. A hooded man rushed toward them. Head down, he was five feet behind them. He was really built and tall. His hoodie shadowed his face as he looked at the ground.

A warning raced through her brain, and she reached for Jace's hand again.

Don't be silly, she chastised herself. The man carried a bag of groceries. Just a guy in a hurry. She was being ridiculous. Still, she tugged Jace closer, firmed her grip, and got them moving at a fast clip toward her car.

"Ouch," Jace complained. "You're hurting my hand."

"Sorry." She relaxed her fingers but kept up her speed.

The footsteps moved closer. Faster. Almost frantic now, sharp thumps echoing into the fog.

She quickly moved Jace to the side closest to her car now only twenty feet away.

The footsteps shifted. Started in a run. A grocery bag hit the ground. Jace's hand was torn from hers. The man rushed past, Jace locked in his arms.

"Mommy," Jace screamed.

"Stop!" Kelsey yelled, her heart racing. "Stop! My son! Stop!"

Shocked, she stood frozen for a moment then bolted after them.

The man ran. Fast. Furious. Toward the busy road. Jace's body was clamped tightly in the man's arms, his little legs dangling.

She screamed and tossed her bag to the ground. "Someone, help! He has my son."

She ran full out, her heart thundering in her chest. She took a quick look around the lot. Looking for someone. Anyone who could help them.

It was dark. Empty. Only a few cars. No one in sight.

"Help! Oh, help!" she screamed at the top of her lungs.

She ran harder. Faster. Her feet struck the asphalt, the shock traveling from her sandals up her legs.

Her foot caught in a pothole. Her ankle twisted. She lost her balance. Her arms flailed out, trying to right herself. She couldn't. She pitched forward and tumbled. Landed hard on her shoulder and her knees razored over the rough pavement.

Her breath left her body. She gulped one in and rolled. Raised her head. Saw the man hauling Jace toward a white delivery van.

"No-o-o," she screamed and pushed to her feet. "Stop. Don't take him. Please. Don't. Please."

She started running again. The fall had cost her precious time. She was too far behind them now. She would never catch them. Never. He simply had to open a door, floor the gas, and her son would be gone. Long gone.

∽

DEA Agent Devon Dunbar's mouth hung open as he watched Bruno Cruz barreling across the parking lot toward his dilapidated old van. The lowlife drug dealer had snatched up a child. A child, for crying out loud. Right out of his mother's arms.

Cruz was a drug mule for a Portland gang connected to the Sotos Cartel out of Mexico and hadn't been involved in their child trafficking exploits to this point. Now, Devon had to reassess his take on the situation.

But first...the kid.

Devon had to save the boy, despite the fact that he would likely blow his cover and put an end to his six-month undercover op. An op that could stop child trafficking and keep children with their parents.

But a boy in imminent danger came first. It had to.

Adrenaline licked along Devon's body as he eased through the fog falling heavy on the parking lot and between the parked vehicles. He wanted to draw his weapon, but he needed both hands to catch the child. Still, he flicked off the holster strap just in case.

Keeping hidden in an SUV's shadow, he assessed Cruz's timing. Caught his rhythm and estimated his arrival. Started counting it down.

Ten. Nine. Eight.

Devon took another step closer, making sure to remain hidden in the misty fog so he didn't spook Cruz into doing something stupid.

Seven. Six. Five.

He braced himself.

Four. Three. Two.

Devon came even with Cruz. He launched his body forward. Slid an arm around the child. Grabbed hold of the trembling little body. Snatched him free and held him tight.

"Hey," Cruz complained.

"Mommy," the terrified child screamed.

Devon had no time to offer comfort. He turned. Swept out his foot. Took Cruz down in one swift kick to the knees.

He put the boy down. "Run back to your mom. Hurry. Run!"

The child took off, his little feet pitter-pattering over the concrete.

Devon's heart soared over the rescue. No time to celebrate. Not yet.

He planted a knee in Cruz's back and wrenched his arms into a tight hold.

"Jace, oh, Jace," the mother cried out.

Devon looked up in time to see her drop to her knees and sweep the boy into her arms. In Devon's job, he didn't often get to see happy endings, and he wished he could see the joy on her face, but the fog obscured his view.

Thank you, God for putting me here at the right time.

Keeping his knee planted, Devon searched the man and found a 9mm Glock lodged in his waistband. Devon tucked the gun in the back of his jeans.

"Get off me, man," Cruz complained as he bucked. "You have no right to do this."

"But I do." Devon disguised his voice as best as he could so he didn't risk his undercover status and pressed his knee harder in Cruz's muscled back. "You're the one without rights here. Attempted kidnapping is going to put you away for a long time. And I'm going to assume you don't have a carry permit, so possessing a firearm won't go so well for you either."

"You some kind of cop or something?" Cruz asked.

"Or something." Devon looked at the woman again and raised his voice so she could hear him, but kept it disguised. "Are you two all right, ma'am?"

"Yes, yes." A long sigh filtered out of her mouth. "I think so."

"Hang tight while I call 911." Devon kept Cruz facedown to prevent him from getting a good look at his face and dialed 911. When the operator came on the line, he avoided mentioning his name and explained the situation. "Please tell the responding officer that I'm a law enforcement officer, and I've restrained the suspect."

"Your name and agency, sir?" the operator asked.

"I'll provide officers with ID when they arrive." No way he was going to give out that information in front of Cruz. And honestly, he couldn't give legit ID to the cops either as he didn't carry his credentials while undercover. But that was something to work out with the responding officers. He disconnected before she demanded additional information and turned his attention to the woman and boy.

"Hold tight," he yelled. "Officers are on the way."

"Thank you." Relief swept through the woman's shaking voice.

Devon had the crazy urge to rush over to the pair and give them a hug. *Odd.* He wasn't a hugger. Not much of a touchy-feely guy at all. Being a SEAL for six years and then an agent for the DEA for two, he'd lost that loving feeling. Or maybe it had more to do with the woman he'd once loved not being able to commit. Either way, he remained in place, pressing Cruz to the ground as sirens sounded in the distance. He shifted his attention to the road and the electric blue lights whirling into the cloudy vapors.

"C'mon, man," Cruz said. "Nobody got hurt. Let me go."

"Not a chance." Devon watched as two Portland police cars screeched into the lot and slammed to a nearby stop. The officers got out and moved together in a cautious approach. The male cop whose name tag declared Zellner was tall and lanky with inky black hair. Devon put the female named Almgren at five foot eight with a muscular build and blond hair pulled back into a ponytail.

"He was armed, but I've searched him and removed the weapon." Devon continued to keep his voice in a high, unrecognizable tone for Cruz. "It's in my waistband in the back if you want to remove it."

"And you are?" Almgren asked.

"Law enforcement just like you. Take this guy away, and I'll get my ID."

"I'll just grab that gun." Zellner moved toward Devon, Almgren stood, hand on weapon prepared to act if Devon made a move. Zellner tugged the gun free.

"I'll secure this guy." Almgren strode to Cruz, pulling her cuffs free as she moved.

She clamped the cuffs on Cruz, and Devon slowly got up, making sure they could see his hands the whole time to keep them from overreacting and doing something stupid.

Cruz jerked to his knees in an effort to take off, but Almgren grabbed his cuffs and hauled him toward her cruiser. Devon tipped his head for Zellner to join him out of Cruz's earshot.

"I'm Devon Dunbar," he said, keeping his voice low. "Undercover for the DEA. Guy's name is Bruno Cruz. Had my eye on him when he suddenly grabbed the woman's child and bolted for his vehicle. I don't carry my official ID on assignment, and I hope not to blow my cover, so if you'll wait until he's in the car, I'll give you a contact number to call and confirm I'm legit."

Zellner gave Devon a quick once-over, and he knew what the officer was seeing. A rough-looking guy with a scraggly beard. Longer-than-normal hair, messed up and shaggy. Clothes that were too shoddy for even a thrift store and should've been washed a few days ago. A tattoo on his forearm with an S scrolling in ruby red and ending with a vivid green snake's head, mouth open and tongue extended. The hallmark for the Sotos Cartel who exported cocaine to the U.S. The tattoo was fake, but Zellner wouldn't have any idea about that. The semi-permanent ink lasted for two weeks or so and then Devon had to update it. When it was a problem in his private life, he simply covered it with a large bandage.

Zellner nodded, and Devon quickly looked at the woman again. She'd gotten to her feet, holding the child tightly in her arms even though he was too big for her to easily handle, and was coming toward them. He didn't need her knowing his ID either, so he lifted a hand to tell her to stay put.

"But I..."

"Everything okay, ma'am?" Zellner asked.

"Yes. I just need to tell you what happened so I can get my stepson home."

Zellner gave her a friendly smile, but his eyes remained fixed in the assessing cop stare Devon knew so well. "If you could just hold tight for a little longer, I'll be with you in a minute."

"Sure, fine." She didn't sound so sure, but she stayed put.

Devon checked on Cruz, glad to see the other officer was settling him in the back seat of her cruiser. The moment she slammed the door, Devon turned back to Zellner. "The number I'm going to give you is my supervisor's cell. His name is Bud Hurst. I go by Dillan Webb when on assignment."

Zellner snapped his phone from a holder on his body armor, and Devon shared the phone number. The cop made the call and gave his identifying information. "I have a Devon Dunbar here who is claiming to be one of your agents. I'm going to send you his picture for confirmation."

The officer snapped Devon's picture then lifted the phone back to his ear.

Devon had no idea what Hurst was saying, but as Zellner listened, his tight expression loosened. "Thank you, sir."

He stowed his phone. "You're clear."

"Thanks for working with me on this."

Zellner nodded. "I'm going to talk to the woman and boy. Hang tight and I'll come back for your statement."

Devon wanted to ask to leave before Cruz caught sight of him, but it was dark and foggy enough at this distance that Cruz couldn't likely make out any identifying details. Still, Devon made sure he kept his back to the car.

Almgren marched across the lot and joined Zellner. Devon followed, but then hung back to listen in and gather additional details on the child and her mother.

She wore a flirty little skirt that skimmed her knees and a very feminine blouse. Her shoes were those stylish chunky sandals he thought he'd heard women refer to as wedges, likely for the hunk of cork shaped like a wedge in the heel area. He never got why women tortured themselves with these kinds of shoes, but as a guy, he had to admit it stretched out her shapely legs. Sadly, her knees were bloody from her fall.

"I'm Officer Zellner and this is Officer Almgren," Zellner said to her. "And you are?"

"Kelsey." She ran her free hand over curly hair that rested just above her shoulders. It was full and lush, coffee brown, and looked like it should be in a shampoo commercial. "Kelsey Moore, and this is my stepson, Jace."

Zellner nodded. "Could I see your ID please?"

She fished in a handbag, the strap slung crossbody, and pulled out a wallet. Zellner examined the ID and handed it back, but Devon couldn't seem to take his focus from her for very long. She had this wispy vulnerable vibe going on that always brought out the protector in him. He searched her finger for a wedding ring, but didn't find one.

Divorced? Widowed? Never married? Or maybe just a woman who didn't believe in wearing a ring.

She shoved her license into the purse and grabbed the child's hand again, drawing him tight against her leg. She was still afraid, and Devon didn't blame her. It was going to take quite some time before she got over her shock and fully processed the near abduction.

Almgren squatted in front of the child. "Would you like to see the inside of the police car, young man?"

He cast an excited look up at Kelsey. "Can I, Mom?"

She bit her lip and shifted her feet. "I don't—"

"It'll be the empty vehicle, and I'll stay with him." Almgren smiled, her eyes lighting with it and offering a friendly vibe. "It's better for him not to relive things."

"Oh, right. Thanks. Yes. Please." Kelsey bent down to the boy. "Listen to the officer and don't touch anything without asking first."

"Don't worry. We'll be fine." Almgren held out her hand, and the boy quickly slipped his free hand into hers.

"My mom works with police," he announced. "And I want to be a cop when I grow up."

Devon saw the woman cringe. He doubted any parent wanted their child to go into a dangerous field of work. He knew for sure his own mother still worried about him on a daily basis. Maybe hourly. He couldn't check in with her very often, and she didn't know how he was doing. He hated putting her through that and planned to get out of the undercover work after completing this assignment. If his cover was blown, tonight's incident might speed that change along.

"How exactly do you work with the police?" Zellner asked.

"I'm a forensic anthropologist," she replied, not taking her eyes off of the boy. "I'm a partner at the Veritas Center."

Wow. The Veritas Center—a private forensic lab with a stellar reputation. They started out running DNA to connect adopted and missing loved ones to their families. Since then, they'd branched out to become a full-service lab for law enforcement, too, and most everyone in the local law enforcement field had heard of them and respected their work.

Zellner looked impressed, too. "Do you think tonight's incident has something to do with the center?"

Kelsey tilted her head, her soft-looking hair framing her face. "I can't imagine it's related. I think that jerk just seized the moment. I was coming out of the store, and he grabbed my stepson and ran away with him." Her voice broke on a sob. "I ran after them, but fell. I called for help, and that man over there saved Jace."

She pointed at Devon, her expression relieved and thankful, sending a warm feeling through Devon that he rarely felt these days, thanks to the Sotos Cartel.

"Saved him how, exactly?" Zellner glanced at Devon.

"He jerked Jace out of the creep's arms, and then took his feet out from under him with a swift kick." She shuddered, but respect gleamed from her heart-shaped face. "It was amazing. Like he's trained in martial arts or something."

Or something. Hand-to-hand combat via his years as a SEAL, but no one needed to know that.

"And then he let Jace come back to me while he held the creep down until you got here. That's it." She ran her hand over her face, her tortured expression remaining.

"Do you have any idea why that man might want to abduct your stepson?"

She shook her head hard. "I can't imagine anyone I know would do that."

"And do you? Know this man, I mean?"

She shrugged. "I didn't get a look at his face."

"Have you called the boy's father?"

Her eyes scrunched up, and her chin wobbled. "Todd died a little over a year ago."

Ah, the reason for a lack of ring.

"I'm sorry for your loss," Zellner said.

"Thank you." She lifted her shoulders. "We were only married for two years. It was so sudden."

"You call Jace your stepson. Does this mean you haven't adopted him?"

"Not yet. I wanted to." She frowned. "We just never got around to it when Todd was alive. I'm Jace's legal guardian, and now that Todd's estate is settled, the adoption paperwork is underway."

"When the detective is assigned to this case, he'll need a copy of your guardianship papers for the files."

She nodded. "I don't carry them with me, but have them in my safe at home."

"I'm sure after Jace confirms your story, our detective can wait on the official papers."

Kelsey fired a look at the patrol car. "Officer Almgren shouldn't be questioning him without me."

"Sorry." Zellner held up his hand. "She's not. She really just took him to the car to spare him from hearing my questions. I just meant after the detective talks to him with you present."

"Oh, okay."

Devon's law enforcement training had him on full alert at the woman's protest. Could she be hiding something or was this just motherly concern? Listen to him suspecting her. He'd been undercover for too long and didn't trust anyone. She was likely acting as any concerned mother might behave.

"Do you think the attempted abduction has to do with the adoption?" Zellner asked. "Maybe someone doesn't want you to adopt the boy?"

She tilted her head in a cute puppy dog questioning look. "I don't see how. Jace's mother is deceased, as are her parents, and she was an only child. And Todd's parents are all for me adopting Jace as long as I keep them in his life. Which, of course, I would do. He has every right to know his grandparents."

Zellner nodded. "Does the name Bruno Cruz mean anything to you?"

"No. Why? Should it?"

"Not necessarily."

She shot a look at Almgren's patrol car. "Is that the name of the man who tried to take Jace?"

Zellner didn't answer. "Okay, is there anything else you think I need to know?"

She bit her lower lip and shifted her stance. "No. No. I don't think so. I just want to get Jace, go home, and forget all about this."

"And testify against the suspect when he comes to trial."

"Yes…oh…yes. Absolutely. He may not have gotten away with kidnapping, but I want to see him pay for trying to abduct Jace."

Zellner gave a clipped nod. "I'll get a detective out here. He'll question both of you and then you'll be free to go home."

"Good. Good. My bag." She spun on those high heels and looked around. "Cupcakes."

"Cupcakes?"

"I have to bake cupcakes for school tomorrow. It's Jace's sixth birthday."

"Oh, right. Okay," Zellner said, lifting his cell phone to his ear.

Devon wanted to step over to this distraught woman. Offer her additional comfort, but she'd take one look at his attire and sorry state and likely run the other way. He usually didn't care what people thought of him, but with her, it seemed to matter. Mattered more than he could have imagined, and that surprised him almost as much as the near abduction.

2

Kelsey rested on the bumper of the ambulance. She'd told Officer Zellner that she and Jace were fine, but he decided that they needed to be checked out. Likely to keep her from suing the department later for negligence. She would never do that. Never. But Zellner had no way of knowing that.

"Mom," Jace said.

She shifted to look at the boy she called her stepson when required, but in her heart, she thought of him as her son. "Yeah, bud."

"Why'd that guy grab me?" His little chin trembled.

Her heart broke for him, and she wished she had an answer, but she didn't, and she wouldn't lie. "I honestly don't know."

Jace scrunched up his face. "Will he come after me again?"

"Oh, no. No. He's off to jail, and he won't get out until you're a grown-up. If even then."

Jace nodded. "Good."

"Sounds like you might still be afraid," the man who rescued him said as he stepped up to them.

She appreciated this man's quick thinking to save Jace,

but gosh, he was rough looking, and she inched closer to Jace.

He gave her a knowing look, and her face flooded with heat at being called out on her instant assessment of him. But come on. She'd just seen her stepson almost stolen from her, and she couldn't trust this man. For all she knew, he could've been part of the abduction and at the last minute changed his mind. He sure looked like the kind of man who would break the law. Scraggly beard and hair. Worn jeans that looked like they might stand up in a corner on their own.

"I can totally see why you might still be afraid." He smiled at Jace, and she got a look at even white teeth. He might be a mess otherwise, but he took care of his teeth.

"You can?" Jace gazed up at the man. "But you're big and tough. Like you totally beat that guy."

"Yeah, sure. But it's natural to feel fear. Part of the instincts God gave us."

"You believe in God?" Jace asked. "I do, too."

"Then you have to trust Him to have your back and forget all about this."

"I'll try." Jace rubbed a hand over his face.

Kelsey had always searched that little face trying to find a resemblance to Todd, but never did. Not in his features or expressions or even mannerisms. Jace's hair was dark, nearly black, like hers. His eyes were deep brown while Todd had blond hair with blue eyes. She'd only seen one picture of his former wife that they kept on Jace's nightstand, and his coloring more resembled hers.

"I know you can do it." The deep confidence in the man's voice sounded almost like a command that couldn't be broken.

When he'd first spoken, she'd been surprised by his high-pitched tone. It didn't go with his solid and muscular build, but now it was deep, nearly bass. Perhaps shock had taken it higher, though honestly, he didn't look the least bit shocked or unsettled by the incident.

"I didn't think you'd still be here," she said. "But I'm glad you are as I wanted to thank you, Mr.—"

"Webb. It's Dillan Webb." He waved a hand. "And no thanks necessary. I'm just glad I was here to help."

"Where did you learn to react like that?" she asked, trying to keep the suspicion from her tone.

"Navy."

"Ah, military. That explains it." And maybe explained the really scary tattoo of an S turning into a snake on his arm that she'd seen earlier. Thankfully he kept that arm behind his back as Jace might freak out at seeing the scary thing.

Detective Frost joined them. She'd never met this detective in her work at the Veritas Center, but she'd taken comfort from the lines near his eyes and deep crevices by his mouth when he smiled. She thought they reflected years of experience, and he would handle this investigation well and the abductor would indeed be going to prison for a long time to come.

Jace yawned, and his eyelids drooped.

"Well, young man." Frost gave Jace a kindly smile. "We're all done here, and it looks like you and your mom are good to go home."

"I got to sit in the patrol car," he said, perking up a bit. "It was fun."

"I know. I had many years of fun in my own squad car." He smiled again and shifted his focus to Kelsey. "I'll follow you home to get a look at that guardianship paperwork."

Kelsey hated that this detective was suspicious of her, but she thought it was a good thing too. Always better to be more cautious at first and pull back than the other way around.

She stood and looked at Mr. Webb. "Thank you again for coming to our help. If you'd give me your phone number, I'd like to do something nice for you."

He looked like he was about to comply then shook his head. "That's not necessary. Seeing the boy with you again is all the thanks I need."

"Are you sure?"

He gave a firm nod, but there was something in his eyes that she couldn't read, and oddly, she wanted to.

"Well, thanks again." She held her hand out to Jace.

As she walked toward her car, she felt that mysterious man's gaze on her, and for some reason she liked it. He'd come to their rescue. Their knight in shining armor, and she was likely transferring her thanks into another meaning. What, she didn't know, because it surely wasn't attraction. She could imagine he might be good looking if he cleaned up. He was built. Muscle on muscle like he worked out. But his clothes? Beard? Didn't he bathe? Do laundry?

She shuddered at the thought.

"Everything okay, ma'am?" Frost asked.

"Fine," she said, but something in her gut—the place where she often got hunches on the job—told her nothing was ever going to be okay again. No matter how hard she tried to suppress that feeling, it lingered in the pit of her stomach, and as she stepped through the foggy night, she was on full alert for danger.

Devon watched Kelsey leave, and despite finding her quite enticing, he didn't trust her. His gut told him not to, and his gut was what had kept him alive as a SEAL and in his undercover work, so he would never, *never* go against it.

First red flag for him? She didn't have full custody of this boy. Did it mean anything—indicate that Cruz's near abduction meant she had some connection to their child trafficking business?

Devon didn't know, but he wasn't going to let it go and allow it to come back to bite him. Not when his life depended on keeping his identity a secret with a ruthless drug cartel who also dealt in human trafficking. They trafficked all ages of children, but their main focus was selling babies taken from girls and women who found themselves in unfortunate situations and unable to care for themselves, much less a child. It was a natural offshoot of their drug business. Get the females hooked on their drugs, pimp them out, and if they became pregnant, take them in, help them kick the habit, and care for them—only to rip the child away from them. The women were so disenfranchised that they never thought to complain or report it.

Until tonight, Cruz had only been part of the drug side of the business, but looked like he was branching out and grabbing a kid to sell on the black market. Maybe, anyway. It wasn't the gang's usual method of operating, so there might be more at play here, and Devon couldn't jump to any conclusions.

Kelsey glanced back at him, gave him a firm nod, and climbed into her car. He waited for her to drive off, noting her plate number as she did, then headed for his vehicle to drive to the east side of the city where he'd lived in a fleabag apartment for the last six months. He wanted to call his supervisor from the car, but he couldn't use the burner phone he carried to make that call. Could mean the end of his life if any members of the Rickey Vargas Gang, an offshoot of the Sotos Cartel, grabbed Devon's phone and discovered the call.

Devon drove downtown, circled a few blocks, making left turns and watching his rearview mirrors. Positive no one tailed him, he swung into a parking area where he rented a bike storage locker to keep personal items close by that he didn't want connected to him. He turned the padlock combination until the lock dropped down, and he opened the door. He grabbed a tote holding his real phone and laptop and took it to his truck parked deep in the shadows. He dialed his supervisor.

Bud Hurst answered on the third ring. "After hearing from Detective Frost, I was hoping you'd call sooner rather than later."

"You're not going to be glad I'm calling once you hear what I have to say." Devon quickly brought Hurst up to speed on the incident. "I don't think my cover's blown, but I won't know until Vargas sends his lawyer in to talk to Cruz."

Hurst issued a muffled curse, his tone dark and deep. "Just when we were ready to bring them down."

"Yeah, I know." Devon had to work hard to keep the frustration from his tone.

Hurst didn't speak for a long, tortured silence. "Do *not* go back to your undercover apartment until we know if you've been compromised."

"Wasn't planning on it. I can't go home either. Not if they know my true ID. Thought I'd check into a hotel for the night."

"Could take us longer than a night to figure it out. We'll need to get a wire on you and send you in while we have eyes and ears on you and can pull you out."

"Then tick tock. I can't spend more than a day out of contact with them, or they'll get suspicious. Then my cover might as well be blown because I won't be able to do a thing."

"I'm sure we can get this organized for tomorrow night, which should give Vargas plenty of time to hear back from Cruz. Go ahead and arrange a meet. Choose a public location that we can defend."

"What's the point? You know they're going to change it."

"Can't hurt to try."

Devon didn't agree. "The day I begin dictating terms to Vargas is the day he gets suspicious. I'll meet with him, but only on his terms."

"Fine," Hurst grumbled. "Just get back to me with the location so I can plan the op."

"Will do." Before hanging up, Devon took a moment to consider other items that Hurst could provide assistance on. "I have no idea why Cruz would go after Jace Moore, but I'm going to check into that. Starting with getting a warrant for the birth certificate and the protective order."

"You think Jace is somehow connected to the trafficking ring?"

"Only Cruz knows that. I can't interview him and neither can anyone in the agency without making him suspicious. So we'll just have to hope Detective Frost is skilled at his job and will share."

"I'll get on the phone to his lieutenant to request an update. And if you give me the kid's details, I'll expedite the warrant request."

"Roger that." Devon shared the boy's and mother's names, and after Hurst promised to get the warrant to Devon within the hour, he hung up.

On his other phone, he fired off a text to Vargas making up an excuse to meet, then got out his computer and connected to his secured wireless connection to plug *Kelsey Moore Portland, Oregon* into a search engine. He found several women with the same name but also found links to the Veritas Center where he learned that the word Veritas meant truth. He clicked on the first link and the picture of the woman he'd just met populated the screen. Good. He was glad that she was who she said she was.

He took a moment to study her face and was struck by her eyes' unique blend of green and blue coloring. He couldn't put a name to the color close to turquoise, but he'd never encountered it before. She had a smattering of freckles over her nose, and that along with a shy smile, made him think "vulnerable" again.

Had she posed for this picture near the time her husband died? Was that why Devon found her looking defenseless?

He read her bio, and instantly felt like a loser in the education department. She held a B.A. and M.A. from the University of Chicago and a PhD from the University of California, Santa Barbara. And if that didn't speak highly enough about her credentials, she also interned at the Smithsonian.

He, on the other hand, finished his B.A. in criminal justice since leaving the SEALs. Sure, he liked to think with his on-the-job experience in the navy that he had an advanced degree in life, but that didn't work very well on a resume or qualify him for his DEA position.

He read down the rest of her bio, and at the last item, he sat back. She was far from vulnerable. She possessed a black belt in karate. She didn't need his protection. If she hadn't fallen, she could likely have taken Cruz down.

He didn't want her to be vulnerable—liked her strength even—but he liked thinking she might need him even more.

"Seriously." He groaned. "Let it go. Find out if she's telling the truth about the kid and move on."

He opened the Regional Information Sharing System

for the western states and plugged in her name. WISN returned her voter's registration, every car ever registered in her name—including the Honda she drove off in tonight, every driver's license she ever possessed, every address she ever used, names of every person in her household—her deceased husband, Todd Adam Moore, along with his son Jace Alan Moore, her neighbors' names, and so much more. No criminal offenses displayed, but he wouldn't count on this database for that information.

On the surface she seemed on the up and up, but he wouldn't believe it until he checked criminal data. He logged into the DEA database and ran her name, including her middle name of Elizabeth that he'd gotten from the first search. It came back clean and revealed her age at thirty-four, the same as him. He ran the husband. He came back clean, too. Then the child. Nothing.

Devon jotted down the trio's social security numbers to look up and completed a search for a protective proceeding where the appointment of a guardian was sought for Jace. He found references to the proceedings but would have to go to the county to get the records first thing in the morning. He would request a birth certificate at the same time.

Then and only then would he believe Kelsey Moore's story, check her off his suspicious person's list, and hopefully erase the image of a vulnerable woman that kept tormenting his brain.

3

Kelsey paced her living room the next morning as Jace played in his bedroom. She needed to get to work, but there was no way she would leave him alone with his nanny, Ahn, for protection. Absolutely no way. Sure they lived in a secure building, but she didn't trust state-of-the-art locks alone to protect her son, and nearing sixty and petite, Ahn couldn't put up much of a fight.

The doorbell rang, and Kelsey jumped.

"Relax, it's Jackson," she told herself as she hurried to the door to let in one of the protection experts on the Blackwell Tactical team out of Cold Harbor. She'd met the owner, Gage Blackwell when she recently helped find her coworker Emory's abducted sister, and Kelsey had called him last night the moment Jace was asleep in his room.

She looked through the peephole to confirm her visitor. She instantly recognized Jackson Lockhart. He was married to Maggie, a fellow anthropologist who Kelsey knew from attending many of the same lectures and conferences. Jackson looked much like the other men of Blackwell Tactical—tall and well-built with dark hair, a strong jaw, and rugged appearance. Riley was the only fair-haired guy in the group.

She released a relieved breath and pulled open the door. "I'm so glad you finally got here."

"Sorry I'm late." He smiled, but it was tight and professional. "Pete here was giving me the lay of the land."

The silvery-haired Veritas Center security guard stood next to Jackson. Pete was short and stocky, but built like a tank. He looked even shorter next to Jackson who was six-two, but as a former police officer, Pete possessed some of the same training as Jackson and a strong sixth sense about people and situations.

She gave him a genuine smile. "Morning, Pete."

"Morning, Ms. Kelsey." He smiled, but his eyes were tired from his night shift. "How's our boy this morning? Hope last night's excitement hasn't affected him too much."

"He's doing much better than I am."

"Kids are pretty resilient. Now OG's like me? Another story." He laughed.

"You're not an old guy," Kelsey said, recognizing his cop lingo.

He snorted. "I'm off for the day, but if you need anything else, I'll be back tonight."

He turned and walked away, his footfalls echoing in the long hall.

"Come in," Kelsey said to Jackson and stood back.

Several bags swinging from his shoulder, Jackson strode into the condo. She secured the door and having this man in her home, she instantly felt more at ease with Jace's safety.

He set his bags down on the floor and faced her. "Okay, so the plan is to have one of us on duty at all times. Trey Sawyer will relieve me tonight."

"Eryn's husband," Kelsey said, referencing Blackwell's cyber expert.

Jackson nodded. "You should know, someone might need to stand in for me or Trey. Maggie's expecting. Baby's not due for six weeks. Trey's child is due in a month. But we like to prepare for any eventuality."

"Congratulations." Kelsey clapped her hands. "I hadn't heard."

"We're pretty excited." A genuine smile crossed his face. "It's a boy."

"Welcome to the club. I may just be Jace's stepmother, but I love him as much as if he was my own."

Jackson's smile fled. "And I'll do my best to be sure he stays safe. I've reviewed the building's security, and I'm satisfied it's strong. Not a fortified compound like Blackwell, but then I know clients visit here, and it's not practical to erect an exterior fence and gate."

She'd been to Blackwell's compound and such a fortress was not the business model the partners believed in here at Veritas. "That would turn them off for sure."

He nodded. "Pete set me up with access to every area via your print readers and access to your video cameras. I'll get my computer set up, so I have a live feed of all the exits."

"Thank you. You don't know how much it means to me that you came on such short notice."

He shrugged. "No biggie. That's what we do."

He said no biggie, but it was a big deal for her, and she was so glad she'd called Gage. Sure, their protection didn't come cheap, but she couldn't put a price on keeping Jace safe. He was the most important thing in her life, and she didn't know what she would do if she ever lost him.

Devon clearly wasn't the only one who planned to be at the Oregon Vital Records Office the moment the doors opened, but he was the only one with a badge and warrant who could skip to the front of the long line.

"Excuse me, official police business." He held out his badge while easing past the people who looked like they'd rather be home in bed for a few more hours.

He received a few stink eyes and grumbles but he didn't let it deter him and slipped into place with three minutes to spare. Thankfully he kept a change of clothing and personal hygiene items in his locker allowing him to clean up his appearance at the hotel, to cover the snake tat, and put on presentable clothes, or they might not have believed he was law enforcement. He'd worked various levels of undercover the last five years, from going in and doing his thing for one meet and getting out just as quickly compared with this assignment where he lived and breathed the life of a drug gang. When he finished this one, he was never going deep undercover again. He was getting tired of living a lie.

His phone dinged, and he glanced at the text from Hurst.

Vargas meeting on target for tonight. Frost's interview with Cruz mostly a bust. Cruz claimed he did this for someone else. Vargas attorney showed up. Cruz clammed up and wouldn't say who asked him to take Jace.

Devon figured this would happen. Cruz had to be too afraid of cartel payback to talk. Devon acknowledged the text and stowed his phone in time for the clerk to open the door. Middle-aged, she was tall, willowy thin with a long face and hair down to her waist. She wore khaki pants and a denim shirt that had seen years of laundering and was frayed at the collar, and her nametag read Wilma Jones.

He held out his credentials. "DEA Agent Devon Dunbar. I have a warrant needing priority processing."

She took a deep breath and blew it out slowly. "You really know how to start a girl's day, don't you?"

"Sorry, but it's a simple request."

"C'mon then, let's get it done." She spun so quickly he was afraid her rail-thin body didn't have the support needed to remain upright. But she hurried behind the counter, slid onto a stool by a computer, and flapped out her hand.

He placed the warrant on her slender fingers. "I'd like the birth certificate for this child."

She studied the warrant, her lips covered in a pale pink lipstick moving with the words. She took her time, and thankfully, there were two other clerks helping the line of people or Devon would be getting even more dirty looks than he was receiving now.

She carefully set down the warrant and started typing on her keyboard. "I assume you need a certified certificate."

Devon nodded.

She clicked her mouse and looked up. "It's printing now and the notary will bring it up. If you have a seat I'll call you back when it's ready."

Devon sat on a hard plastic chair to wait. The moment he had the certificate in hand he would head over to the Multnomah County Courthouse for a copy of the guardianship paperwork.

Until then, he plugged in the child's social security number in the fed's site and waited for the record to populate. When it did, he sat forward and stared at his phone. The number belonged to a deceased child named Finn Zehr. He died twenty years prior.

Devon blinked and checked the number. Yeah, he'd put the right one in. Was there a mistake in the name? He entered Jace Alan Moore. Three additional names came up, but they were all adults.

Devon sat back, his mind a whirl of thoughts, but the one that twirled up and settled on the top of the funnel was that Cruz's near abduction of Jace last night wasn't a coincidence and this child had been sold to Todd Moore. He and his wife Kelsey seemed on the up and up, but then no one knew what secrets lingered behind closed doors.

"Agent Dunbar," the clerk called out.

He went back to the counter, and she slid a birth certificate over to him. He gave it a quick review to note the names were correct then thanked her and exited the building. Outside, he paused in the building's shade to study the paper. Jace Alan Moore born to father Todd Adam Moore and mother Margo Carol Bradley. He was born the twelfth of April six years earlier at the Rugged Point Community Hospital, with a Dr. Wallace Harriman the doctor of record.

Okay, something odd was going on. The certificate was official, but the social security number wrong. If the Moores had an official certificate, they could easily have gotten the child a legitimate social security number. So why use a false number?

He got out his phone, located the phone number for the Rugged Point Community Hospital and dialed.

"Records please," he said when the operator came on.

He was transferred, and when the woman answered, he identified himself. "I'm looking into the birth of a Jace Alan Moore with an e, and just need to know if he was born at your hospital to a Margo and Todd Moore."

"I can't—"

"Please. I'll get a warrant for additional information, but don't want to make the trek all the way out there if he wasn't born in your hospital. Can't you just give me a yes or no?"

"I don't know."

"Just a yes he was born there or a no. Simple as that."

Silence stretched out, then a sigh, and he heard fingers clicking over the keyboard. "You said Moore with an e?"

"Yes," he said and gave her Jace's birthdate.

"No," she said clearly.

"He wasn't born there?" Devon clarified.

"No."

"You're certain?"

"Look, mister. You asked. I checked. Don't push it."

"Thank you."

Okay, something was up with this kid, and Devon needed more information. Starting with getting the guardianship paperwork and then questioning Kelsey Moore. He wouldn't call ahead. Wouldn't alert her in any way giving her time to concoct a story. That is, if she didn't already live in fear of this day and had one made up for just such an occasion.

Kelsey held Jane Doe's hyoid bone in her hand, staring at it and looking for a cause of death, but nothing registered. Despite having Jackson holding down the fort, she couldn't quit thinking about nearly losing Jace yesterday. In a flash, a beat, a mere moment, he could have been taken from her, and her life would have spiraled out of control again as it had when Todd was murdered.

And that was with her marriage on the rocks. She'd caught Todd in lies more than once in their two years together. She'd eventually lost respect for him and was sure she'd fallen out of love with him. But Jace? She loved him as if he were her own, and that's why she'd stayed with Todd. If she lost Jace…she couldn't even fathom the thought of living without him.

"Earth to Kelsey," Maya Glass's voice cut through Kelsey's fog.

She looked up to find the center's managing partner and

head of the Toxicology and Controlled Substance Unit standing over her. She was dressed in her typical jeans, T-shirt, and white lab coat. Her deep blue eyes were locked on Kelsey.

"Sorry." Kelsey smiled at her partner. "I didn't hear you come in."

"You're still thinking about last night." Maya ran a hand over her glossy blond hair that curled near her shoulders. "I imagine that's going to trouble you for a while, but just remember, Jace is fine."

Tears pricked Kelsey's eyes, which had been happening every time she thought about the incident. "If that man, Dillan Webb, hadn't been there...I..."

Maya patted Kelsey's hand. "But he was and the abductor is behind bars where he can't get to Jace."

Kelsey had been trying to find comfort in that thought, but... "What if it wasn't a random thing? What if he was specifically targeting Jace?"

Maya tilted her head. "Why would you think that?"

"I don't know. My intuition says it's possible."

"Possible, but why? No one wants to take Jace from you."

"And I need to make sure no one can. At least legally." Kelsey pushed to her feet.

"Where are you going?"

"To see my attorney." She set the hyoid on the stainless steel table holding Jane Doe's other bones laid out in an anatomically correct order. "He's been working on the adoption paperwork and called a few days ago saying he needed to see me. I was going to hold off meeting with him until after Jace's birthday parties were all over, but now I think it's a good idea to go over there."

Maya's eyes narrowed. "Do you want me to come with you?"

Kelsey shook her head. "I'll be fine."

Maya continued to watch Kelsey, but didn't speak.

"Did you need something?" Kelsey asked.

"What?"

"You came in here for a reason."

"Oh, yeah, right." She tapped the table. "I was wondering if you were done with Jane's bones so I could run my toxicology tests on them."

"Sorry, no." Kelsey frowned as she looked at the skeleton laid out on the table. "This one is tough. I still don't have a cause of death. Maybe the missing bones hold the key, but with the scavenger activity, it's not likely we'll recover them."

"The detective is really pushing me for results." Maya frowned. "Any idea when you might finish?"

Guilt peppered Kelsey, and she gnawed on her lip. "Maybe I should stay instead of going to the attorney."

Maya shook her head. "No. Go. You won't get any work done unless you do."

"Right. Okay. So I shouldn't be gone longer than an hour. Then I promise to buckle down here until lunch at Jace's school for his birthday."

Maya shook her head. "I don't know how you handle being a single parent, but you do it so well. I can barely feed my fish and keep up with my workload."

"Yeah, but you also manage the business. That's a full-time job in itself, and we should think about hiring a manager to take it over."

Maya waved a hand. "No sense in creating more over-head when I've got it for now."

Kelsey studied her friend and partner for five years. She looked refreshed, but that was more a factor of strategically-placed makeup than the required amount of sleep. All seven of the partners worked long hours and were often sleep deprived, but it was hard not to be when they were responsible for locating a killer or someone's parent. "Stop looking at me like one of your bones and get out of here already." Maya grabbed Kelsey's purse and shoved it into her hands.

Kelsey took her handbag and they stepped into the hallway.

"I'm taking the stairs," Kelsey said.

"I'm with you."

Kelsey's lab took up the full basement, and Maya's lab was on the second floor. The elevator would be faster, but their jobs were pretty sedentary, and they liked to get in every step they could in a day.

"Let me know the minute you finish with Jane Doe," Maya said at the first floor.

"I will." Kelsey waited for Maya to continue up the stairs then pulled open the door and hurried down a hallway to the back exit of the six-story building.

Outside in the bright April sunlight, she stared for a moment at the main floor that was all glass and sharp angles. She ran her gaze up the other glass-enclosed floors, sunlight glinting in sharp points. She loved the sparkling glass, but didn't mind that she was stuck in the basement all day. In fact, she preferred it as there were no windows to distract her from her work.

Maya inherited the building from her grandfather when he passed away. It was supposed to be a mixed-use building. Retail on the ground floor, offices in the east tower and condos in west tower, but when he died, it hadn't yet been leased. So the partners pooled their money, built out the labs, and the single partners moved into the condos. Kelsey lived there until she married Todd and returned again after he died. She found living and working in the same building a very symbiotic relationship that she was grateful for.

Despite Maya thinking Kelsey had it altogether as a single parent, she was so far from it some days she could cry.

She slipped into her car and made the twenty-minute drive to Vern Beal's office in Lake Oswego. She didn't have an appointment, but Vern readily agreed to see her, and the receptionist ushered Kelsey into his office. He sat behind his desk, his silvery head bent over paperwork. He stood and slipped into his suit jacket then tucked a yellow-and-black-dotted tie inside.

"I'm glad you decided to stop by instead of putting this off." His deep tone held concern.

A fresh wave of anxiety joined the residual feelings from last night. She took a breath and moved closer. "What's wrong?"

"Go ahead and have a seat." His expression was intense as he gestured at a burgundy leather chair by his desk.

Her stomach cramped as she sat. "You're scaring me, Vern."

"Sorry. I don't mean to, but this is serious."

"Please. Just tell me."

His unwavering gaze held hers. "I don't think Jace is Todd's biological son."

"What?" She shot to her feet. "That's impossible."

"I'm afraid it's altogether quite possible," he said, ice blue eyes sober.

Thoughts raced through her brain, and she took a calming breath. "So Jace is adopted?"

"No. As far as I can determine, Todd didn't have any legal rights to Jace at all."

Her mouth dropped open. "None. But how? Why? I don't understand. We provided his birth certificate for the guardianship proceedings, and it wasn't contested then. Everything went through okay." The panic in her own voice scared her even more.

"That's because the judge had no reason to question the validity of the certificate." Vern's eyes narrowed, and he pointed at the chair for her to sit again. "I need you to remain calm and hear me out. That's the only way we can resolve this."

She could hardly think, and her knees were weak, so she dropped back into the chair.

He came around the desk and rested on the corner. "Let's back up to what has transpired since you asked me to start formal adoption proceedings."

"Okay." She clutched her hands together, not at all surprised to find them clammy and shaking.

"As you know, I was closing out Todd's financial dealings. In my review, I noticed something highly irregular."

"What?"

"He wasn't claiming Jace as a dependent on his tax records. He was a CPA and a frugal man. That raised a red flag for me and got me questioning what was going on. Only one thing came to my mind."

Her heart dropped to her stomach. "Todd didn't claim Jace because he had no legal right to do so."

Vern nodded. "So I did some digging. The certificate is real enough, and Jace was listed in vital records as Todd and Margo's son, but then I looked up Jace's social security number."

"And?" She held her breath to wait for the answer.

"And, it belongs to a child who died twenty years ago. His name was Finn Zehr."

"No. No." She shook her head hard. "It's just an error in the system. I'm sure of it."

"It's crazy, but I doubt it's an error, and we need to consider that Todd became Jace's parent under suspicious circumstances."

Queasiness claimed her stomach in full, but she swallowed hard to will it away. "So what do we do now?"

"Now?" He tapped his chin as if he hadn't quite gotten to that point. "Now we put the adoption on hold until we figure out how Jace came into Todd's life, and hopefully..."

He paused and locked gazes. "Hopefully, I find a way for you to keep Jace."

4
———————

Dazed and confused, Kelsey sat across the small cafeteria table from Jace and couldn't help but stare at him. *Are you Todd's child?* she wanted to blurt out. To beg him to clarify. But he knew even less than she did. And he certainly didn't know that if anyone found out about his false social security number, he would be ripped from her arms and taken into custody until the misunderstanding could be straightened out.

She couldn't let that happen. She couldn't lose him. Not for even one night. She clutched his hand.

"Ouch, Mom," he grumbled. "You're hurting me."

She relaxed her hold and forced a smile into her tone. "Sorry. I'm just so happy to be having lunch with you that I got carried away."

His sweet twenty-something teacher, Miss Olsen, cast Kelsey a questioning look. Kelsey managed to smile at her. "Should I get the cupcakes?"

Miss Olsen nodded.

Kelsey nearly leapt from the table and bolted across the room to the container she'd carried in with her. Just looking at the chocolate cupcakes with bright blue icing and dinosaur toppers brought tears to her eyes. It felt like a life-time ago that she'd baked the cupcakes.

Wait. Last night. Could this Cruz man have played a part in how Jace had come to live with Todd? Or was that an unrelated event? Was Vern right that Todd had not gotten Jace through legitimate means?

Vern didn't make mistakes, and he wouldn't have brought this to her attention if he thought Jace was Todd's biological child. Not that they had proof. But she could find that proof. She'd take samples of their DNA to expert Emory Steele to process. Kelsey would have to go to her storage unit to find something from Todd, and hopefully something in his boxes contained DNA from his deceased wife, too.

"Mrs. Moore," Miss Olsen called out. "The children are getting antsy."

Kelsey plastered a smile on her face and turned with the container and stack of paper plates. She handed out the cupcakes to the wiggly kids. Then she took pictures of gooey frosting-coated faces alive with smiles from the sugary treats, Jace's face flashing the biggest smile of all as his class-mates sang "Happy Birthday."

Would this be his last happy birthday celebration with her? Tears pricked her eyes, and she swiped at them.

"It's so sweet how choked up you're getting over his special day," Miss Olsen said. "A lot of parents by this age are less emotionally involved, and I love that you feel so strongly about him."

If she only knew what was motivating Kelsey's tears.

"Being his stepmother, I don't take even a moment for granted." And now—even less so.

She needed to get to that storage unit and hunt for any records that might help her understand what was going on. Todd had told her many lies over the years, but this was the granddaddy of them all. And it probably explained every lie he'd had to tell, now that she thought about it, since they were all related to adopting Jace or about Jace.

Oh, God, no. Please. Please don't let this be true. I don't know what I'll do if it is.

"Okay, children," Miss Olsen called out. "Let's get your places cleared, wash up, and line up for recess."

The next ten minutes were organized chaos until Kelsey could hug Jace to her. He squirmed. "Come on, Mom. I gotta go outside."

"I know. Just one more birthday hug." She clutched him tightly.

He groaned and eased out of her hold to run after his class. She watched until she could no longer see him on the playground and then turned to head back to the lab. She had to spend the rest of the workday evaluating Jane Doe's bones, and then she would have Jace's grandparents watch him after his birthday dinner so she could search the storage unit for those DNA samples.

The thought brought her feet to a stop. Surely Todd's parents would've known if Todd's former wife had been pregnant. Todd couldn't have just sprung a baby on them out of the blue, could he? They had to be in on this, and Kelsey would question them tonight, too.

She got her car on the road and somehow managed to drive to the lab, though she remembered very little of the drive. She would be going out again tonight, so she parked in the front and entered the lobby. The cool blues and muted lobby colors always brought her comfort, but today the sight of the man sitting on the sofa near the stairs raised her apprehension even more.

He was the guy from last night. Dillan Webb. She was sure of that, but he looked completely different. He'd trimmed his beard, revealing his chiseled bone structure.

Amazing structure. As an anthropologist she had a thing for good bones, and she appreciated his high cheeks and rugged jaw. His deep brown hair was tamed into a sleek look, and he wore black tactical pants with a gray polo that molded to his toned body. And a big bandage covered that awful snake tattoo. He looked up, his gaze locking on hers, and she had to remember to breathe.

He pushed smoothly to his feet. She kept watching him. Respectable and dangerous were the words that came to mind. Handsome, too. And confident—his stride powerful as he met her near the stairway. Her heart did a weird hop, and she swallowed hard.

She noted a gun at his hip and badge on his belt. What was going on here?

"This is a surprise." She tried to smile but her chin trembled, and she didn't manage to move her lips even a fraction of an inch upward.

"For me, too."

"Excuse me?" She stared at him. "How can being here be a surprise to you?"

"I never imagined I'd be coming over here to see you today."

"And yet, here you are."

"Yes. Here I am."

"How can I help you Mr. Webb?"

"Actually, it's Devon Dunbar, and I need to talk to you in private."

"But last night you said your name was Dillan Webb."

"So I did."

She didn't like his evasive answer, but clearly he was law enforcement of some kind. Explained his change in attire and how he could morph into this powerful-looking man so easily. "What's this regarding?"

"Your stepson."

He knows. How, she didn't know, but he did. Was he here to report her? To take Jace?

Her heart constricted, and she felt the blood drain from her head. She had to grab the railing to stay upright.

He clutched her elbow. "Are you okay?"

She shook his hand off. "Just a little lightheaded for some reason."

"Maybe you should sit down."

"Maybe I should. Let's get you signed in, and then we can talk in the conference room." She took off, nearly running, to the front desk, wishing she didn't hear his footsteps clipping along behind her, but she did. Loud and clear. Footsteps of the man who was going to report Jace's suspicious parentage.

"I need to sign in my visitor," she told their receptionist Lily.

The blond in her early twenties smiled at Kelsey then changed her focus to Devon and gave him an iPad. "Go ahead and fill in the form."

Devon cocked an eyebrow. "Is this really necessary when you're with me?"

Kelsey nodded. "We don't ever want anyone to be able to call our results into question, so we make sure every visitor is registered and escorted at all times."

"Makes sense, I guess." He filled in the form and clipped the visitor badge to his shirt.

"Follow me." Kelsey used the fingerprint reader to access the secured area of the main floor, and once in the conference room, she dropped onto a white leather chair. She took in long breaths and let them out slowly as he sat across from her. She felt him study her, and yet, she couldn't look him in the eye.

"Seems like you know why I'm here," he said.

"Go ahead and tell me," she sidestepped.

"First I need to tell you I'm an undercover DEA agent."

Drugs. What in the world? Her gaze shot up. "DEA?"

"Sounds like you think that's a bad thing."

Oh, yeah. The worst. Because as a law enforcement officer, if you know about Jace, you'll have to report him. "No. Go on."

"I was tailing Bruno Cruz last night. He works for a gang that's part of a notorious drug cartel. I've been undercover investigating them for six months."

"Drugs," she said, feeling relieved that he was dealing with drugs and not babies obtained in unusual, maybe illegal, ways.

"Yeah, that and they're big players in a child trafficking ring."

Her heart plummeted.

"Child trafficking," she managed to eke out.

"They're involved in many criminal enterprises, one of which is selling babies from drug-addicted mothers."

She looked at him then and hoped he thought her shock was simply due to the horror of the act. "How exactly does that work?"

"When one of their customers who's fallen on hard times gets pregnant, they basically kidnap the woman and help her get clean. They support her during the pregnancy, and when she gives birth they take the child."

"How horrible," she said, honestly disgusted and not thinking about Jace at the moment. "But can't the women report them?"

"They're so alienated from everything good and decent that they think no one will listen to them." He clenched his hands on the table. "And the gang's enforcers threaten them. Plus as soon as a woman gives birth, they provide her with her drug of choice and plenty of it. She's soon medicating away her problems and loses clarity."

"That's awful. Just awful." *But why are you telling me this? Is that how Todd got Jace?*

Devon nodded. "So when I saw Cruz try to grab Jace last night, I had to wonder if it was related to the child trafficking business."

"And do you think it is?" She held her breath because it would be unfathomable that her precious son had come into her life due to a gang of drug dealers.

"I do," he said. "Jace's social security number belongs to a deceased child, and there's no record of Margo Moore ever giving birth at the hospital listed on his birth certificate."

"It's all likely a mistake," Kelsey said, her avoidance of the truth so obvious to her that he had to be picking up on it, too.

He kept his gaze trained on her, and it took everything she was made of not to squirm and look away. Instead, she dug deep for resolve and looked at his crystal blue eyes.

He firmed his shoulders. "Something tells me you already knew all about this."

"No," she said automatically then realized she'd lied. "I mean sort of. My lawyer just told me about the social security number this morning, but I had no idea before that."

His eyebrow went up. "Explain."

She shared her conversation with Vern. "So you see, we're looking into it and will report our findings to the appropriate authorities." She waited, holding her breath and hoping that he would just depart and leave this alone.

"You know I can't ignore this. Walk away."

"No. I know. But could you maybe hold off for just a day or two. Give me a chance to look in my husband's records. Run DNA. Question my in-laws and get the team here looking into it."

He sat back and propped his leg on his knee. "I can't

have you all come bursting into my investigation and ruin six months of undercover work."

She'd worked with enough law enforcement officers over the years to know he wouldn't agree to her request, but she'd had to try.

Panic started in the pit of her stomach, ran up her throat, and nearly choked her.

What was she going to do? She couldn't lose Jace, but this man—someone she would likely respect in any other situation—was going to take him away from her, and she didn't know how to stop him.

Devon should be digging out his phone right now and dialing social services, but Kelsey looked like she might pass out on the spot. Surprisingly, Devon was trying to come up with a solution to her problem instead of making that call. To figure out how she could continue her guardianship of this child while they looked into the conditions of his birth.

"Work with us, Agent Dunbar," she pleaded. "We won't make a move without your approval, but you'll have some of the top forensic minds in the country at your disposal at no cost to your agency. We could make your job so much easier, and you could probably wrap up your investigation faster."

She had a point. It was all true. But could he keep quiet about the boy?

No. He couldn't do that. Still, he hadn't told Hurst yet, and Devon could hold off at least until the afternoon.

"First, it's *Devon*, and second, do you swear to me that you had no idea Jace wasn't your husband's child?"

"Yes. Yes I do." She clutched the ruffles on her flowery blouse. "I knew nothing until today, and honestly, we still don't have concrete proof he's not Todd's son. Or Margo's child. Only DNA will prove that."

"Then we need to get the DNA running."

"That's one of my reasons for looking in my husband's files. They're all at a storage unit. I'm sure the boxes there will have a sample for both of them."

"Okay, fine. We start there. Now."

Hope brightened her expression. "Does that mean you won't report this?"

"I assume you all can rush this DNA."

"Yes and no," she said. "We can put it at the front of the queue, but it's still going to take at least twenty-four hours to process. Likely more."

"Then I guess you have a twenty-four-hour reprieve."

"Thank you. Thank you." She sagged in her chair and gulped in air, her whole body heaving with the effort.

He was glad to help her. More than glad, but... "Just don't make me regret waiting."

"I won't. I promise." She shot to her feet, her full skirt skimming the knees of her long, slender legs. "Let me check in with the team, and then we can go straight to the storage unit."

"Just so you know," he said as he got up, "I won't be letting you out of my sight before the DNA results come in."

"Sure. Fine. Whatever you need. Come on. You can come up with me to check in." She didn't even look at him but rushed from the room toward an elevator. Her spiky heels clicked on the tile floor drawing his attention to those amazing legs again.

He jerked his gaze away and caught up to her as she was pressing her fingers on a fingerprint reader outside the elevator. She punched the up button, and the car whirred into motion, descending down to them.

He looked back down the hall at the richly decorated

lobby that made him think of a spa. As he'd waited for her to return, he'd paced the lobby admiring every inch of the décor. The staircase seemed to float above a seating area where the center's logo—"Connecting Loved Ones Around the World"—was painted in fire-engine-red letters circling a black globe on the wall above photos of happy smiling people. He assumed the pictures were of people the lab helped reunite through their DNA testing.

The elevator door parted.

"Never thought I'd see what goes on behind these walls," he said.

She cast him a surprised look. "So you're familiar with our work, then."

"What law enforcement officer in the area isn't?"

"I suppose that's true." She boarded the car.

He trailed her inside and caught a hint of her perfume. Flowery, but he couldn't name which one. The scent was understated and feminine just like she was.

She stabbed the button for the second floor. "We'll stop at the toxicology lab to report to Maya Glass, our managing partner. Then I'll have her talk with our DNA expert and get her on board with running the tests right away."

He arched a brow.

"What?" she asked, suspicion lingering her tone.

"I thought you might try to stonewall that," he said bluntly. "You know, to buy more time with the boy."

She jutted out her jaw. "I may not want to lose Jace, but I want to know the circumstances of my stepson's birth as badly as you do. Probably more so."

He respected her forthright answer. She seemed like an honest woman, but then he'd never been real good at reading women he was attracted to. Case in point, his former fiancée. He'd left the SEALs because his frequent dangerous deployments scared her and she wouldn't be with him under those conditions. Turned out Tara didn't want to be with him at all, and he'd left the team for no reason. Given up what he loved. Given up everything. Now he had to think long and hard before he bought a woman's story.

So how was he letting this woman worm her way into his good graces without trying, and he wasn't doing a good job of keeping her out? He had to do better. Especially since he was going out on a limb here to help her.

They exited on the second floor and marched straight past the DNA lab to the front of the building where the sign read Toxicology and Controlled Substance Unit. She used another print reader to gain access.

"Maya. This is DEA Agent Devon Dunbar." She succinctly explained about his undercover work.

Maya ran a quick assessing gaze over him, and he felt like he was left wanting.

"How can we help you, Agent Dunbar?" she asked.

Devon opened his mouth to explain but then thought better of it. "I'll let Ms. Moore tell you."

"Kelsey," she said to him then looked at Maya. "You might want to sit down."

Maya's gaze wary now, she dropped onto a stool. "What's going on?"

"You remember my visit to my lawyer."

"Sure, yeah. You went to see him this morning."

Kelsey nodded and then launched into explaining what they knew about Jace.

"This is some kind of joke, right?" Maya crinkled her nose. "You're punking me or something."

Kelsey shook her head. "No joke. We're headed over to the storage unit right now to try to find DNA samples for Todd and Margo."

Maya nodded and firmed her shoulders. "What can we do?"

"Get Emory ready to run the DNA tests ASAP, and arrange a partner's brainstorming meeting. I want everyone's help, and since I only have twenty-four hours I need it to be top priority."

"Of course. No question about that." Maya gave a firm bob of her head. "But I'll just tell them to stand by and let you share about Jace."

Kelsey's eyes narrowed. "I can't believe Todd was lying to me all this time. Not just the lies I knew about. Those pale in comparison to this monstrous one."

So all was not well in her former marriage. Interesting.

Maya's expression tightened. "We'll get to the bottom of this."

"A word of warning," Devon said, making sure his tone conveyed that he meant business. "I can't have the undercover assignment compromised, so Kelsey has agreed not to take any steps without my approval."

"He's right," Kelsey said. "We'll be taking all direction from him."

Maya bristled. "Don't much like that."

Kelsey's voice rose. "It's either that or he reports Jace to social services."

Maya glared at him. "Blackmail?"

Devon started to defend himself, but Kelsey jumped in. "It's not like that. Devon's doing me a favor, and in return, I'm doing one for him."

Maya looked between them both. "Okay, if you say so."

"I do." She squeezed her friend's arm. "Now I need to go, and I'm assuming you realize that this means I'll only be able to work on my search for Jane Doe's cause of death in down times."

"Of course, and don't worry about that. It's a cold case,

and it's not like there's a suspect fleeing as we speak. I'll call the detective and let him know something has come up." She made shooing motions with her hands. "Now get out of here."

"I need to grab some supplies." She quickly retrieved evidence bags and swabs from a cupboard and packed them in her large purse. She slung it over her shoulder before rushing into the hallway.

Devon got the idea that she was a little dynamo though she wasn't so little. More like a tall dynamo. He pegged her at five-nine or so without the shoes. At six-one himself, he'd always been attracted to taller women.

They stopped in the lobby for him to turn in his visitor pass and stepped into the parking lot, misty rain now falling and dampening the sidewalk.

"We'll take my vehicle." He clicked his key fob to unlock his stone gray F-150 pickup truck, thankful he'd had it detailed yesterday or she might find a mess from his undercover work where he used his own vehicle instead of a company SUV.

He opened the passenger door for her and after she settled in, he took his place behind the wheel. "Where to?"

She gave him directions to a storage company he remembered passing just down the road.

Once he had the vehicle pointed in the right direction, he glanced at her. "You mentioned your husband lying to you."

She sighed. "He did. Often. Not big things, but it all added up. When I look back on it now, I can see that most of it was related to Jace."

"How so?"

"When Jace turned four he started asking a lot of questions about his mother and about when he was a baby. So I asked Todd to share about those early days and to give me more pictures of her than the one on Jace's nightstand. Todd said the pictures were lost in a flood, but then I found some hidden in our closet. I don't know why he wanted to hide them, but he did. Then I'd been wanting to officially adopt Jace since I married Todd, but he kept telling me his attorney was working on it, and when he resolved a few complications he'd let me know. It never happened, and I got different stories every time I asked."

Devon didn't say anything. Best to let her give him as much information as possible.

"Looks like we know the reason now." She sighed again, long, low, frustrated. "Then there were times he said he was one place, but in reality, he was somewhere else. He would never tell me where, though."

She seemed like a nice person and didn't deserve to be lied to. Didn't deserve being strung along. He hated that it happened. Maybe because he had to lie so often on the job and really didn't like doing so. But it was his job. This guy lied to the woman he promised to love and cherish.

"Maybe he was trying to find a way to work it out so you could adopt the boy," he suggested, trying to make things better.

She seemed to consider it, but then shook her head. "If he stole Jace from his mother, that would never happen." She didn't sound bitter, just hurt. Deeply hurt.

He wanted to reach out. Take her hand. Squeeze it and assure her that not all men were like this Todd guy—Devon sure wasn't—but the truth was, there were many men who would do what Todd did. Devon ran into guys like that on a daily basis.

Maybe it was better to face facts so she could move on. "Okay, so maybe he was doing the opposite. Putting things in place so you would never find out about Jace's birth."

"Yeah, that sounds more likely." She wrapped her arms around her slender waist and sagged into the seat.

Her increased suffering cut Devon to the quick. He suspected she'd suffered just as much when Todd was alive, too. He wondered if she would have left him if he lived. Or if she would've stayed for the child she seemed to love so much. He didn't know her at all, but he suspected she would have stayed.

But that was a moot point because her husband was gone. "How did Todd die, if you don't mind me asking?"

She sat up, her back rigid. "He was mugged—gunned down—in the parking lot of his hotel when he was traveling for business in Tucson."

Gunned down? He shot her a questioning look. "Did they arrest the shooter?"

She shook her head. "The detectives had few leads. They think it was just a random mugging."

Random muggings *did* happen, and they were often hard to solve, but Devon had to wonder if the murder had to do with the boy. Devon made a mental note to get the case files for review.

"And what about Margo?" he asked. "How did she die?"

"Cancer ultimately took her, but she also had early-onset Alzheimer's. Todd described it as pretty advanced for her age. She didn't know Jace a lot of the time, so they never really bonded, and she used to wander and get lost. Todd had to hire a full-time caregiver." Kelsey shook her head. "I can't even imagine that in my old age, but at my current age? That's just crazy to think about, and then to get cancer on top of it? Unfair."

Devon totally understood her reaction. "It's hard to see people suffer like that. One thing then another. I see it all the time in my work, and I admit I gotta wonder what God is thinking. Piling it on so heavy for some people and others skate by with far less. Usually, the lowlifes I'm arresting are unaffected while the innocent victims suffer." He shook his head. "Listen to me. I sound bitter and jaded."

She sat forward and solidly met his gaze. He was hard-pressed to look away. "It's a challenge not to be jaded in your line of work."

"And in yours." He looked back at the road.

"Yeah, mine, too, but I try not to let it get me down."

He liked her positive attitude. "Did you always want to be a forensic anthropologist?"

"Pretty much. I mean, not the forensic part, but I wanted to be an archeologist and go on digs in exotic places to unearth treasures." Enthusiasm rang through her words.

He liked seeing this up side of her. "What changed that?"

"Going on a dig and living in tough conditions. My idea of roughing it is a hotel without room service so living in the wild for months on end? No way." She grinned at him, her unusual eyes coming alive and sparkling.

Her beauty caught him unaware, and he drew in a sharp breath to counterbalance it.

She frowned. "Something wrong?"

He shook his head, shaking off his reaction and fixing his eyes on the road.

What was with this woman? How did she seem to pull things out of him that he hadn't felt in years? Especially when he didn't even know if she really was telling him the truth. He hadn't been able to prove that yet, and he was a facts-first kind of guy, not wear-your-heart-on-your-sleeve kind. About the only time he let his emotions go these days was with music. He was nearly addicted to jazz and used it to settle his soul from all the horrible things he witnessed.

Maybe jazz would wipe out this feeling he was getting from her.

He reached for the radio and turned on his favorite station, letting the music wash over him.

"You're into jazz?" she asked.

"You sound surprised?"

"No, I mean...yeah, I guess I am. You seem like a pretty straight shooter, and jazz is kind of moody."

She had a point. But... "I started listening to it after I made a SEAL team. Wiped out all the horrific things I saw and cleared my head."

She gaped at him. "You were a SEAL?"

"Don't look so horrified." He chuckled. "It's just a job like any other."

"Hardly. You...I mean...wow. I've read about the job, and it's *not* just like any other. Starting with the endurance test to get into it."

"Yeah. It's brutal."

"If it makes it any better, I appreciate your service."

He felt his chest start to puff out and quickly stopped it. He'd never been one to brag about getting into the SEALs, but he was proud of his service. When he first made the team, he'd accepted compliments with more swagger than he should, but the other guys quickly wiped that out of him.

"That's it." She pointed across the street at the storage facility.

Thankful to get out of the truck and forget about all these crazy thoughts, he swung into the place. She provided the code to lift the gate, and he drove back to Unit Eight and parked. She was out of the car before he removed the keys. She was like an Energizer Bunny, and he was going to have to get faster if he wanted to keep up with her.

He joined her at the door, and after she released the padlock, he bent to raise it up. She flipped on the bare overhead lightbulb, and the harsh glare highlighted stacks and stacks of boxes along with a few pieces of furniture.

He waited for her to enter and show him where to start looking. She didn't move but stood staring ahead.

"You okay?" he asked.

She shook her head, her curls swishing over her shoulders. She looked up at him. Her eyes were wary and almost terrified. Her raw emotions cut him to the core.

"Now that I'm here," she said, her voice almost a whisper. "I'm afraid of what I'm going to find, and I don't even want to step inside to look."

5

Kelsey took a fortifying breath, but still couldn't move. The single bare bulb cast a harsh shadow on the space, raising her unease to a level she never imagined possible from simply looking through her deceased husband's possessions.

Devon rested a hand on her shoulder, surprising her with the way his nearby presence comforted her. For some reason, she believed he was an honest and forthright man. A what-you-see-is-what-you-get kind of guy. But then she couldn't trust her instincts when it came to assessing a man. Not after Todd. Shoot, she probably couldn't trust her assessment of anyone. Man or not.

He met her gaze, his holding a healthy measure of compassion and was almost her undoing. She couldn't look away. Didn't want to look away.

"Are there particular boxes that belonged to your husband that we should start with?" he asked.

His comment snapped the hold he had on her, and she shook her head. "Everything in here is his."

Devon's forehead furrowed. "Everything?"

She nodded. "After he died I couldn't deal with his things, so it was all brought here."

"Because of his lies?" he asked.

Surprisingly, she wasn't at all upset over the many personal questions he kept asking. She'd never shared all of this with anyone. Not her family or her friends. But a compassionate stranger seemed to be the right person to tell.

"Yes. A specific lie actually. He'd been gone from work all day. He didn't know I knew. When I asked where he'd been, he lied. Said he was at work. I was *so* mad at him, and we had a terrible argument. Then he left on his trip." The pain of their brutal last words washed over her. "And that's how we left things."

"This was the trip where he was shot?"

She nodded. "After that, I couldn't bear to touch his things. I couldn't stand to look at them either. So my partners at Veritas packed it all up and brought it here. Then they packed up the rest of our things, and Jace and I moved back into my old condo at Veritas, and I sold our house."

His eyes widened. "I don't understand. There are condos at the lab?"

She was feeling like she'd known him for some time and forgot that he didn't know all about her work. "The upper floors of the west tower are condos where the partners live. With the hours we keep, it's great to live so close."

He frowned. "I couldn't imagine living that close to my job. There's the undercover thing, but when I'm on regular assignment, I need time to forget all about it and decompress." He frowned. "The last six months haven't given me much time to do that."

She faced him. "Would you tell me what that's like while we look through the boxes? Might help keep my mind off the past."

"Sure. I guess. I mean I can't give you details of the op." He pressed his lips together.

"I'm more interested in how it works."

"Okay," he said, but still sounded reluctant.

"Let's start in the back," she said. "Those boxes are from a former move, and if Todd kept any of Margo's things, we'll find them there."

They eased through the stacks to the back, Kelsey's heart hammering in her chest. She didn't know why she was so emotional here. Sure, she hadn't been in here since her friends moved Todd's things, but it had been a year now. She would never fully get over losing him to such violence, but she'd moved on. That she was sure of. So why the angst? Probably because she was reminded again how often he'd lied to her.

Devon whipped out a pocket knife and sliced open two boxes. She lifted the flaps of the closest box and needed that distraction. "So, your assignment. You looked pretty rough last night when I saw you. Was that because you were living in the same area as these guys?"

"Sorry for my appearance."

She waved a hand and met his gaze. "Didn't really matter what you looked like. You saved Jace, and that's all that mattered."

He watched her carefully for a long moment as if looking for a deeper meaning in her statement, but she couldn't begin to imagine what he was searching for. She did imagine it would be hard to have to go around looking so scruffy.

"How come you were able to...you know...clean up since last night? You look great now." She realized she'd inadvertently told him she thought he looked good, and the heat of a blush rose over her face.

His mouth opened, but no words came out. He rubbed a

hand over his beard that he'd trimmed to a heavy stubble. "I work hard to keep enough of my regular look to be presentable when away from the job. It's mostly about the clothes and hair on the job. I try for the just-got-out-of-bed look when I meet with gang members. I keep clothes in a pile on the floor for that very reason." He laughed and shook his head.

"What?"

He opened his box and paused, flap in hand. "The first time I got my hair cut before going undercover, I asked for a haircut that could make me look respectable at times and at other times like a druggie. The stylist's expression was priceless."

He laughed, his face coming alive.

She liked his sense of humor and grinned along with him.

He tapped the bandage on his arm. "And you should know. The tattoo isn't permanent. Lasts for a few weeks then fades and I have to replace it. It's a scary-looking thing, so I cover it when I'm not working."

"Yeah. That's what I thought last night." She turned back to the box. "So tell me more about your assignment. My only experience with undercover work is what I see on TV and in movies."

"This op is a little different than that."

"How's that?" She pulled out a stack of folders and started flipping through them, looking for any paperwork that might tell her more about how Jace had come to be Todd and Margo's child.

"On shows and in movies you see the undercover officer basically give up his life and immerse himself in the gang. Living with the gang for months without any contact with his agency. Doesn't often happen that way. Officers don't usually go deep into the criminal environment around the clock. You get in, do your thing, and get out. This is done over and over, building trust over time. We have a life just like everyone else."

"So it's more like you make contacts and work them, but you don't give up your personal life to do it."

"Exactly. But my current assignment is kind of a cross between them. I have an apartment in the gang's area that I use when needed, but I do go home some nights."

She spotted Todd's license to marry Margo and forgot all about Devon. She studied the paper, looking for what, she didn't know. Perhaps she expected it to say something that would let her know he was a liar, but that was impossible.

"What's that?" Devon asked.

She handed the certificate to him. "Nothing earth-shattering."

He ran his gaze over the paper. "Let's pull out any official documents we come across and set them aside."

"You think Todd might have lied about this, too?"

He shrugged. "But put together, the documents could tell a story."

Or they could tell her that he'd duped her over something else. Still, she set the license on another box.

"And it'll be interesting to see if Jace's birth certificate matches the official one I obtained at the records office this morning."

She flashed her gaze to him. "You did that?"

"I wouldn't have approached you without first doing some digging." He took a long breath. "And speaking of the certificate, I'm going to have to visit the hospital listed on it."

"I'm coming with you when you do." She jutted out her chin before he could tell her no.

"Okay," he said, surprising her at his easy acquiesce.

She knew better than to question a decision made in her favor and turned her attention back to the stacks of financial documents from years prior to Jace's birth. "I still can't believe Todd didn't claim Jace on our taxes. And I didn't notice that." She felt a flush steal up over her face. "I'm embarrassed to admit I didn't know anything about our finances except where our accounts were located."

"He was a CPA, right? So it was natural to leave it all to him."

"It was, but still, I should have paid more attention. It's not good to be ignorant in any area of marriage. Not when your spouse can lie so easily."

"Don't beat yourself up about it. Just learn and move on."

She held her hand in place in the box but looked at him. "You sound so wise."

"You know it's easier to give advice than live what you preach." He huffed a laugh.

"Sounds like you're speaking from experience."

"Of course. We all have our things we wished we had or hadn't done."

"Like what?"

"Like leave the SEALs for a woman who then decides she's not actually ready for a commitment." His eyes glinted with surprise as if he didn't believe he'd said that, and he clamped his mouth closed.

She appreciated his honesty. "Oh, yeah, that would sting."

"Still does," he said and reached into the box to lift out a jar labeled "Scent Evidence."

She forgot all about his issues and stared at the jar. "What's that?"

"I'm not sure, but I think it's a scent preservation kit." He turned it around to display a label holding Margo's name, the date, and her address. "I've heard about these but have never seen one. People who suffer from dementia take a gauze pad and wipe their armpit area and seal the pad in a jar capturing their unique scent. If they go missing, the jar is used for K-9s to search for them."

"Wow. I had no idea that was a thing."

He nodded. "Parents also can do this with their children."

"Well in our case, it will be perfect to recover Margo's DNA."

"Exactly." He looked around the space. "Let me grab the empty box over there, and we can put the items we locate in it."

She nodded, and he picked his way through the stacks. She'd been so irritated when he'd shown up at the lab, and now she was thankful for his help and simply for his presence. Maybe thankful for these warm feelings he was stirring inside her.

But she shouldn't—couldn't—be thankful for that. She needed to be watchful. For deceit and lies. She had one agenda here. He had another. And if she learned anything from her time married to Todd, those separate agendas led to lies and pain. Something she wasn't about to go through ever again.

"My lab's in the basement," Kelsey said in the Vertitas Center's elevator. "It's been dubbed 'The Tomb' by others because of all the bones."

Devon was surprised she offered this information, but she'd shared quite a bit in the storage unit, and he found her to be honest and pretty forthcoming. "And how do you feel about that?"

"Feel?" She shrugged. "I've never really thought about it. It just is. I need a special air filtration system, and it was easier to install in the basement, but I guess being underground is fitting for my work."

The doors opened to a brightly lit hallway, and she stepped briskly to a door marked Osteology Lab. He spotted a print reader mounted at this door just like all the others, and she quickly got them inside and went to a neatly organized desk in the corner.

Holding the box of items they'd collected at the storage unit, Devon took a look around, and the space left him feeling uneasy. Could be the animal bones in the display case with their names on labels. More likely the human skeleton laying on one of the long stainless steel tables was the reason for his unease.

As if she could read his mind, she waved a hand at the bones. "My latest investigation. I'm struggling to find a cause of death."

Devon went to the table and looked at all of the bones, but one of the arms and part of a leg was missing. "This isn't a complete skeleton."

"No." She frowned. "We recovered a hundred thirty-seven bones, which is good for a body left exposed to the elements, but I have a feeling the missing bones in this case are what I need to determine the cause of death."

"How many bones in the body?" he asked, surprised he was finding this interesting and gross.

"We're born with around two hundred seventy, but bones fuse together as we age so an adult will have two hundred six."

"Interesting." He took another look around at the clinically clean room. "So this is where you spend all your time."

"This is only my dry lab," she said as she dropped her purse on the desk.

"Okay," he said. "Then I assume you have a wet lab, too."

"Over there." She pointed at a glass-and-metal door sealed tight.

He set down the evidence box on an empty table and took a look inside. He spotted a pair of the same metal tables, but they were connected to large stainless sinks against a wall. On the other wall was a huge burner and large pots. Another wall held tools. Some he recognized like trowels, others he didn't.

He looked at her. "I'm also afraid to ask why you need this wet lab."

"It really is the most obnoxious part of the job unless you consider maggots and other insects obnoxious." She gave a nervous laugh.

"Um, yeah, I do. Especially at a murder scene." He mocked a shudder. "So what do you do in there?"

"Are you sure you want to know?"

Her hesitancy left him questioning, but he did want to know what her job entailed, so he nodded.

"Before bones can be examined or analyzed, the remains almost always must be macerated or boiled to remove flesh and connective tissue clinging to the bones." She held up a hand. "And yes, before you ask, the smell is awful. Which is why we have an industrial exhaust and clean air system installed."

He shook his head and kept shaking it as he stared at her.

"What?" she asked.

"You." He paused for a moment. "Please don't take offense at this, but you're so delicate and fragile-looking, and it's not the kind of thing I see you doing."

She gritted her teeth. "I've heard that plenty of times before, along with the fact that I look too young to hold a PhD. But as a law enforcement officer, you should know that looks can be deceiving."

"Yeah, you're right. I *should* know that." But when it came to her, he didn't know much of anything except he liked what he was learning about her and that he found her very appealing.

"You might be interested to know I hold a black belt in karate." She met his gaze, and he saw her struggle to remain serious, but her lips tipped up. "So you won't want to cross me."

"Duly warned." He smiled at her, and her face lit with humor.

He wondered if she used humor to block out bad things like law enforcement officers often did. He suspected she would, as would her teammates, as they encountered many of the same horrific things officers witnessed on the job.

He looked back into the wet lab. "And the tools?"

"Used for recovering remains. We sterilize them in the wet lab as well."

"Sterilize?" He eyed her. "Digging tools?"

She leaned away from him, her eyes narrowing. "Just like any other crime scene, we don't want to contaminate it with soil or debris from a past scene."

"Right. Yeah. I don't know why I would think this was any different. That makes sense."

She smiled, but underneath it there was an edge, and he wondered if he offended her.

"Go ahead and spread out the items we collected on one of the tables while I grab evidence bags," she said.

He obeyed before he said anything else that might be questionable, and she stepped to a storage cabinet on the far wall. She moved in her quick, efficient way and returned with bags before he had everything out of the box. She pulled out three bags and inserted Todd's hairbrush in one, the scent jar in another, and cut fingernails from Jace that she'd stopped in her condo to retrieve from his bathroom trash in the third.

Devon had gone to her condo with her and was shocked to see she'd hired Blackwell Tactical to protect the boy. Devon would probably do the same thing if he were her, but he had to wonder if she knew something she wasn't telling him and that's why Jace required a full-time bodyguard. Devon needed to watch for any hint that might reveal something she was hiding.

She grabbed a marker and filled out the labels. She bit the edge of her lip and wrote in neat block letters. She was concentrating so hard, he knew she had no idea he was watching her slender fingers move over the bag. He'd nearly insulted her saying how feminine she was, but in addition to her fine bone structure, she dressed in a short skirt and frilly blouse again today, adding to that impression.

The door opened, and a woman with shoulder-length red hair and black glasses entered the room.

Kelsey looked up and relief spread across her face. "Emory, good. Come in and meet DEA Agent Devon Dunbar."

Emory smiled while holding out her hand. "Emory Steele. DNA."

As he grasped her warm hand, he made what he liked to call his cop sweep and noticed her Chuck Taylor sneakers and an engagement ring on her other hand. "Nice to meet you."

She released his hand and looked at Kelsey. "Maya said you had some DNA samples that you need run ASAP for personal reasons. What's going on?"

Kelsey stood for a moment, her eyes narrowed. "You'll hear all about it at the meeting, but time is of the essence, and I wanted your team to get started on processing the samples right away."

Emory's brown eyes narrowed behind the lenses, and she looked like she wanted to ask for more information but looked at the bags. "What do you have?"

Kelsey handed Emory the bagged samples and Devon wondered if Emory would connect Margo's name to Todd or if Kelsey would have to explain. "We're looking for a relationship between the three individuals."

She picked up the bagged jar. "Interesting. I've heard of these but haven't seen one before. Should work great." She turned her attention to the brush. "As long as we have a full follicle here, we're good. And of course, the fingernails are perfect."

"Thanks for agreeing to rush these samples," Kelsey said, sounding very relieved.

Emory waved a hand. "Are you kidding? After what you did for me and Cait?"

Kelsey turned to Devon. "Emory's twin sister, Cait, was abducted, and we all worked the investigation to find her."

Interesting. "It must be great to have the support of such talented people when needed."

"You can't even imagine." Emory sighed and picked up the other bags. "I'll personally get these started and see you in the conference room later."

Eyes suddenly glistening with tears, Kelsey hugged her friend. Seeing her tears raised Devon's protective instinct again, and he had to clamp down on his mouth not to say something that would give away his growing interest in this woman. He'd just stood by her side for hours as she searched through her life with her husband, tears flowing much of the time, and he'd witnessed her strength, her profound sense of loss and residual anger. And he wanted to help her in any way he could.

He didn't know how she handled life while feeling such intense emotions. Probably anger was the hardest because with her husband dead she couldn't direct it anywhere to relieve the pressure. And worse yet, she likely felt guilty for being angry. At least that's how he felt about Tara. Not the guilt, but the anger. He'd tried to let it go, but it was hard to realize he gave up his dream job only to be dumped.

"I'll see you at the meeting." Emory grabbed the bags and left the room, the soles of her shoes squeaking as she turned.

Devon glanced at his watch. Fifteen minutes until their meeting. He had just enough time to make a quick review of the paperwork they'd brought back. He lifted the stack from the box to spread the pages out on the table in chronological order.

First up, Todd's birth certificate, then his college degrees and CPA license. Next his marriage license. Then sadly his wife's death certificate, but oddly there was no birth certificate for her in the files. He would have to check into that to look for any oddities. Last, he laid out the tax files for the year Jace was born.

Kelsey joined him. "I don't get why you only wanted that particular tax year."

"Having a baby is expensive and medical bills are tax deductible. I saw that Todd deducted medical expenses in prior years so he surely would've done the same for Margo and Jace if his birth was legit."

She picked up the tax form. "No medical deductions."

"Exactly."

Kelsey dropped onto a stool. "I don't know why I keep thinking we're going to locate something to prove Jace is Todd's son. Not when there are so many red flags pointing in the opposite direction."

"Hey, I get it," he said with conviction. "It's hard to believe someone you loved lied to you like this."

"And hard to believe he might have been involved in

something illegal," she added, her tone dismal. "If this turns out to be true, do you think I have any hope of keeping Jace?"

Man, what a question to ask. He thought to lie to her, but what good would that do. "Honestly?"

She nodded, her eyes filled with pain.

"Not if we find his biological parents, and they want him. In that case, I don't think you stand a chance."

"But if he was sold by his mother then surely I'll have a chance."

"Yes, then I think you might." He should stop right there, but she deserved the truth. "*If* you can prove you didn't know about it."

"Well, I didn't even know Todd when Jace was born, so that's easy to prove. But not knowing since I got involved with him?" She rubbed the back of her neck. "I don't see how I can prove that."

"Yeah, that's going to be tough. But I'd be glad to testify about your surprise, and how once you learned about it, you cooperated in finding out if it was true."

She gave him a pained stare. "Cooperate, right. All except giving Jace up right away."

"That's understandable, too. You have to be sure he's not Margo or Todd's biological son before disrupting his life and potentially traumatizing him."

"I don't know if I can even tell him about this." Tears wet her eyes. "My poor sweet little boy lost his mom. Then his dad. Now he has to learn they weren't actually his mom or dad, and he'll lose me, too. I...I..." She started crying, big tears running down her face, her body shaking with the anguish.

Life was so unfair. In so many ways. Good people like Kelsey suffering. A sweet boy suffering. Everything God could prevent but He allowed.

Why?

Devon had asked that question often enough in his job after seeing the ravages of drugs on families. He could never find an answer nor could he help those people, but maybe he could do something here. One thing was clear. He couldn't sit by and not offer comfort.

He pressed a hand on her shoulder to let her know he was there for her. Her body convulsed under her sobs. She swiveled and looked up at him. Her tear-streaked face took the last of his ability not to do more. He reached out and drew her into his arms.

"*Shh*," he said feeling at once awkward and at home as she settled against him.

He stroked her back in little circles like his mom did to him when he was a boy. She was the perfect example of a wonderful mother, and if she did this for him, he knew it would help Kelsey.

Her crying slowed, and she eased back. She swiped at her tears with an angry frenzy. "I shouldn't be crying like this. It says I believe I'm going to lose Jace, and I can't think like that. I have to believe God brought him into my life for a reason, and that He plans to keep Jace with me."

"We could pray together if you want."

She flashed him a surprised look.

"What? You don't think undercover agents pray? Let me tell you. It's a hard job, but without faith it could destroy a person."

"I guess I've run into so many cynical law enforcement officers that I didn't stop to think about faith in relation to your job. I didn't mean to offend you."

"Don't worry. No offense taken. My skin is far too thick for that." He smiled at her.

Her lips turned up in a sweet smile and tripped his pulse into gear. A strand of hair had dropped over her forehead, and he lifted his hand to brush it back, but an alarm sounded from her phone stopping him.

"That's for the meeting." She silenced the ringing. "You ready to meet our full team?"

"Looking forward to it." He stepped back to let her go first and offered a silent prayer for her since they'd been interrupted.

"Mind if we take the stairs?" she asked in the hallway. "When I'm in the lab, I need to get in as many steps as I can throughout the day."

"Sure," he said. "Do you spend more time in the lab or the field?"

"Lab more often than not. I'm called in on body retrievals and law enforcement delivers bones to me."

"It's a full-time job?" he asked, as he couldn't imagine her services were needed very often.

She opened the stairwell door. "You'd be surprised at how often bones are found. Most of the time they're animal bones, but it happens a lot. And there isn't a tremendous number of board-certified forensic anthropologists across the country."

He took the door so she could enter. "I assume you're board-certified."

"By the American Board of Forensic Anthropology. The field isn't licensed, but you can earn a certification." She jogged up the stairs at her usual rapid clip.

He started after her. "I've always wondered how easy it is to tell animal bones from human ones."

"For the most part, a trained person finds it very easy to tell," she called over her shoulder. "The biggest challenge is bones from bears. They're often difficult to distinguish from humans. Especially from their paws. Many of their bones have initially been mistaken for human by those who aren't forensic anthropologists."

He couldn't begin to imagine the knowledge she needed to possess to do her job, and he was even more impressed with her.

She reached the main floor and pulled open a heavy fire door before he could offer to help. She led him down a long hallway to the same glass-enclosed conference room where they'd met earlier that day. With all he'd learned about Kelsey already, it seemed like days since they'd met.

Three men and three women were already seated at the table, and they turned to look when he and Kelsey entered.

"Everyone," Kelsey announced as she strode to the long polished table. "This is Devon Dunbar, DEA Agent, and the guy who stopped Jace's abduction last night. Please introduce yourselves."

"I know I speak for everyone when I say we're all so thankful for what you did for Jace and Kelsey," Emory said. She still wore her white lab coat and sat close to a dark-haired man. Too close for a professional relationship in Devon's opinion.

"Blake Jenkins," the man said. "Former sheriff and now team investigator." He touched Emory's hand. "Also fiancé of this amazing woman."

"Congratulations on the engagement and job change," Devon said and meant it. He hated to lose a quality law enforcement officer to the private sector, but the man looked content and Devon wouldn't begrudge anyone that.

Blake nodded. "I've heard good things about you from the Blackwell Tactical team in Cold Harbor. Gage and I have been friends since high school."

Small world. "I've known Alex Hamilton for years. Met Gage through him."

Blake gave a clipped nod, and Devon took it to mean that meant Blake had accepted him.

The man next to him stood and shoved out a large hand.

Redheaded with a close-cut beard, he was ruggedly dressed in tactical pants and a performance polo shirt, a favorite of law enforcement professionals. "Grady Houston. You want to shoot someone or blow them up, I'm your guy."

He didn't crack a smile, likely because this was a line he used all the time, but Devon laughed.

"Once you get to know him, you'll learn he means it, and then you won't laugh." The next woman sitting on the other side of the table chuckled, and Devon was struck with how perfectly straight her blond bangs were above large brown eyes. "Sierra Byrd. Trace evidence and fingerprint analysis."

"Good to meet you." Devon turned his attention to Maya seated next to Sierra, her striking blue eyes fixed on him. Since they'd already met, he nodded his greeting.

The man seated next to her had brown hair with a short beard and an intense focus. He wore jeans and a T-shirt that said *Prayer, world's largest wireless connection*. "Nick Thorn, computer cybercrimes."

"Nice to meet you," Devon said and took another look around the group, noting that Emory was the only one wearing a ring. Not surprising. The partner's workload likely took up all of their free time. Or in the case of Kelsey, Jace *and* her work.

"Go ahead and sit," Kelsey told him as she walked to the head of the table. "I know you're all wondering why we're here."

"Is it about last night?" Emory asked. "The attempt to take Jace, I mean?"

"Sort of. And before we get started, Nick, I would like to ask you to run a background check on Bruno Cruz. He's the man who grabbed Jace."

"I don't see this guy as being the mastermind behind the abduction," Devon offered. "He's not a thinker, but a take-orders kind of guy. My supervisor is following up on Detective Frost's interview with him, but I doubt Cruz will offer up the name of the person who ordered the abduction. I'll keep you updated on any progress on that front."

Nick gave a tight nod, but suspicion lingered in his gaze. Devon got it. He was going to have to prove himself to these people. He'd be doing the same thing in their position.

"Okay, moving on." Kelsey took a deep breath. "First, I wanted to mention that I hired Blackwell Tactical to provide protection for Jace until I know he's in the clear. Jackson Lockhart is already here, and Trey Sawyer will take night shift."

"Good thinking," Blake said. "This place is pretty secure, but if someone wanted to get in they could find a way. Sure, we'd likely know they breached security right away, but they could do some damage in a short time, and you can never be too careful."

She appreciated his support, but his comment unsettled her even more. She couldn't dwell on that. "Now, I don't know how to say this without coming right out with it, so that's what I'll do. It's come to my attention that Jace may not be Todd or Margo's biological child."

Sierra tilted her head, those straight bangs shifting. "Adopted?"

Tears glistened in Kelsey's eyes again, and she shook her head. "It's possible that Todd and Margo bought Jace through a child trafficking ring."

Sierra gasped.

Kelsey held up her hand. "I should say we have no proof of this, but there's also no evidence that Jace was born to either of them or adopted by them. My attorney started questioning their parentage when he noticed that Todd didn't take a deduction for Jace on our taxes. For a CPA, that's like a huge red flag. And then on top of that, the man who tried to take Jace last night is involved with a drug cartel that's also into child trafficking. Devon was watching the man, and that's how we learned about the potential connection."

"What about DNA?" Grady asked. "That's an easy and quick way to prove parentage."

"My team is running it now," Emory said, obviously figuring out who the samples belonged to.

"You checked all the avenues for adoption?" Nick asked. "It's not just through the State of Oregon but could've been a licensed private adoption agency or directly from the birth parent as an independent adoption with the assistance of an attorney. Or even from foreign countries."

"All of which are legitimate," Devon said. "And if he used any of these methods, I would have found legal adoption proceedings in my searches, but didn't."

"Still," Kelsey said. "I'd appreciate it, Nick, if you would do a deep dive on Todd and Margo to see if we've missed something."

Nick cocked his head, his focus fixed on Kelsey. "You may not like what I find."

"I know, but it has to be done." She took a long breath. "I can't have Jace taken away from me, and I fully intend to be armed with as much information as possible so I can stop that from happening."

"Oh, sweetie." Sierra squeezed Kelsey's hand. "I didn't even think about that aspect. Do you really think you might lose him?"

Kelsey took a deep breath and let it out slowly. "It's a strong possibility."

"Then we need to keep you both in our prayers," Sierra said looking around the table.

Her partners nodded their agreement.

"Thank you." Kelsey's voice broke, and she looked up at the ceiling, breathing in and out for a long moment.

"You can count on us," Maya said. "We're here for you in any way you need."

Devon wondered what it must feel like to have this kind of support. Sure, he had buddies at the agency who had his back on the job, but they didn't hang out much outside of work. He honestly didn't do much outside of work because he worked a lot. And he handled his issues alone. Could be why they still affected him so much.

"Do you still have Todd's computer?" Nick asked. "If so, I can look for files that could tell us something."

Kelsey dropped her gaze to Nick. "It's in our storage unit. I should have thought to grab it when I was there, but I'll go back for it."

Blake sat up straighter. "Do you want me to coordinate this investigation?"

"Absolutely." Kelsey smiled at him and then looked at Devon. "When our lab works all aspects of an investigation, Blake now coordinates the investigation so we keep everything on track. Means we'll need to report all of our findings to him."

"Duly noted." Devon wasn't used to having someone looking over his shoulder, but he could see the advantage to it and would cooperate.

Kelsey turned to the whiteboard and jotted down *hospital*. "Devon and I will visit the hospital where Jace's birth certificate claims he was born. A town called Rugged Point."

"That drive will take hours." Blake sat forward. "Why don't I call Gage, and ask if he'll send his helicopter for you?"

"Would you?" Kelsey asked.

"Of course he will." Emory smiled at her fiancé. "I've gotten to know Gage better, and I know he'll say yes."

"A helo would be perfect so I can be back in time for a

meeting I have late tonight." Devon was used to working his investigations on a budget and could easily get used to having such resources at his disposal.

"I'll call right now." Blake got up and stepped into the hallway.

Kelsey smiled, and Devon wished he was the one to give her a reason to smile instead of all the reasons he'd provided for her to be disappointed. "I've already served a warrant for all male children born on the same day as Jace's birthday along with a list of birth certificates applied for."

"You're assuming the birthdate is correct," Nick said.

"I am, but I made sure the warrant included a wider date range."

Kelsey looked at Nick. "Once we have a list of names for males born there, can you run background checks on the children to see if they are living with their birth parents?"

"Sure. And since the births are a matter of public record with the county, I'll get those records for you to compare with the hospital files in case they give you an incomplete file."

"Thank you." Kelsey wrote the names *Valerie and Zachary Moore* on the board. "My in-laws might know something, and I'll interview them after the hospital visit."

"We'll interview them," Devon said.

"Right. Yeah." She frowned. "So you all know, this is very time sensitive. Devon should report the situation with Jace to social services, but because we don't know definitively that he's not Margo or Todd's child, he's given me until the time the DNA comes in to figure this out before he'll report it."

"But that'll only be a day or so," Emory said. "Maybe less."

Grady eyed Devon, his gaze as deadly as any gun he might possess. "Seriously, man, can't you hold off longer?"

Devon didn't want to answer, but he had to. "If the DNA says he's not their child, and we haven't found they became his parents legally, then I have to report it." He held up a hand. "And before you think I want to do that to Kelsey or Jace, you're wrong. It's clear they love each other and seems like Jace would be best left with Kelsey. But that's not my decision to make."

"And please," Kelsey said. "Don't be upset with Devon. He has to do it. It's his job."

Maya muttered something under her breath and glared at him. He tried not to take offense at her or the others' attitudes as he would probably feel the same way if he was part of their team.

Shoving his phone into his pocket, Blake returned. "Helicopter's on its way. I can give you directions to the nearby helipad Blackwell uses."

Kelsey smiled, and Devon took a moment to enjoy it, because he suspected once they arrived in Rugged Point, everything in her world was going to change.

6

Kelsey had been to Blackwell Tactical's compound only once before, but the compound had impressed her, and she was equally awestruck today as Cooper Ashcroft landed on the private helipad and quickly escorted them to a black SUV.

Coop was well over six feet tall, all muscles, and had deep brown hair and intense dark brown—almost black—eyes. Kelsey knew all of the Blackwell team members were former military or law enforcement and had to leave their jobs due to an injury, but she didn't know his injury or where he served before coming here.

Devon opened the passenger door for her, and he got in the back.

Coop slid behind the wheel and nodded ahead at a small village with false storefronts. "We use our little town for urban tactical training."

"Looks like you have a training going on today." Devon's face was nearly pressed against the window, eyes wide, as he took in the town.

Kelsey knew this was a first-rate operation, but as a law

enforcement officer, Devon probably appreciated the quality even more.

"Yeah," Coop answered. "It's a mock hostage situation at the bank."

Dressed in riot gear, several officers approached the bank storefront, and in unison they turned with their guns and pointed them at the vehicle.

"They think we're part of the training." Coop laughed and waved them down. "Don't worry. We don't use live ammo."

He continued on down the road. "Training facility is on the right and next you'll see the cabins for the trainees."

"Alex told me about this place, but I thought he was exaggerating," Devon said, gawking at the setup. "He wasn't."

"Oh, right, yeah, I forgot you and Alex are friends." Coop looked in the rearview mirror. "He's got a group out in the woods right now doing tactical tracking, or we could check in with him."

"Maybe I'll catch him on the way back."

Coop drove past a group of unique cabins. "Team cabins. Gage's house is straight ahead."

"Could we stop at his place for a minute?" Kelsey asked. "I'd like to thank him for letting us use the helicopter and for freeing you up to fly it."

"Sure, why not?" Coop said. "I know he's home this morning."

He pulled up to a well-maintained ranch house, parked, and handed her the keys. "Gage will open the gate for you. Just call me when you're ready to head back. I have a baby girl at home, and I like to be there for her at night, so depending on the time, Riley might fly you back to Portland." He smiled broadly, and Kelsey liked how this big, tough guy sounded so smitten with his daughter.

He got out and so did they. Coop waved and jogged down the drive. Kelsey suspected he was racing home to stop in and see the daughter he was so in love with.

Kelsey went to the door and rang the bell. Devon stood beside her. She soon heard solid footsteps coming toward the door. It opened, and Gage faced them, a small baby with a button nose and fiery red hair in his arms.

Gage was nearly Coop's size, buff, with dark hair, and a warm smile. "Devon. Kelsey. I see Coop got you here okay."

"I'm sorry to interrupt." Kelsey nodded at the baby, dressed in a pink onesie. "But I wanted to stop by and thank you for the use of the helicopter and for providing a pilot."

"You're not interrupting. Evie here has been colicky, and I'm just giving Hannah a chance to take a nap."

There was nothing more endearing to Kelsey than a strong guy like Gage with a sweet baby in his arms, but *man*, one who was also letting his wife nap? Kelsey had always respected him, but he just went up another notch in her book.

"Congratulations, man." Devon offered his hand for a fist pump, and if Kelsey was right, a hint of jealousy lingered in his eyes.

"Thanks," Gage said beaming. "You guys want to come in for a minute?"

Kelsey waved her hand. "We just wanted to say thanks for the use of your helicopter and a pilot."

"No worries. I can't even imagine what you're going through." He shifted Evie closer and took her little hand in his. "You need the helo, it's yours. No questions asked. You got it."

"Thank you," Kelsey said, tears threatening over his kindness as she knew she couldn't afford that cost on top of paying for protection services. "Say hi to Hannah for me."

Gage nodded, and Evie started fussing. He lifted her

onto his shoulder and patted her back. "I'll unlock the gate from my office. Hope your interview goes well."

"Thank you." She went to the SUV, the house door closing behind them. "He sure seems happy."

Devon nodded, but he frowned.

"Did I say something wrong?" she asked as he opened the passenger door.

"No. Not at all. I'm glad he's doing so well."

Devon took the keys from her hand, obviously thinking he would drive. She didn't argue as she really didn't care who drove. She just wanted to get to the hospital and get some answers.

He crossed in front of the SUV and slipped behind the wheel. He adjusted the seat and got them moving.

The gate slid open, and he turned onto the rural road, his foot pressing down harder on the gas pedal than she would have liked for the winding road. She assumed he had mad driving skills from his SEAL days, but still, she'd be more comfortable at a lower speed. Not that she'd ask him to slow down. Not when he was letting her come along to the interview.

Maybe talking would keep her mind off his lead foot. "Seems like you were impressed with the compound. I am, but I know nothing about the things they do, so it wouldn't take much to impress me."

He nodded enthusiastically. "They're first-rate. I used to joke with Alex that I wanted to get injured so I could work with them and play with all their cool stuff. I didn't really mean it. I like my job just fine."

She shook her head. "I could never do what you do. I'd be terrified all the time."

"I won't lie and say I'm not afraid half the time. I am. Just learned as a SEAL how to manage it."

"Why did you choose to work for the DEA?"

"I saw a lot of guys get addicted to drugs in the navy. Great guys. Ruined their lives. I want to do my part in keeping drugs out of our country. If I have to be scared some of the time to do it, then that's what I'll do."

What an amazing attitude. "I admire that."

"Hey, before you put me on some sort of pedestal, you should know I also like the adrenaline rush of being on the edge of getting caught all the time. Reminds me of my SEAL days."

"Another job I don't know how anyone can do." She smiled at him. "But I'm thankful there are people like you who are willing to do it."

"You have a job that most people couldn't do."

"But there's no comparison. I don't risk my life. Unless you think working around creepy crawlies is risky." She laughed.

He locked gazes and smiled. A moment passed between them. An electrically charged moment. Shocked at her visceral reaction to him, she jerked her gaze away and made sure to keep looking out the window until he parked by the hospital.

She climbed out and breathed in the ocean air. She never expected to find a hospital with an ocean view, but on the way inside she watched the waves rolling in under the setting sun. Thankfully, she'd arranged for Ahn to transport Jace to and from his birthday party with Todd's parents tonight. She hated missing the party, especially when she could potentially lose him, but this hospital visit could give her the information she needed to ensure she was with him for all future birthdays.

She approached the contemporary structure with odd lines and angles and smaller buildings connected by glass breezeways sitting not more than a few hundred yards from the sand dunes. The exterior had been etched by sand over the years, and the inside revealed the facility's age—walls dull and faded, worn-out furniture, the air a combo of antiseptic and a musty ocean odor.

Devon identified himself to a receptionist, and they were quickly escorted to the hospital administrator's small office.

She was a middle-aged woman with leathery skin and too much makeup. She wore a black pantsuit with an aqua scarf at the neck. She stood and held out a hand covered in age spots. "Gloria Clark. Welcome."

They exchanged introductions.

"Please have a seat." She dropped into the black leather chair behind her desk.

Devon stood by a side chair, and once Kelsey sat, he did also. She was coming to learn he had impeccable manners that didn't at all go with the scruffy-looking guy she'd met last night. She had to admit to loving the contradictions in his personality. If she ever met his parents, Kelsey would compliment them in raising such a gentleman.

"How can I help you?" Gloria asked.

Devon took the warrant from his pocket and laid it on her desk. "We need this information immediately."

Gloria's penciled-in eyebrows rose, but she didn't speak as she extended her red nails toward the warrant. She unfolded the paper and seemed to read every word as it took her forever to look up. "What's this about?"

Devon sat calmly, not at all bothered by her question. "I'm afraid I'm not at liberty to say."

Gloria pursed her lips. "I understand your need for discretion, but if a scandal is about to hit my hospital I need to know about it."

"I can appreciate that," Devon said. "But my hands are tied. Now if you'll give me the information stated in the warrant, we won't waste any more of your time."

"I'm sure you know that I'll need to run this request past

our attorney." She glanced at her watch. "I doubt I can make that happen today."

Kelsey didn't like the way Gloria was stalling, and it was obvious by Devon's intake of air that he didn't either. Kelsey thought to plead with the woman, but on the helicopter ride Devon had asked her to let him handle the interview, and she'd agreed, so she clamped down on her lips to resist the urge to speak.

"We can do this one of two ways," he said, his tone as piercing as a bullet. "If a scandal results in relationship to my warrant request, I can put a positive spin on it for the press. Or if you insist on stonewalling the investigation, I can make sure reporters know that you failed to cooperate." He leaned back and propped a leg on his knee, looking relaxed and not at all bothered by her reticence. "Either way I get what I need. Your choice on how it goes down."

She glared at him. "Blackmail?"

"Of course not. I'm just presenting possible scenarios to you." He didn't move a muscle, and Kelsey could easily see him negotiating with a drug kingpin and getting his way.

Perhaps that was the former SEAL in him. She knew to become a SEAL he had to be nearly fearless and used to commanding respect so the bluffing of a small-town hospital administrator was nothing to him.

"Fine." Gloria snatched up her phone handset and dialed. She barked in commands to have the attorney come to her office, never once asking but assuming compliance with her orders. She hung up. "If you'll follow me, I'll take you to a conference room where you can wait while I review the warrant with counsel."

"Thank you, Ms. Clark," Devon said. "Your cooperation is noted."

"Coerced cooperation." She scowled and marched to the door.

Kelsey got up, and he gave her a quick smile. Not only was he good at this, he enjoyed it. She, on the other hand, did her best to avoid confrontation and would have handled the request much differently. But then, they wouldn't be heading down the dingy hall to a small conference room waiting for a ruling on the warrant.

Gloria opened the door and stood back to let them enter. Kelsey passed the woman and could feel the anger radiating from her.

"I'll send my assistant in with some water and coffee." Gloria spun on her heels to march away.

"That was uncomfortable." Kelsey sat at the far end of the table, already imagining the administrator returning with the report they needed. Hopefully the report would confirm Jace's birth to Margo at this hospital, making all of this ugly business go away.

"I'm sorry if I was the one who made it so, but when serving a warrant I often have to play hardball. And maybe with so many months on this undercover assignment, my finesse has disappeared." He sat next to her and released a smile that hit her right in the heart.

"Trust me," she said. "Your charm is quite intact right now."

His eyebrows shot up. "So you find me charming?"

"Yes, and handsome," she said without thinking.

His already-big eyes widened, and his smile vanished. He locked gazes with her, and the fact that he returned her interest radiated from his face. Kelsey had to admit enjoying the warmth traveling between them.

A young woman suddenly appeared at the door carrying a tray with a water pitcher, glasses, carafe, and mugs. "Ms. Clark asked me to bring this in to you."

"Thank you." Kelsey gave the woman props for not

having an attitude, but then maybe Gloria didn't tell her about Devon's demands.

"Appreciate it." Devon gave the young woman a devastatingly potent smile.

She stopped the tray midair for a moment, then quickly set it down and backed from the room while giving him a coy smile. Kelsey had no problem seeing why the young woman was smitten.

His smile was a megawatt number with the slightest of gap between his top teeth. Otherwise she would claim it the perfect smile.

She shook her head, smiling.

"What?" he asked.

"You are quite the charmer."

"Seriously, what?" His eyes narrowed.

She noticed the tiniest of lines between his eyes, but quickly snapped her gaze away before she fell prey to his charms, too. "The way you smiled at her. She didn't have a chance."

He shook his head. "It wasn't anything intentional. Just a thank you for the coffee."

Kelsey nodded, but wondered if he didn't know how good-looking he was. Or maybe he'd gotten what he'd wanted so many times because of his looks that he wasn't aware of turning on the charm.

He got up to pour steaming coffee into a serviceable white mug. "Want some?"

She shook her head. "If I drink coffee this late in the day, I'll be up all night, so I'll stick with water."

She reached for the pitcher, but he took hold before she could and tipped it over a glass, the ice clinking as it poured.

He set the glass in front of her and sat back down. "You should know this could be a long wait for nothing."

"How so?"

"The attorney might decide to fight the warrant."

"Is that likely?"

He lifted the mug to his full lips that she admired. "Happens more often than you might think."

"Then maybe we should have told her this is about a potentially stolen baby."

He shook his head. "We do that, and they'll close ranks even more. Which is why the warrant doesn't specify Jace or his supposed parents' names."

"Supposed. That sounds so bad." She shook her head. "How could I not know the man I was married to for two years was lying to me the entire time? I feel so dumb."

"Hey." Devon lifted a hand as if he planned to put it over hers then thought better of it and let it drop. "There's no way you could know."

"I should have been interested enough to look at our taxes."

"He was a CPA, for crying out loud. I'm suspicious by nature and even I wouldn't ask a CPA spouse about that."

"Thank you for trying to make me feel better." She smiled at him.

"I'm not. Just stating facts."

Footsteps sounded in the hallway, and they looked at the door. Gloria appeared, forehead furrowed, but she held a packet of papers. She crossed the room and slapped it on the table. "The information you demanded."

"Great." That smile that Devon used on the assistant made an appearance. "Thanks for your cooperation."

Gloria was totally immune to his charms, and she started to leave without a word.

"Hold up," Devon said. "I need to take a quick look to be sure this is actually the information I requested."

She sighed but stopped and glared down on him.

Devon studied the top page, then started flipping

through, pausing on one particular page. He set down the report then got a folded paper from one of his cargo pockets. "I'll also be needing the following information."

"Now come on," Gloria snapped. "You could have given me this at the same time."

"I didn't know if it would be necessary until I looked at the data."

"I'll be right back." She grabbed the paper then stormed from the room.

"What is it?" Kelsey asked after Gloria disappeared. "What's on the report?"

He turned to a page near the end with a heading of Birth Certificate Applications. He ran his finger down the page to the middle where it listed Todd, Margo, and Jace's names.

Kelsey shot him a shocked look. "So Jace *was* born here and they *are* his parents?"

Devon didn't answer but turned to another page titled Births. "They're not on this list so I asked for Jace's medical file."

"But what does this mean?"

"My guess?" he asked. "Though Jace wasn't born at the hospital someone on the staff sent in a request for a birth certificate and claimed he was. And if we're going to resolve this, we'll have to figure out why."

Kelsey's in-laws embraced her in the plush foyer of their house, and it wasn't hard for Devon to see they were fond of her. He could understand why. He could already tell she was a kind and compassionate woman who gave people the benefit of the doubt where he was suspicious of nearly everyone. Well, maybe she wasn't so trusting of men anymore. Not after the number her former husband did on her. He couldn't believe any man could lie to such an amazing woman like that. But he could believe that a man would do everything he could to remain married to her.

She pulled back, anxiety in those large eyes where he could read her every emotion. "Devon, meet Todd's parents, Valerie and Zachary Moore."

He took a quick look at the stylishly dressed fifty-something pair. The woman's hair was short and dark and her face narrow. The man had red hair cut close to the scalp, a goatee, and wide face. They were of similar height at around five foot eight and physically fit.

Kelsey gave them a tight smile. "This is Devon Dunbar, a DEA agent who has some questions for you."

Devon held out his hand, but Zachary gaped at him. "Drugs? Does this have to do with Todd?"

"Why don't we all sit down, and I'll explain," Kelsey said and stepped toward the back of the house without asking permission.

A tight scowl on his face, Zachary gestured for Devon to follow her. He found Kelsey in a large room with a roaring fire blazing in a gas fireplace. The room held two boxy white sofas with bright orange pillows and two black leather-and-chrome chairs. Soaring windows looked over a large yard, and the contemporary space seemed to fit the couple.

"Please, sit." Valerie pointed at a sofa where Kelsey perched on the edge of a cushion. "I'm sorry you had to miss our little party with Jace tonight, but I assume Ahn got him home okay."

"I wish I could've been here," Kelsey said. "And yes, Ahn arrived home safely."

Devon preferred to stand, but he wanted to put this couple at ease, so he sat next to Kelsey. Her knee was shaking in a nervous cadence, and if he was with anyone but her deceased husband's family, he might press a hand on her leg to stop it, but doing something so familiar in front of this pair might send the wrong message. Shoot, it might send the wrong message to her, too.

Valerie and Zachary sat on the other sofa with a narrow glass coffee table filling the space between the sofas.

"Now what's this all about?" Zachary asked, but it was more of a demand.

Kelsey clutched her hands together. "As you know, I am in the process of adopting Jace."

"Yes, of course." Valerie smiled. "Something we fully support."

"In the process, my attorney has come to question whether Jace is Todd's biological son."

Valerie's mouth dropped open.

"That's preposterous," Zachary said. "How can you even question that?"

"Other than a birth certificate, we've been unable to find any proof of his birth," Devon said.

"Really, and you call yourself a law enforcement officer." Zachary scoffed. "Just go to the hospital where he was born and request the records."

Under these conditions, Devon cut the man some slack for his rudeness. "We did, and the records don't exist."

Valerie gasped. "But of course they do."

"I'm sorry, Valerie," Kelsey said. "Devon is right. We found a request for his birth certificate but no birthing records for him and Margo."

Zachary crossed his arms. "Then they simply lost them. After all, they're a Podunk hospital in a Podunk town."

"Misplacing the records is always a possibility," Devon admitted. "But highly unlikely. Especially with electronic records."

"Did you see Margo when she was pregnant?" Kelsey asked warily.

"Yes, of course. They lived in Rugged Point so we didn't get over there often, and she didn't like to travel while pregnant. But yes, we saw her."

"In all stages of her pregnancy?"

"I mean...well...not in the later months. She couldn't travel, and Todd said she didn't want visitors."

"So how pregnant was she the last time you saw her?" Devon asked to clarify.

Valerie looked at her husband. "Five, six months?"

He gave a firm nod.

"And did you go to the hospital for the birth?"

They both shook their heads, and Devon saw a flicker of unease in the father's eyes.

"When did you first see Jace?" Kelsey asked.

"He was almost a week old by the time Margo felt up to having visitors," Valerie said. "We went to their house."

"Did Todd send you any pictures of Margo in her later stages of pregnancy or from the actual birth?" Devon asked.

Valerie shot her husband a questioning look. "Could it be true, do you think? Is Jace not Todd's son?"

Zachary lifted his shoulders into an even straighter line than the already good posture he'd displayed. "This is all just conjecture."

Valerie nipped her lip for a moment. "But remember when we asked for pictures? Todd kept saying he'd send them, but he never did. Claimed he was just too busy."

That sounded an awful lot like the fabricated stories Kelsey mentioned that Todd told to keep her from adopting Jace.

Zachary took his wife's hands, but looked at Kelsey. "It's easy enough to find out, right? You could have your DNA person run tests."

Kelsey nodded, and Devon waited for her to admit that

they were already running them, but she didn't. He waited, wondering why she wouldn't tell them.

"Then you have our permission to run them," Zachary said.

Kelsey nodded, though Devon knew she didn't need their permission. She was just trying to make this easier on the couple, proving again what a kind person she was.

Devon had no additional questions for the pair, and he started to rise.

Zachary held out a hand stilling him. "You're not leaving before you tell us what a DEA agent has to do with this."

Devon had hoped the guy wouldn't ask since Devon couldn't share details, and this man seemed like the kind of person who would press for them. And Devon didn't want to mention the near abduction either. That was Kelsey's story to tell if she wanted to.

"I can't discuss my investigation," he said, dropping back down on the cushion. "But suffice it to say, Jace's parentage came up in the course of it."

"Was Todd into drugs?" Zachary asked.

"What?" Kelsey gaped at him. "No. Of course not."

"But..."

Devon held up a hand. "My investigation goes beyond drugs into other areas, so please don't assume anything."

Zachary crossed his arms. "We wouldn't have to if you would give us details."

"I apologize for not being able to do so." Devon got up because this conversation was going nowhere.

Kelsey came to her feet, slowly and with a cautious gaze.

"Do you know what all of this is about?" Valerie asked her.

"Not all of it, no."

Valerie shot to her feet and clutched Kelsey's arm. "Please tell me you won't destroy my son's reputation."

Kelsey took a long breath and locked her gaze on the older woman. "I'll do everything within my power to be sure that doesn't happen, but if Todd lied about Jace's parentage, I'm not sure I can stop it."

Valerie pulled her hand free and fired a combative look at Kelsey. "You know we can fight Jace's adoption."

Devon took a step closer to Kelsey. "Are you threatening Kelsey?"

"No, no...of course not. No. I'm...it's just..." Valerie wrung her hands. "I don't know what to do here, and I can't bear the thought that Todd might have lied to all of us. Jace might not be our grandson. How does one come to grips with something like that?"

Kelsey patted Valerie's shoulder.

"Trust me—I know exactly what you are feeling." Her voice cracked.

"We should get going," Devon said.

Valerie grabbed Kelsey's hand again. "You'll keep us informed."

Kelsey nodded. "If I can."

Devon started out of the room, and then paused to wait for Kelsey as he was afraid Valerie might try to keep her there.

On the front porch, Kelsey whooshed out a long breath, dragged in another, and sagged against a thick metal column.

"I'm sorry that was so hard for you," Devon said, wanting to comfort her with more than words, but not letting himself do so.

"Yeah, it was hard." She fixed her gaze on him. "But what will be even harder is if they decide I've betrayed them and speak against the adoption."

"But it's looking like Jace isn't their biological grandson, and they may not have any standing in the matter."

"Maybe not legally, but they're influential people, and they could sway the outcome for me." She wrapped her arms around her stomach. "So can you please keep that in mind going forward?"

He nodded, but honestly, that couldn't influence his investigation. He had to follow the clues wherever they led, even if it meant this couple made it hard for this very special woman to keep custody of the boy she loved.

7

While Devon jogged around front of his truck, Kelsey took a moment to offer a prayer for Valerie and Zachary. And for Jace and that she could keep custody of him. Feeling a smidgen of calm after the contentious conversation, she opened her eyes to see Devon grip the wheel and turn the key.

"We need to go back to the storage unit," she said, hoping her tone sounded as confident as he seemed to be all the time.

He glanced at her. "For the computer?"

"Yeah, that, but your question to my in-laws made me remember a box of pictures I saw there. They might show us something that could help."

"Sounds like a plan." He shifted into gear and had them back at the unit in no time.

She slid out and turned the key in the lock, her unease ramping up as she pulled up the garage-style door. She hadn't looked at these files before today, and now she was going to go through them a second time. It felt wrong somehow.

"Everything okay?" Devon asked

She shook her head. "I feel like I'm invading Todd's privacy."

"*I* should be feeling that way, but you? You were married to him for two years and have every right to look through his belongings."

"Yeah, but they were belongings he kept from me. He didn't want me to see them."

"True, but it has to be done if you want to keep Jace."

"I know, and I will do it. It's just disturbing."

"Do you want me to check them out while you wait in the truck?"

She shook her head. "I don't run away from my challenges."

"That's my girl." He grinned at her.

What? She wasn't his girl. Not hardly. She should point that out to him, but oddly enough she liked hearing him say it.

But she wouldn't let it distract her. She marched inside and went straight to a computer in the corner. "Would you mind putting this in your truck while I find the pictures again?"

"Glad to." He picked up the machine and carried it out the door.

She went to a box where she thought she'd seen pictures and lifted out a large shoebox. She took out the first few pictures of Jace as a precious toddler and heard Devon return.

Jace's chubby face and legs melted her mother's heart on the spot. She wished she'd known him then and had been able to cuddle him and help raise him into the child he was now. But at least Todd had done a good job of that as Jace was an amazing boy.

She held out a picture of Jace smiling for the camera, four shiny new teeth in his mouth. "Wasn't he adorable?"

Devon smiled and nodded. "I don't get why Todd couldn't have shared pictures like this with you."

"Maybe he thought I would ask for birth photos, and he couldn't produce those." She retrieved an older box and continued through the pictures, tears lingering just behind her eyes as she worked her way to the earliest pictures. She perched on a short stack of boxes and lifted out the newborn photos.

Devon peered over her shoulder. "These were definitely taken at home, not the hospital."

"Yeah," was all Kelsey could say as this was another item that pointed to Todd not being Jace's father. She flipped the picture over to look at the date stamped on the back. "One week after his birthdate."

Devon tapped a photo of Margo. "And Margo doesn't look like she's recently given birth. Unless she starved herself during the pregnancy."

Kelsey should be paying attention to all of the details that were proving her husband was a liar, but she was more interested in the way she felt with Devon's arm lifted over her shoulder, and his breath on her neck. She liked the warm feeling enveloping her. Liked it too much. She shoved the photos back in the box, hoping he would back off, and he did.

She took out the next few and flipped through them. Some were taken by a third party of Todd, Margo, and Jace. The love and joy on their faces over an event she missed in her son's young life hurt as much as the lie.

"When did Margo die?" Devon asked.

That question brought things into perspective for Kelsey, and she shut down the ache of not knowing Jace as a baby. "Jace was around a year and a half old when she died. Todd had been alone for about a year when I met him, and we only dated for six months before getting married. I suppose we should've dated longer, but if all of this is true, he was already lying to me, so I don't suppose more time would have mattered."

Devon didn't respond, so she kept going through the pictures, not noting anything of interest. She put the shoebox back where she found it and lifted out a smaller box, the contents shifting as she did.

She opened it to find a pair of old iPhones and a charger. She put the lid back on the box and started to return it to the stack.

"Wait," Devon said. "Those are early model iPhones. Looks like a 5s. I had one about the time Jace was born. These could contain important information, and we need to look at them."

"I didn't think of that." She felt the excitement of a potential lead. "We can drop these off with Nick so he can take an image and then share any pertinent information."

Devon shook his head, a smile on his face. "What's it like to have experts in every area that a crime investigator might need at your beck and call who can give you information that would take me days to get through my channels?"

"I guess I haven't really thought much about it," she replied honestly. "I've never been involved in an investigation with personal stakes. But yeah...I can see how it *is* an incredible advantage, and I shouldn't take it for granted."

He gave a firm nod. "What about the phone he had when he died?"

"The mugger took it."

He frowned. "Anything else you think we should look at here?"

"What about the boxes of baby clothes? Maybe they kept a hospital bracelet or baby book with more details. Or even a T-shirt or onesie with the hospital's name."

"Sounds like we should take a look." He led the way to

the other side of the unit where they'd set aside the boxes of clothing on their first visit. He flipped up the flaps and started holding up then setting items on another box. Onesies, undershirts, tiny jeans, sleep sacks, and swaddling blankets were soon all mounded up. Kelsey took one of the blankets and rubbed it over her cheek.

Devon looked at her, his eyes filled with compassion. "In addition to feeling like you're violating Todd's privacy, it must really be hard on you to see Jace's life before you knew him."

"It is, but yet, it's nice, too. I think when this is all over, I'm going to bring some of these things home for him. He might get a kick out of it."

"Um, sure."

"You don't think so?"

"I can only base it on what I would've liked when I was his age, and it would've been guns and sports equipment, not soft little baby blankets." He grinned.

She chuckled. "Yeah, you might be right. Jace isn't into guns, but Legos and almost anything you can build with."

"I loved Legos, too. My mom still has mine, and my nieces and nephews play with them. It's also possible I build a few things with them when I'm over there."

"So you're a little boy at heart."

"You know it." He laughed. "Most guys are, aren't they?"

"Hmm," she said. "Todd was pretty serious. Numbers and spreadsheets. He spent a lot of time with Jace but didn't play much."

Devon frowned as if he didn't understand that kind of guy. Or maybe he didn't understand how she could have fallen for such a reserved man. She didn't really understand it either. She wasn't an overly adventurous type. Sure, archeology digs fascinated her, but she didn't like risky things like hang gliding or parachuting.

They say opposites attract, yet Todd was more similar to her than dissimilar. She'd wondered after their marriage had settled into a predictable pattern if she'd been more attracted to having a son than being married to Todd. Not that she didn't love him. She did. But in a safe kind of way. Not like he was her one true love—the kind she'd read about or saw in movies.

Now, Devon was definitely her opposite, and there definitely was attraction. Way too much to be good for her.

She grabbed a few photos, then tucked the box and blanket under her arm. "Let's get the phones to Nick, and then we can start researching the information we got from Gloria."

Devon stepped back so she could get through the aisle, and still, she brushed against his side, raising her awareness of him even more.

Stop it. Just stop it.

She exited the building, vowing to keep a lid on these crazy emotions before she found herself falling for this man she knew nothing about. For all she knew, he could have his own agenda and be lying to her just like Todd. She could never survive a relationship like that again.

Devon expected Kelsey would want to head straight to her lab so they could review the lists from Gloria in private, but Kelsey wanted to check in with Jace first. She sat with Jace while he ate his dinner at the kitchen counter, and love for her stepson poured from her expressions and actions.

Devon took a moment to look around her home. The open kitchen faced a great room with a beige sectional and a stone fireplace with a large TV mounted above. A plush navy blue rug covered the dark wood floor on that end of the room, and a large dining table and chairs sat on the other end.

Her choice in frilly clothing didn't extend to her home décor. It all looked comfortable and homey, like you could come by for a visit, kick off your shoes, and then not want to leave. He knew she would be a good hostess, making her guests feel welcome as she'd done when they'd arrived tonight.

He turned back to the trio. The nanny, a plump woman with gray hair and kind eyes smiled at Jace. How could you not smile at the kid? He was downright adorable. He had big brown eyes, dark hair that was messed up at the top, a wide smile, tons of freckles, and pudgy bare feet sticking out of jeans.

He suddenly looked up at Devon wide-eyed. "You're really a cop?"

"Law enforcement officer," Kelsey corrected.

"Same thing, right?" He took a bite of a chicken nugget.

"Sort of," Devon said. "And yes. That's what I do for a living."

Jace swallowed. "Do you have a gun?"

Devon nodded, but was thankful he'd put on a light jacket or he thought the kid might ask to hold it.

"Now? Here?" He gaped at Devon.

Devon nodded again. Kelsey and the nanny scowled, so he moved on. "What do you want to be when you grow up?"

"Don't know. Maybe a cop." Jace shoved the rest of his chicken nugget into his mouth and chewed. "Mom says I can be whatever I want."

"She's right."

"I like to dig in the dirt. Maybe I'll do what she does. Or build buildings. Lots of buildings. Zillions of them." He spread his arms wide. "Big ones. Really big ones. Bigger than this one." He dipped a fry into ketchup and pushed it into his mouth to chew thoughtfully.

Devon liked the boy's enthusiasm. "That sounds like a fun job."

"So does being a cop. Shooting bad guys."

Kelsey's deepening frown said she didn't want him to talk about shooting people, but he couldn't leave Jace with the wrong impression. "Being a law enforcement officer is much more than shooting guys. In fact, we do our best not to have to shoot anyone."

He tilted his head, his eyes narrowing. "You do? Why? I'd shoot my gun all the time."

"Because, Mr. Nosey." Kelsey tweaked Jace's nose. "When you shoot someone, they get hurt and sometimes they die."

His smile disappeared. "Like Dad."

"Yes. Like your dad."

He looked up at Devon, his gaze searching for something. "But you'd never shoot a good guy like my dad, right?"

"Right," Devon said and hoped he never had to shoot a good person who found themselves on the wrong side of the law.

"You'd protect people like him."

"I would."

Jace nodded and grabbed another nugget, dipping it in the ketchup until the red sauce covered most of the crispy breading.

"Okay, bud." Kelsey stood. "You need to finish your dinner, and Devon and I have to go to my lab."

He swallowed and focused on Devon again. "She doesn't let me go in there, but I know there are bones. People's bones."

She bent to kiss him on the head and then hug him. He grabbed onto her and left a big ketchup stain on her shoulder. Devon didn't know her well, but he suspected when she discovered it, she wouldn't care. She might even wear the stain as a badge of motherhood. He'd never met a woman who seemed so suited for the job. Well, maybe except his own mom. She totally rocked being a mom.

Kelsey set off down the hallway, taking out her phone on the way, but he had no idea who she was calling.

"Blake, good," she said as she pressed her fingers on the elevator's print reader. "Can you meet me in my lab? I want to give you an update on my day."

Right. Blake. They had to keep him informed so he could coordinate the investigation.

She finished her call and boarded the elevator. "Blake will be joining us."

Devon nodded and didn't honestly know how he felt about that. Blake wouldn't be part of this team if he wasn't a top-notch investigator. Having him on board was a good thing, but Devon was used to keeping investigative details close to the vest. Maybe his reluctance also had to do with the fact that he'd enjoyed his time alone with Kelsey today, and he wanted it to continue.

The elevator doors slid open in the basement, and she started down the brightly lit hallway. She sped to her lab like she was eager to start work. Or maybe she just didn't know how to move at an average person's pace.

"You really love this stuff, don't you?" he asked. "The bones I mean."

She nodded and unlocked the door. "I find it all interesting. I'm a science geek at heart, so that makes sense. But mostly I love helping bring closure to families desperate for any news on their missing loved ones."

"Yeah, I can see that about you." He stepped into the large room behind her and got the same unsettled feeling as the first time he visited her lab. "I have to admit it kind of creeps me out. The bones and all. I mean, that's a *person* laying on the table."

She shrugged. "I get that a lot. But think of it this way. I may work with the dead, but I do what I do for the living. To help innocent families who lost so much at the hands of violence find peace."

"Oh, I get that part. That's why I got into law enforcement. To stop the drugs and violence." He shook his head. "In a way we have the same job."

"And horrific hours." She frowned and tipped her head in a pensive gaze. "I sure hope a judge isn't going to hold that against me. Or what I do. I mean you're freaked out by all of this, and you're this big tough guy who I suspect doesn't freak out over much."

"Bees," he said before thinking.

"What?"

"I'm afraid of bees. Have been since I was a kid and got stung three times," he added, feeling like he needed to explain.

"That's understandable."

"But irrational. I know it. You know it." He scrubbed a hand over his face. "And honestly, I'm embarrassed. Not sure why I even told you."

She met his gaze, her expression soft. "I'm glad you did. Makes you more approachable."

"I'm approachable."

"Um…yeah…sure, but you have this air of confidence that makes it harder. It's an unapproachable confidence I find in most law enforcement professionals."

"You need it to stay alive. I mean, a suspect isn't going to respond to me asking, 'pretty please will you stop breaking the law and let me put handcuffs on you.'"

She held up a hand. "I'm not criticizing, just saying it makes you a little less accessible."

"Sorry," he said, as he was overreacting. "With the way LEOs are under scrutiny right now, we can get kind of defensive."

"I totally get it." She smiled. "As I said before, I'm appreciative of what you do."

He returned her smile. "I never knew I was thankful for what you do, but now that I see the details of your job, the law enforcement community is blessed to have you on our side."

"My pleasure." A genuine smile lit her face.

His heart raced at that amazing smile that was just for him.

An undercurrent of attraction ebbed around them, and he didn't want it to end. In fact, he wanted more. To explore it. But even if he was looking for a woman in his life right now, what kind of an agent was he if he got involved with the woman who he should still be suspicious of? Not a very good one, that was for sure.

The door clicked open, and Devon heaved a sigh. She tilted her head, watching him, but he wasn't about to explain his relief over the interruption.

Blake stepped in. His gaze went from one to the other. "Am I interrupting something?"

"No," they both said quickly.

"No," Kelsey said again. "Let's grab a seat at the table, and we can review the day."

Blake took a chair by the small conference table in the corner opposite her desk, and Devon waited for Kelsey to sit before turning a chair and straddling it.

Kelsey brought Blake up to speed on the birth report conflicting with the requested birth certificates.

Blake frowned. "Sounds like the hospital employee in charge of the records falsified the birth."

"Jace isn't the only one." Kelsey got out the report and

laid it in front of Blake then tapped two additional names. "We're going to follow up on these as we suspect the children were sold, too."

Blake looked up from the report. "How do you plan to do that?"

"Nick is running one of his famous algorithms to gather information on the children. But we're also going to do a manual search online."

"I suggest interviewing these parents." Blake frowned. "But not yet. If these parents bought their children, I doubt they'll tell you anything, and you don't want them to know you're on to them until you have more proof."

"Agreed," Devon said. "We'll hold off on those interviews for now."

Blake took a long breath. "Anything else I need to know to keep things moving forward?"

"We found a pair of old phones in Todd's storage unit," Devon said. "They're an iPhone model that came out around the time that Jace was born. Nick's imaging them now, and hopefully they'll contain information to help us move forward."

Kelsey folded her hands on the table. "That's our day in a nutshell."

"Let me follow up with the others to see if they've made progress today. I'll get back to you." Blake got up.

"Thanks, Blake," Kelsey said. "I'm so glad you joined our team."

Looking embarrassed at the compliment, he gave a sharp nod and strode out of the room.

Devon liked this guy and was appreciative of his assistance. In fact, Devon liked all of the Veritas partners. Especially the one sitting across from him.

8

Devon had left the morning drizzle behind, and the Veritas security guard, Pete escorted him to their elevator and up to the fifth-floor condo tower. Devon had planned to meet Kelsey in the lobby so they could begin their day, but she texted telling him she was running late and that Pete would bring him to her condo.

Devon knocked on the door, and Jackson opened it, his gaze checking Devon out before going up and down the hallway.

"Catch you later." Pete saluted Jackson, and yawning from his night shift, he strode down the hall.

Jackson stepped back, his focus still laser intense. "Kelsey said she's expecting you, so come in."

Devon had met Jackson through Alex but knew little about Jackson except that he was a former Green Beret. That's all Devon needed to know—this guy was well-qualified for the job of protecting Jace. Jackson secured the door and double-checked it.

Jace came running into the room and smiled up at Devon. The innocent excitement of a child happy to see him melted Devon's heart.

"Hi." Jace's grin widened.

"Hey, bud." Devon had the urge to ruffle the adorable boy's hair, but didn't know how that would be received by Jace or Kelsey, so Devon shoved his hands into his pockets.

Jace stuck out his hand to Devon. "C'mon. I have something to show you."

Devon took the soft little hand, surprised at how much he enjoyed the trust Jace was placing in him. He was so used to having to earn trust that he'd forgotten how children innately trusted people until they learned otherwise. He hated to think this little boy would have to experience such a thing in his life, but like every child, he eventually would.

Jace tugged Devon down a hallway.

"Mom, Devon is here." Jace's excitement bounced off the walls.

"I'll be right out," Kelsey yelled from a room further down the hallway.

"She spilled orange juice on her shirt and had to change," Jace informed him. "And she takes a *really* long time to choose her clothes."

And every second of that time was worth it in Devon's book, as the result was spectacular. "I guess she just likes to look nice."

"And smell nice. Girl stuff." Jace plugged his freckled nose.

"Yeah, girl stuff," Devon said and could easily conjure up the flowery scent of her perfume and couldn't wait to see her.

Jace pulled Devon into a room with a twin-size bed holding a blue-and-orange comforter covered with a variety of robots. The curtains were made from matching fabric, and his walls held giant robot cutouts.

He let go of Devon's hand and ran to a cardboard conglomeration in the corner. "This is WALL-E's house. I made it." He scooped up an orange robot that Devon recognized from the Disney movie he'd seen several years ago with one of his nephews. "He likes it. I even made a mom."

He shoved WALL-E into Devon's hand and brought out a robot made from a toilet paper tube. He frowned. "WALL-E doesn't have a dad. He wants one. And a brother. So do I. But Mom says I have to have a dad to have a brother. No fair."

Devon hated to see the boy's pain, especially knowing that Devon could soon have to report his suspicious parentage to social services and be responsible for taking the boy away from Kelsey.

Father, please work this out. Don't let Jace suffer any more. He's already had too much pain in his young life. Please let this be the time You hear me and respond with a yes. Please.

"They live in the same house and their own rooms." He lifted his little shoulders in pride.

Devon squatted by the house and opened the taped-on doors to look inside. "Sounds like you thought of everything."

"Uh-huh. I like to build."

Devon heard footsteps coming down the hallway so he stood.

"Tape and cardboard are Jace's best friends," Kelsey said as she stepped into the room.

Devon ran his gaze over her, the wait worth every moment not only in getting to know Jace more, but seeing the striking outfit Kelsey had chosen. She wore a black skirt with large white polka dots paired with a solid black blouse gathered on her upper arms. And pointy black shoes with spiky heels brought her eye-to-eye with him. She was so incredibly feminine. Soft with all the curves and a fashion sense he'd only seen on TV and in movies. And a style that was totally at odds with the unnerving field she worked in.

He couldn't begin to imagine her digging in the dirt and unearthing a body. But he knew she did so. Her lab proved that.

She met his gaze, and a sweet blush stole over her face. "Sorry about the delay."

"No problem. Jace told me about the orange juice."

"Did he mention that a little boy who wasn't supposed to be running inside bumped into me and upended my glass?"

Devon glanced at Jace. "Ah, no, that he didn't tell me."

"Sorry," he said and bolted for Kelsey to hug her. "I didn't mean to do it."

"I know you didn't." She wrapped her arms around him and kissed the top of his head. "And what did you learn?"

"Not to run inside."

She brushed his hair from his forehead, pure love consuming her face. Devon could only begin to imagine what that kind of love would feel like coming from her. Powerful, that he was sure of.

"Remember that, okay?" She kept her gaze locked on Jace.

He gave a serious nod.

"Good." She smiled. "Now, Agent Dunbar and I need to go to work."

"Aw, do you have to?" His lower lip came out in a cute pout. "I wanted to play robots with him."

"Maybe another time," Devon said, and when Kelsey frowned, he realized he shouldn't have said anything about another time without asking her first. There might be this sizzling connection between the two of them, but he didn't know if she was interested in pursuing anything with him. He didn't like it, but he didn't take it personally. She was still reeling from what Todd had done to her—and nothing was resolved yet with Jace.

So why did Devon want to change that? Especially when he was still smarting from Tara's brutal rejection?

Kelsey's phone chimed, and she pulled it from her skirt pocket. "A text from Nick. He found something important on the old phones from the storage unit."

Devon nodded and tried to control his enthusiasm for a potential lead. He'd been an agent long enough to know that few leads actually took them straight to the suspect they sought. They were more likely not to pan out or only give him enough information to point him in the general direction of the actual answer.

Kelsey gathered Jace into a hug. "I'm going to miss you bunches."

"Aw, Mom." He squirmed and pushed free to glance up at Devon. "I'm not a baby anymore."

"You're right." She looked so sad that Devon wanted to hold her hand and assure her everything would be all right. "But you'll always be my baby."

Still looking at Devon, Jace shook his head, looking so grown-up, and yet, a child at the same time that Devon couldn't look away from the boy.

"Okay, I get it. Let you grow up." Kelsey laughed. "I might be really late tonight, but I'll check in with you later."

"I'm going to build a deck and a sandbox for WALL-E." He dropped to the floor by the robot house and grabbed a piece of cardboard and scissors.

"See you later, Jace," Devon said.

His surprised gaze flashed up to Devon. "Really, you're gonna come back?"

Devon hated getting Jace's hopes up when Devon might never see the boy again, but he also couldn't dash them to the ground. "I could stop in with your mom. You never know."

He smiled widely, his little nose wrinkling. "Cool."

Kelsey left the room, and Devon exited behind her.

"I'm leaving, Ahn," she called out to the nanny who was drinking tea in the kitchen.

Ahn bowed her head. "Have a blessed day."

Kelsey marched over to Jackson by the door. "I'll be gone all day. Call me if you need me."

"Understood." He held up his hand, opened the door, and checked the hallway. He turned and gave Kelsey a firm nod then stood back.

"Later, man," Devon said as he passed the powerhouse of a guy.

In the hallway, Kelsey met Devon's gaze. "Jace really wants you to think he's a big boy."

"Yeah, I got that."

"He's desperate for a male role model, and he doesn't hide it very well. Nick and Grady help, but I know Jace wants something more permanent. Breaks my heart." She pressed her fingers on the elevator reader. "If we find out he was taken from his biological parents, I can't see how any judge would leave him with me, and honestly, he deserves a father."

Devon wanted to say something to comfort her, but what could he say?

She rested against the elevator wall and patted her hair that she'd swept up in the back with a sparkly clip, showing off her slender neck. "How did it go with the drug kingpin you were meeting last night?"

He was thankful for the question that brought him back to a topic he could do something about. "Went off without a hitch and my cover's still intact. For now anyway. I'll meet up with the guy while wearing a wire as often as needed until we can be sure I'm in the clear. Or until we bring down the trafficking ring."

Her full lips covered in a coral lipstick dipped in a frown. "Do you really think they're somehow connected to Jace?"

"I do, but I have nothing to prove my theory. Just that it would be a big coincidence to have a guy working for a trafficking ring try to take your son if there's no connection. And I don't believe in coincidences."

"Yeah," she said sounding so sad. "Me, either."

The elevator dinged on the third floor, and she stepped out. "Nick shares this floor with Blake."

They passed the sign announcing Investigations to the back of the building and entered a room with dim lighting. The place felt more like a cave than the brightly lit labs he'd visited. Monitors sat on tables that ringed the walls and machines hummed on the floor beneath them. Devon figured this guy had far more computing power than anyone might need, but a top-notch cyber expert like Nick probably needed every bit of it.

"Nick likes things dark for some reason that he has failed to explain to us," Kelsey said, her voice raised. "But then we don't often understand the way his computer geek brain works."

"I heard that," Nick called out from behind an open door on the far side of the room.

Kelsey chuckled and stepped into what Devon thought served as Nick's office. He sat behind a desk with multiple monitors covered in sticky notes in all colors, but predominantly blue. His posture was perfect, his chest broad, and Devon figured the guy pumped iron on a regular basis to stay so fit.

Devon looked around the rest of the room, a chaos of computer parts stacked everywhere.

Kelsey grinned at Nick. "I wanted you to hear me."

"I know. Still hurts." He mocked a knife to the chest then burst out laughing.

Kelsey's smile widened, and Devon loved seeing the lighthearted woman in front of him. He could easily imagine how fun she could be when she wasn't worried about losing Jace. And surprisingly, Devon wanted to see her laugh and find joy in her son. To see Jace return the happiness. They both deserved it so much.

"So about the phones," Nick said, all business now. "One belonged to Todd, the other to Margo. No surprise there. But I was pleasantly surprised to find texts and pictures still in the files I recovered. Of course, the texts stopped with Margo when she died, but Todd's went on for another year until he probably bought a new phone."

Kelsey's smile evaporated. "I'm guessing since you called us down here, that you found something suspicious in the texts or pictures?"

"No. Just wanted you to know what was on them." He handed each of them a thick packet of papers. "I printed everything for you to review. I didn't see anything odd, but you never know. These things could mean something later on in the investigation."

Kelsey held the papers like she might a dirty diaper and dropped them on the desk. "I can't look at this. It feels like spying on Todd."

"I'll review it all," Devon offered, glad for once to be able to do something to help her. "But maybe you should take the packet. If at a later date you decide to look at them, you'll have a copy."

She shook her head hard, a tendril of hair coming free from her clip and dangling by her ear. "I won't change my mind. I promise you that."

Devon watched her carefully, but she firmed her stance and lifted her chin. He wished she would look at the files. There might not be anything to help with the investigation, but they could hold something to help her get over her trust issues. Still, that was personal, and Devon wouldn't press her any further.

"Anyway," Nick said drawing them back. "That's not why I asked you to stop by. I found something interesting in Snapchat."

"Snapchat?" Devon gaped at the man. "But how? Those pictures disappear in less than ten seconds. That's the whole point behind the app, right? Share a picture or conversation and then it's gone. So how can you have located anything there?"

"See, that's what people count on, but they don't know what guys with mad skills can do." A cocky smile slid across Nick's mouth. "The files aren't really gone. At least not in the short term. The phone deletes the file, but performs no wipe function such as overwriting the old messages. They remain until they're overwritten by the natural function of hard drive memory space. On most phones, that's a long time."

Devon didn't understand all of that, but as long as Nick did, that was the only important thing. "And what do these messages say?"

"See for yourself." Nick handed over another pile of papers and sat back with a satisfied grin.

Devon scanned the messages. His mouth fell open, and he stared at Nick. "Todd's conversation with the guy who sold Jace to him."

"Oh." Kelsey's face paled. "Oh, my. He…" She grabbed the edge of the desk and wobbled.

Nick quickly wheeled a chair over to her and urged her into it. His tight expression held concern for his partner.

"So it's true then." She gripped the chair's arms, her fingers turning white. "Todd got Jace under illegal circumstances and some poor mother lost her baby."

Nick's shoulders tensed. "I'm afraid so."

"I didn't know Todd. Not at all. And I still married him." She balled up the papers and threw them across the room. "How could I fall for him? Just how?" She buried her face in her hands and started crying.

Devon started to lift a hand to comfort her, but Nick beat him to it by patting her arm. "Hey, Kels. You couldn't know. And shoot, maybe Todd didn't know the child had been taken from his mother. I mean, it doesn't say anything about that in the conversation."

She hiccupped and her tears soon stopped. She dropped her hands, her face tear streaked, but anger was lodged in her eyes. "Thanks for trying to cheer me up, but people don't sell people. Todd had to know that was wrong."

Nick tensed. "Yeah. You're right."

Devon didn't think it was healthy for Kelsey to continue focusing on Todd's reprehensible behavior, and Devon hoped focusing on the investigation could stop that. "Can we get the name and contact information for the man Todd was chatting with?"

Nick's self-assured smile returned. "Already did."

Devon continued to be impressed by this guy's thorough work and nodded his approval. "So what's his name?"

"Simon Kilroy. Lives in El Paso."

Kelsey swiped at residual tears. "As in Texas?"

Nick nodded. "Moved from Rugged Point to El Paso three years ago. He's a portrait photographer in a mall studio. Mainly children. And before you ask, I wondered if that's how he discovered babies to take, but there haven't been any abductions reported in Rugged Point, so that wouldn't be the case."

"But he *could* find parents looking for another child that way," Devon suggested.

Kelsey shuddered. "It's so creepy that the man who works with kids sells them, too."

"True that." Nick lifted another smaller report. "Details on the guy."

Devon took the papers but looked at Kelsey. "We'll need to get to El Paso to interview him."

"Figured you'd want to do that," Nick said. "So I called in a favor with a buddy of mine who owns a small jet. The plane will be ready for you first thing in the morning, and the pilot will wait on the other end to bring you home the same day."

Devon gave a slow disbelieving shake of his head. "Seriously?"

"Yeah, man." Nick handed him yet another piece of paper with flight information. "Oren made a killing in Silicon Valley and moved out here to get away from the congestion of the valley. We met at a white hat hacker convention."

Devon looked up. "A what?"

"A conference for tech people who hack for good and not evil."

"So a computer superhero convention?" Kelsey teased. Her eyes were still wounded, but Devon was glad to see she recovered enough to joke with Nick.

Nick nodded and laughed.

Devon couldn't believe the way these experts kept surprising him. "You people move in circles that makes my head spin."

Nick sobered. "We have developed some amazing contacts over the years."

"Might those contacts help you figure out the identity of Jace's birth mother?" Devon asked.

Nick frowned. "I'm good at what I do, but I'm not sure I can pull that one off. I can try, though."

"Thanks for that." Kelsey smiled at her partner. "And for making these phones a priority."

Nick reached over to his inbox and grabbed a stack of paper clipped pages. "In my search, I made copies of the birth certificates for the children in question. These aren't official, but notice anything similar between their certs and Jace's?"

Devon took the papers and held them out so Kelsey could see. He read the details and shot Nick a look. "Dr. Harriman signed all three."

"Bingo." Nick's expression brightened. "Here's Harriman's contact information so you can interview him. And I took the liberty of arranging for Gage's helo to take you there this morning. Coop's waiting at the helipad for you now."

Devon didn't bother expressing his amazement again. He was beginning to think there was nothing the team couldn't overcome with the flick of a finger. "Keep us updated if you locate any other information. And as Kelsey said, thanks." Devon held out his hand for a fist bump.

"Anytime, man." Nick pounded his fist. "Now you do your thing and make sure Kelsey gets to keep our boy Jace."

Devon couldn't even begin to promise that he could deliver on that, so he kept his mouth shut and led the way to the door. In the hallway, he opened the stairwell door, and they quickly headed outside, jogging through spitting rain to his truck. He got them on the road and Kelsey called Jace's nanny to confirm she was available tomorrow and perhaps late into the night so they could travel to Texas.

Of course, she had to do that. She had people counting on her. Devon? Not so much. He didn't need to tell anyone his plans. No one would notice he was gone for the day. Okay, maybe his supervisor might, but that was work. His personal life was a different story. He'd never really noticed how alone he was until now. Until Kelsey. The thought made his gut hurt.

She hung up and shoved her phone into her large canvas purse.

He glanced at her to find her lips pursed. "Something wrong?"

"I was just thinking. If this interview turns out the way we think it will, we're going to end up ruining the lives of two families." She shook her head in sorrowful arcs. "I don't want to be responsible for that."

It was just like her to think of the other families who may have been involved in the trafficking ring when she was hurting herself. "They bought their children. That's not on us and makes them the responsible parties."

She swiveled to face him. "Yes, but their worlds are still going to be rocked. And the real victims here are the children. These parents will likely go to jail and the children will be reunited with their birth parents if the police can find them. And if not, then what? Foster care?" She sighed. "I just know how devastated I am, and they'll be even more so because these families have been together since the child's birth."

He knew he shouldn't, but he reached for her hand. As he closed his fingers around hers, a warm rush traveled through his body.

Surprise flashed on her face, her mouth falling open. She quickly snapped it closed, freed her hand, and wrapped her arms around her stomach. "I just don't get why God is allowing this to happen. Jace is as happy as he can be after losing Todd. He's loved so much, and I'm doing my best to raise him in faith."

"I totally understand that. I've questioned God's plan enough times myself." He desperately wanted to help her here. "I don't have an answer, but I can tell you what my mom always says."

She released her arms and cocked her head. "What's that?"

"When a crisis comes along, don't make quick judgments. Focus on God instead of the crisis. His ways are higher and wiser than our ways. If we believe that, then we have to trust that He's in control and it'll all work out for our good."

Kelsey sighed. "In theory that all sounds great. But this is *big. So* big and scary."

The pain in her voice cut him to the quick, and he wanted to whip out a solution and fix it. He was a fixer. That's what he did as a SEAL and in his current job. But no way he could fix this any more than he could fix the broken families he encountered in his job, and it made him mad.

He wanted to pound a fist into the wheel, but that wouldn't help Kelsey. Empathizing and telling her about his own issues might. "I've never faced such a life-altering challenge like this. Closest I came to it was when my fiancée, Tara, decided she didn't want to be with me." He paused to swallow down his residual anger so he didn't sound so bitter. "It doesn't even compare, but at the time I thought it was something I would never recover from."

Her posture perked up. "And now?"

"I'm still not sure," he admitted truthfully. "I mean, am I over being in love with her? Yeah, totally. Am I willing to put myself out there again? No, I don't think so. I can't stand the fact that I gave up the thing that mattered most to me when it wasn't necessary. I *do* get that if Tara was so flighty that I'm better off without her."

Kelsey slumped down on the seat again. "I can't imagine I could be better off without Jace."

"Yeah, it's a different thing all together. But still, I know God's got it in hand."

Kelsey leaned her head against the window and didn't

speak. Surprisingly, Devon wanted to keep talking because he wanted to find the right thing to say to make her feel better. But he didn't know what that was, so the best thing he could do for her right now was to pray. The very best thing.

9

Kelsey had ridden in a helicopter a few times. This one in particular—two times just this past year and again yesterday. But still, it took her most of the flight to adjust to the feeling of weightlessness that was different than flying in a big jet.

They hit an air pocket, and the helicopter bounced.

She clutched a nearby strap and glanced at Coop sitting tall and sure behind the controls, not seeming the least bit bothered about the bouncing.

"You worried?" Devon's voice came over her headset.

"Yes and no. I mean not really, but I'm not the calmest of flyers." She peered into his eyes and found a serene calm. "You, on the other hand, probably don't freak out at all."

"I have to admit this is pretty tame from some of the places I've flown into. Or jumped from."

She looked at the door and shook her head. "I can't even imagine jumping out."

"Maybe we should do it sometime. You'd love it if you tried it."

She shook her head so hard her hair threatened to come down so she stopped. "No way."

"We can jump tandem. I'll handle the controls, and you just come along for the ride."

She held up her hands. "No. No way."

He gave her a *we'll see* look, but she knew better. He had zero hope of getting her to leap out of any kind of aircraft with him. He was such a macho, tough guy. Not afraid of anything—except bees—and despite his trained instinct to react with physical strength, he'd been kind and caring toward her. His compassion for her plight was obvious in so many ways. The unusual mix of traits was attractive. *Very* attractive, and she suddenly wished she was free to pursue her interest in him.

She sighed.

"You okay?" he asked, that ongoing concern for her present in his voice.

She nodded and concentrated on not doing anything to draw his attention for the rest of the flight or the drive to Dr. Harriman's office. She was better off focusing solely on figuring out who tried to abduct Jace so Devon could return to his life and she wouldn't be tempted by those compelling eyes.

They entered Harriman's office, and she expected a bigger space, but his waiting area held only three chairs. The room was tidy and the furnishings plush. The reception desk was protected by a glass enclosure. A blond that Kelsey put in her late twenties sat behind it. She wore an Armani silk blouse. If there was one thing other than anthropology that Kelsey knew, it was fashion, and this blouse commanded a price of over six hundred dollars. And a four-thousand-dollar Dolce & Gabbana graffiti leather satchel sat on the desk next to her. Pricey for a receptionist. Shoot, pricey for anyone except the very wealthy. Maybe she was married to someone with money. Kelsey looked at her hand for a wedding ring, but found it empty.

She took one look at them, glanced at her computer, and frowned. "I know you don't have an appointment, but can I help you?"

Devon displayed his credentials and introduced himself. "We'd like to speak to Dr. Harriman."

"DEA, but I don't understand." She batted obviously false lashes at Devon. "Why would you want to speak to the doctor? He would never do anything illegal."

"I didn't say he did," Devon said, but his skeptical expression said that he found the receptionist's vigorous protest interesting.

Kelsey did, too. Could the young woman know about the birth certificates? Maybe she was involved somehow? Was that where she got the money for her expensive things?

"Please let him know we're here." Devon's tone brooked no argument.

She waved a hand with nails lacquered in a vibrant pink color. "He's with a patient."

Devon firmed his stance. "We'll wait."

"Then he'll be going to lunch, and he never misses lunch. Please tell me what this is about, and I'll have him call you back." She rested her nails on her chest and flashed Devon a tight smile.

He squared his shoulders. "He'll be missing lunch today."

"I can't—"

"Please tell him we're here." Devon said please, but his tone declared it wasn't optional. "I know he'll want to speak to us."

She huffed and slid the glass enclosure shut then got up and stomped off on designer heels.

"Odd reaction for a receptionist, right?" Kelsey asked.

Devon nodded. "Something's off."

"At first I thought she might have a thing for the doctor,

but look at the date on his diploma." She pointed at the framed certificate on the wall behind the desk. "He has to be in his sixties and I put her in her twenties."

"Doesn't mean anything."

"No, I suppose not, but..." She mocked a shudder.

"Yeah," he said, but turned away when the receptionist returned and slid the window open.

"Have a seat," she snapped. "He'll see you when he finishes with his patient."

They sat in comfy armchairs, the time ticking by, until the door next to the reception desk opened and a very pregnant woman waddled out. She was accompanied by a thin man with patchy gray hair. He wore black pants and white lab coat, and a stethoscope hung around his neck.

He stepped past the woman, who stopped to make an appointment, and stood looking down at them, his expression neutral. "My daughter said you wanted to see me."

"Ah, that explains it," Kelsey said without thinking.

Dr. Harriman tilted his head. "Explains?"

Embarrassed at speaking her thoughts aloud, Kelsey waved a hand. "Nothing."

Devon flashed his credentials, and introduced both of them as he came to his feet.

Harriman's high forehead furrowed. "What's this about?"

Kelsey expected him to be nervous, but he seemed calm and honestly confused. That would make sense, she supposed, even if he was involved in falsifying birth certificates as he could hardly expect a DEA agent to question that.

Devon stood. "You're going to want to discuss this in private."

Harriman eyed Devon for some time and suddenly spun. "Follow me."

They trailed him down a long hall and into an office holding pricey furniture. He sat behind a large walnut desk and gestured at two leather side chairs.

Devon made a point of looking around. "Nice office. Business must be good."

"I do okay." Harriman sat and steepled his fingers together on the organized desk. "Again, what's this about?"

Kelsey sat, but Devon took out the questionable birth certificates and laid them on the desk in front of the doctor.

Harriman grabbed a pair of silver reading glasses and propped them on the end of a long nose. He quickly looked up. "I pride myself in remembering every child I deliver, and I don't recognize the parents' names. Or the children's names for that matter."

"Odd when you're listed as the doctor," Devon said coolly.

He looked at the certificates again. "I see that, but there has to be some mistake."

"Perhaps you've forgotten," Kelsey suggested. "Maybe you could check your records."

"My daughter will clear this up for you." He snatched up the certificates and went to the door.

"Marissa," he yelled down the hallway. "Come here please."

The receptionist soon appeared at the door, her lips puckered as she looked up at her father.

He held out the pages Devon had given to him. "My name is on these birth certificates but I don't recognize the family names. Can you check the files to see if they were patients?"

Her face paled. "I...I..."

"What's wrong?"

"Nothing." She looked away. "I...I'll just go look them up." She fled from the doorway.

"She's hiding something," Kelsey said.

Harriman rubbed his chin and stared at her. "I beg your pardon."

"She acted weird when we told her who we were and that we were here to see you. And just now, she looked like she might pass out after glancing at the certificates."

"Did she?" Harriman seemed legitimately surprised as if he hadn't noticed. "I can't imagine why."

Kelsey wanted to fill him in on the falsified birth certificates, but that was Devon's job, and if he was remaining quiet about it, she should as well.

Shaking his head, Harriman took a seat. He opened his mouth to speak but the sound of rapid footsteps came down the hallway, and he snapped it closed.

"They're not your patients." Marissa set the certificates on the desk, and Kelsey noted her hand was trembling. "Either there's a mistake or you were at the hospital that day and the women's doctors couldn't make it so you delivered the babies."

"Wouldn't you still have records of that?" Devon asked.

"Typically, yes." Marissa looked at her father. "Do you want me to call the hospital to get to the bottom of it?"

"Yes, please." Harriman gave his daughter an earnest smile then stood and looked at Devon. "If you give me your card, I'll call you once the mix-up is resolved."

Devon pulled out a card and laid it on the desk. "See that you call the minute you learn anything, or I'll be back on your doorstep, and I'm sure you wouldn't want your patients to see a DEA agent questioning the two of you."

The thinly veiled threat caught Kelsey off guard, so the moment they stepped outside she told Devon as much. "Harriman seemed legitimately surprised to me."

"Something's up with the daughter."

"*That* I agree with. Do you think she had something to

do with putting his name on certificates without him knowing about it?"

"Yes."

"Maybe she's getting paid for the certificates. She's spending money that's for sure. Her outfit is designer, and her handbag cost like four thousand dollars."

Devon gaped at her. "No way. A purse can cost that much?" She nodded.

His head shaking, he opened the passenger door for her. "Dare I ask why you even know that?"

"I like clothes, so I keep up with fashion." She slid into the vehicle. "I don't buy the pricey things, but wait for knockoffs to show up in stores I can afford."

"I don't get fashion, but you do always look great." He ran his gaze over her, sincere approval telegraphing from his eyes as he locked onto hers.

The intensity of his interest left her stunned, and she didn't know how to respond. She quickly muttered her thanks then reached for the door handle.

He held it in place and gave her a pointed look.

Did he expect her to say something? To acknowledge this spark between them? She couldn't—wouldn't—and gave a quick shake of her head.

Hurt flashed in his eyes, and he closed the door.

She didn't give him a second to continue this personal conversation when he took his place behind the wheel. "The office was nice, too. Pricey furnishings. So maybe I'm off mark here and Dr. Harriman is behind the certificates and uses the money to spoil his daughter."

Devon put the key in the ignition, but his expression was pinched as if he didn't like Kelsey's choice of topic. She gave him a pointed look, hopefully communicating her wishes to move on.

"You might be right," he finally said. "But that doesn't explain Marissa's cagey behavior."

"True. I guess we just have to wait to hear back from them." Kelsey glanced at the office from their parking spot on the street. "But I hate to have Riley fly us back to Portland only to get a call from the doctor and have to come right back. Gage has been so good about letting us use the helicopter, and I don't want to abuse that."

"I wasn't thinking about leaving yet."

She looked at him. "What did you have in mind?"

"Hanging out here for a little while." A satisfied smile tipped up his full lips. "I think we spooked Marissa enough that she might just lead us to the person who falsified those birth certificates."

Kelsey wouldn't look at Devon as they sat in the SUV watching the doctor's office, and Devon had to believe it was because of that intense study he'd given her as she got into the vehicle. He shouldn't have done it. Should've had more control, but she got to him. Still, he didn't like this tension, and it was time for him to apologize. "I made you uncomfortable when you got in the SUV, didn't I?"

"Uncomfortable?" She tapped her chin as if she didn't really know. "Um…yeah…I guess that's the word."

"Sorry." He made sure his tone and his expression conveyed his sincerity. "I didn't mean to put you on the spot. I might be great at undercover work, but hiding my interest in you isn't something I'm excelling at." He glanced at her to gage her reaction and found her blushing, but he wouldn't leave it alone until he cleared the air. "And I *am* interested in you."

"Um...yeah...that was...ah..." She fanned her face. "Clear."

Her continued unease made his gut tighten. "Sounds like you don't like that thought very much."

"No, I don't mind. In fact, I feel the same way. It's just..." She moved her hand faster and took a long breath. "I'm not in a place to get involved, so I don't want to do anything to lead you on."

Was it the whole Todd thing or something else? "I should have asked if you were with someone else."

"No...I'm not. It's nothing like that." She lowered her hand and clenched it with the other one on her lap. "With everything up in the air about Jace, it's not a good time to start a relationship."

He tried not to stare at her, but he searched her expression to see if it was more than that. "And if that was resolved in your favor?"

"Then..." She let the word sit for a long moment. "Then I'd have to think long and hard about getting involved with someone. I mean, for Jace's sake, I don't want men coming and going in my life. You know, Jace getting attached to them, and then having the guy leave."

"I'm sure you would handle that well by not introducing a guy to Jace until you believe the guy would stick around."

"Yeah, you'd think I would because I never want to hurt Jace, but I don't know if I can trust my judgment anymore. So how am I supposed to know when or if the guy is trustworthy?" She nibbled on her lip and looked away. "I bought into Todd's lies hook, line, and sinker. What if another guy lies to me? I don't know if I could see through it...so I'm better off not getting involved at all."

"I'd never lie to you," he stated plainly and wondered why he kept heading in this direction when he wasn't open for a relationship either. Or did his inability to let this go mean he was finally letting go of the damage Tara had done? He knew Kelsey wouldn't hurt him the same way. At least not intentionally, but what if she started something with him and then all the junk from Todd sent her running in fear?

Could he risk being with another woman who might bail on him?

"I'd like to believe you, but..." She shrugged.

"But you can't."

"Exactly."

"It's okay. I get it." He worked hard to hide his disappointment because the last thing he wanted to do was to add to her distress and challenges.

He pinned his gaze on the building.

Kelsey's phone chimed. She got it out and frowned. "Nick's emailing his reports on Todd, Margo, and Cruz."

"That's good news, so why the frown?"

"I don't want to look at the report on Todd and Margo. Nick says he didn't uncover anything, but we still need to review the reports."

"I can do it for you."

She looked up for a moment then nodded. "I'm glad to have you do it. Thank you. You've really helped me with things related to Todd."

He shouldn't feel anything from her innocent comment, but a warm feeling settled in his heart at being able to help her. He looked away before he took them back to the personal realm.

He stared at the office and Marissa came charging out of the building. She rushed to a small black Mercedes. A black purse with white scribbling all over the leather hung from her arm.

He glanced at Kelsey. "That purse really cost four grand?"

"Around that, yeah."

He shook his head. "Our world is so messed up."

"At least the priorities for sure," Kelsey commented, but her gaze remained on Marissa.

Thankfully, they'd parked on the street so she didn't seem to notice them but whipped her Mercedes onto the road. He started the vehicle and gave her a head start so she wouldn't spot them. He merged into what little traffic there was on Rugged Point's main drag. She was racing well above the speed limit, dodging in and out of vehicles.

Kelsey leaned forward, watching out the front window. "She's in a hurry to get somewhere."

"That she is." Devon kept Marissa in sight, but when she turned into a neighborhood, he laid back even more.

"Hurry," Kelsey encouraged. "You don't want to lose her."

"I won't."

"Yeah, what am I saying? I'll bet you're an expert in covert surveillance."

"I am at that." He grinned at her, but she quickly looked away.

Marissa slowed and turned into a driveway. Devon pulled to the curb and watched as she rang the doorbell. A tall, well-built guy with copious tattoos answered, and she flung herself into his arms.

Kelsey leaned forward. "I wish I knew what they were saying."

"I can call the office and have someone get the property owner's info," Devon said not taking his eyes off the couple. "But Nick could probably get the information faster."

She got out her phone and requested the information from Nick. "Yeah, I can hold."

Marissa and the guy disappeared into the house. Devon shifted into park and turned off the engine.

Kelsey dug out a small notepad and pen from her purse. She suddenly started writing. "Okay, yeah. Text me what you find."

"Owner's name is Neal Zinzman. Get this. He works at Rugged Point Hospital in the records department." She met Devon's gaze, her interest in the latest news written in her rapt expression. "He could be the one falsifying the birth certificates."

Devon jerked the key from the ignition. "Then I need to talk to him."

"Now?"

"Now." He bolted across the street and heard Kelsey rushing to catch up to him. He slowed to make it easier for her, and when she came up next to him, he headed up the walkway.

Before he could knock, the front door opened. Marissa stepped out, took one look at them, and gasped. Neal's gaze narrowed as he assessed them.

"Hello, Marissa." Devon said. "Neal, we know you work at the hospital records office. Suppose you tell me what you're up to with these forged birth certificates, or I'll arrest you both now for kidnapping and selling babies."

10

"Tell him." Marissa nudged Neal, who looked darkly dangerous to Kelsey. His tattoos covered most of his visible body and were of sinister images, and he had several angry-looking scars on his wide face. He wore a ripped T-shirt, torn jeans, and was barefoot. She was surprised a hospital would hire him, but if he didn't work with patients, his appearance might not be a problem.

The neighbors arrived home, parking in their driveway and getting out to cast questioning looks their way.

Neal's face tightened and jerked a thumb over his shoulder. "Inside."

He whirled around and led them into the house.

Kelsey didn't know if the neighbors arrival or the flinty look Devon pinned on him made Neal act, but she was thankful he seemed ready to talk. Still, she had to admit Devon's intensity shocked her. She would never want him to look at her that way. If he did, she didn't know how she would respond.

She trailed Neal into the house that smelled like pizza. Soda cans and paper plates were piled on the living room table. Kelsey sat next to Devon on a leather couch that squeaked under pressure. Marissa perched on a matching chair, and Neal took a seat on the floor, scowling at them.

Surely Marissa wasn't romantically involved with this guy. His sloppy clothing and worn bachelor's furniture was as far from designer as anything could be. She waited for him to say something, but he didn't speak. Instead, he clamped his mouth closed.

"Doesn't make sense to bring us in here and then clam up," Devon said.

"I'm not saying a word." Neal glared at Devon, not seeming at all intimidated. "They'll kill me."

"Who's they?" Devon now sounded like a friend instead of an interrogator.

Neal mocked zipping his mouth shut and shook his head.

Marissa crossed her arms. "I'm not going to prison. I'll tell him. I think it's the Sotos Cartel."

Neal glared at her. "If it is, you just signed our death warrants."

She rolled her eyes. "Don't be so dramatic."

"How did I even hook up with you?" He shook his head. "I mean what would the rich little daddy's girl know about my world?"

She fired him a testy look. "My dad doesn't give me money, and I've told you to stop saying that. I have to make do with my measly income, which is less than yours, and maintaining my appearance isn't cheap."

Devon held up his hands. "Let's not get distracted. I'll need specifics. Who do you deal with in the cartel because I know it's not Sotos. He'd never get his hands dirty."

"I only worked with Neal, here," Marissa said. "But he's mentioned the name Frisco."

"Shut up, Marissa." Neal clenched his fists.

"How did you get connected with them?" Devon asked.

Neal shrugged.

Devon changed his focus to Marissa.

"Don't ask me. I don't know. I met Neal at a bar. We hit it off." She wrinkled her nose as if a foul smell had entered the room. "If you can believe it."

Kelsey wanted to say no she couldn't, but she wouldn't interrupt for that.

"I was complaining about my dad cutting me off." Marissa shook her head, her highlighted blond hair swinging over her shoulder. "Neal told me he had a way for me to make big bucks and no one would get hurt. I should never have listened to him and agreed to help him."

"It was all Daddy's fault for cutting her off." Neal scoffed. "She's twenty-six, and she still lives at home. She likes nice things and Daddy wouldn't buy them anymore. He made her get a job, or he said he'd throw her out." Neal snorted. "Like working for your dad is a real job."

She glared at him.

"Marissa," Devon said taking her attention. "Tell me what you did."

"Just forged my dad's signatures on phony birth certificates that Neal filed through the hospital to sell."

Kelsey couldn't believe that Marissa didn't sound like what she was doing was wrong when she'd ruined lives by her actions. "Did Neal also tell you that these certificates were for babies that were then sold to wealthy parents?"

She shot Neal an incredulous look. "You said no one would get hurt. It was just paper records. Did you really sell babies?"

"Of course not. I just sold the certificates like I said."

"But you knew why they wanted them, didn't you?" Devon asked.

"Actually, I thought they wanted them for their own children. You know, to make them U.S. citizens."

Kelsey didn't believe that. "No way. The parents' names wouldn't fit with their nationality."

"I figured they had that covered, too." He glared at them. "You know they can do anything they want. They make something seem innocent enough, and then once they get their hooks into you, you're theirs for life. And they don't tell you the whole story, either. Just the little bit you need to know at the time."

"Doesn't really matter what you know or didn't know," Devon said. "You'll still go away for accessory to aggravated kidnapping, which carries a life sentence."

"No, wait!" Marissa shot up in her chair. "We didn't know. Honest. Can't we testify against them, and you can cut us a deal?"

Neal grabbed Marissa's hand. "They'll kill us if we testify. I want to help, but I can't. I'd rather rot in prison then die the horrible deaths they inflict."

"Are you still providing birth certificates?" Devon asked.

She nodded. "We just did two more this past week."

"Have you turned them over yet?"

Neal shook his head. "I'm waiting for them to contact me."

"How do they do that?" Devon asked.

"A text on an untraceable phone. Thought I'd hear from Frisco today, but he hasn't texted yet."

"Then we wait for that text, and I go with you to your meet."

"No. No."

"Okay, we do it your way." Devon stood. "Get up. I'm hauling you in."

"Wait," Marissa cried out and looked at Neal. "Please. Please don't let this happen. We could testify and go into witness protection." She shifted her gaze to Devon. "Right?"

"Maybe. Depends on the quality of information you provide."

"We'll get you whatever you need, right, Neal?" She poked his arm. "Right?"

"Yeah, sure. Okay. But we do it my way."

Devon looked skeptical. "We'll see about that when the time comes. Now give me your phone."

"I can't give it to you."

"Why not?"

"They'll know."

"How?"

Neal crossed his arms. "I don't know. They just will."

"No way unless there's a tracker on your phone."

"I'd have Nick check out the phone, but he's in Portland," Kelsey said. "Gage has a computer expert on his team. We can take it to her."

Devon held out his hand and fixed a stare on Neal.

"Fine." He got up and went to a drawer in a small table and took out a cell phone.

Devon grabbed it from his hand as if Neal might chicken out. "You deal solely with this Frisco guy, and he gave you the phone?"

Neal nodded, his greasy hair not moving.

Devon pocketed the phone. "Does the name Simon Kilroy mean anything to you?"

"No."

Kelsey worked hard to hide her disappointment in his answer. "Think again. He was a photographer. Moved to El Paso."

"Nah, don't know him. But if he's involved in this he could work for the cartel. It's not like I know all of them." He gave a snide smile.

Devon gritted his teeth, and his focus intensified. "What about Rickey Vargas? Ever heard of him?"

"Yeah, heard of him. He's like a big gang leader in Portland, but I've never met him."

Kelsey had to assume this was the leader of the gang that Devon had infiltrated and was investigating for child trafficking.

"So you have no affiliation with him?" Devon asked.

Neal shook his head.

"What's Frisco's last name?"

Neal shrugged. "He never said, and when I asked, he clammed up."

Kelsey couldn't believe Neal would go into business with a guy when he didn't even know his full name. What was she thinking? She couldn't believe anyone would even go into business with a member of a notorious drug cartel. That was just plain foolish.

"How long have you had this side business going on?" Devon asked.

"Three years now," Neal said. "Maybe more."

Devon shifted his focus to Marissa. "Then how did you know the certs I brought in today were fake?"

"I didn't at first."

"But you still freaked out."

"I figured they had to be bogus ones or you wouldn't be asking about them."

Devon looked at Neal. "Anyone in your department doing this before you?"

He shrugged. "At least not that I know of."

"Did anyone abruptly quit working about the time you started providing the certificates?"

"Not that I remember."

"I want you to refresh your memory when you go to work tomorrow. Start asking discretely or get a look at employee files if you can."

Neal gaped at Devon. "I could get fired if they catch me

snooping at files."

"Then don't get caught." Devon stood. "Marissa, please don't tell your father about this until I tell you it's okay. The last thing Neal needs is for the DEA involvement to get back to Frisco."

She rolled her eyes. "Are you kidding? I'm never going to tell him."

"He's going to learn about it at some point, and it will be better coming from you."

"I'll be glad to wait on that." She pouted like a toddler.

Devon shifted his gaze to Neal. "You'll be hearing from me."

He gestured for Kelsey to exit before him, and she hurried out. On the way to the SUV, he kept looking around —for what she didn't know, but it raised her apprehension more. He opened her door, and once they were both seated, he called Alex Hamilton on speaker phone.

"Hey loser, that really you?" Alex laughed. "You fly here twice and don't stop in, I figure you don't know how to call."

"Things have been...well...urgent," Devon said. "Speaking of which, I need a favor. I'm in Rugged Point, and I need a computer expert to evaluate a cell phone for a tracking app. And I need it done like yesterday. I know you have someone on your team."

"Yeah, Eryn. She's right here. Let me ask if she's free."

Kelsey heard Alex pose the question, and a female responded, but she didn't hear what Eryn said.

"She'll do it if you can get here soon," Alex said. "Like put the pedal to the metal and don't stop for anything. I'll meet you at the gate and let you in."

"On my way." Devon ended the call and got the vehicle running.

Kelsey's heart was racing after their encounter with Neal, and she was grateful Blackwell was only ten miles away. She buckled her seat belt for what she suspected would be a fast and furious ride. She looked at him. "Thankfully we have Neal's phone so he has no way to report us to his contact, but do you think someone from the cartel was watching Neal's house?"

Devon shook his head. "I scoped it out. Trust me. No one was watching us."

She did trust his skills. As a former SEAL he would know if they were being watched.

"Still, there could be a tracer on the phone," he added. "And until we confirm that there isn't, it's important for us to get behind Blackwell's secured perimeter should they be watching the phone and come after us."

She glanced behind them. "You think they're tailing us?"

"No. If they weren't sitting on Neal's house, they couldn't respond to the tracer in real time and be close enough to put us in danger. But I'd rather err on the side of caution."

She heard his words and believed him, but her stomach clenched. When he swung onto Blackwell's fenced property, Kelsey exhaled deeply. A tall guy stood at the gate. Assuming it was Alex, Kelsey took a good look at him. He had curly brown hair with hints of red, and his eyes were a warm brown, too. He was leaner than the other guys she'd met on the team, but equally intense.

Devon pulled up to the gate and waved at Alex. He punched in a code, and the gate swung open.

"That's Alex." Devon pulled through and stopped on the other side.

Alex jerked open the back door and hopped in. "Hey, man. Good thing you needed a favor, or I'd never see you."

"That's my fault." Kelsey swiveled and introduced herself.

"Is that so?" Alex eyed her.

"I'm sure you know I hired your company to protect my

stepson, but maybe not the details." She explained about the near abduction and Devon's rescue.

"Good job in saving the kid." Alex clapped Devon on the shoulder.

Devon looked embarrassed at the compliment. "Where to?"

"Training center. Just follow the road." He shifted his gaze back to Kelsey. "So do you know yet why someone might want to abduct your stepson?"

She looked at Devon before sharing what might be confidential information.

"There's more to this than Jace," Devon said and told Alex about the trafficking ring.

"Seriously, this is going on in little Rugged Point?" Alex shook his head. "I like to think these small coastal towns are as crime free as they are picturesque, but guess not."

"You don't know the half of it," Devon said.

Kelsey hoped she never had to learn about all the things he witnessed on the job. She saw some pretty horrific things, too, but drug cartels were notoriously ruthless, so Devon's experiences with them and his missions as a SEAL had to take a toll on him.

She glanced at him and saw a fiercely tough, undefeated warrior. And yet, he was thoughtful and empathetic in spite of all of that. A caring man of faith. Under different circumstances, someone she would like to get to know. She suddenly wished he didn't have such a dangerous career. That he worked in a simple nine-to-five job without putting his life on the line. She doubted that would ever happen or that he would ever consider working in an office.

He pulled up to the large building that was the size of a gymnasium and parked out front. Alex hopped out and opened her door.

She smiled her thanks and started for the building. He

held that door for her, too. He and Devon were much like her male partners at Veritas. Gentlemen all the way. Even Nick the jokester was a true gentleman at heart.

Devon eyed Alex. "I thought once you got married you wouldn't try so hard to impress the ladies."

Alex rolled his eyes. "Excuse him. He's undercover so much he forgets what manners are."

Devon socked him in the arm on the way in.

"For what it's worth," she whispered to Devon. "You've been the perfect gentleman with me, and I think your manners are impeccable."

His face colored a tomato red, and he opened and closed his mouth as if he didn't know what to say. She loved being able to catch the very astute lawman off guard.

"What's wrong?" She grinned. "Never been accused of being a gentleman before?"

"Actually, no. I haven't." He smiled back at her, and a long heat-filled moment passed between them.

"Oh, I see," Alex said with a knowing smile as he passed them.

Devon snapped his focus to Alex. "See what?"

"You got it bad for the lady. No wonder you didn't want me opening her doors."

Kelsey expected Devon to argue, but he didn't say a word, and she glanced at him. He was looking straight ahead, but she got the sense that he wasn't the least bit annoyed with Alex's comment. She, on the other hand, didn't know how she felt about it.

Alex strode through a large room and disappeared through an open doorway in the back.

Kelsey took a quick look around the left side of the space boasting a large open area with tables and chairs set up in classroom style. The other side of the building looked like it was divided into smaller rooms and a hallway. They stepped into the room after Alex, and Eryn pushed out of the chair using the arms to lift up her obviously pregnant body.

"Eryn Sawyer." She held out her hand to Devon.

"Devon Dunbar."

She shook hands with Devon. "Hey, Kelsey. Sam raves about your team all the time. One day I'm going to get over there to check it out."

Samantha Willis was Blackwell's crime scene analyst and good friends with Emory so everyone at Veritas knew and respected her. Kelsey had worked investigations with Sam, too.

"You're always welcome to stop by," Kelsey said to Eryn.

Eryn nodded and flipped her long black hair over her shoulders. "So you have a phone for me to look at? I don't mean to push you, but I get tired these days and need a nap."

Devon handed her the phone, and she sat next to a large tool kit.

Kelsey took a seat next to Eryn. "Jackson told me you're due in a month."

"Thirty long days." She sighed. "Trey wants several more kids, but I can promise you, right now there's no way I'd commit to another one."

Kelsey had no idea what it was like to be pregnant, but she'd heard the last few months could be unbearable.

Eryn turned her attention to the phone, and Devon and Alex started catching up. She heard Alex say that his kids were adjusting well, but she had no idea what he meant.

"You have something in common with Kelsey," Devon said. "She's trying to adopt Jace, too."

She looked at Alex. "You're adopting?"

Alex nodded. "Zoey and Isaiah. Four and seven. My wife's sister passed away and Whitney has custody of them.

Not like a piece of paper matters. They're our kids no matter what."

"I feel the same way about Jace." She had slept very little last night, and her emotions rode right near the surface. Just mentioning Jace brought tears to her eyes. "But until all of this is resolved, I don't have the right to adopt him. If we find out he's been taken from his birth mother, I might lose him."

Eryn shifted, the effort seeming a challenge. "As a mother, I can't even imagine what you're going through."

"Thank you." Kelsey took a breath before those ever-present tears kicked in and changed the topic back to the investigation. "And thanks for looking at the phone when I know you'd rather be resting."

"No problem." Eryn tapped the phone. "It's clean, but I can put tracking software on it if you want me to."

Devon shook his head. "I just need to be sure the guy who gave this phone to our suspect can't track the location."

"If he bought the phone, tracking app or not, he'll have administrator privileges for the phone. So if he set up the account and turned on GPS, he has means to track it." She held up a hand. "And before you ask, GPS is disabled right now."

"So as long as it stays that way, we're good?" Devon asked.

"Yeah, I mean, the phone company could ping the phone, but he'd have to have someone in the phone company on his payroll to make that happen."

Devon frowned. "We're dealing with the Sotos Cartel here, so I wouldn't put it past them."

The phone vibrated on the table, and Eryn jumped. "Looks like you got a text."

She handed the phone to Devon. He glanced at it and shot to his feet. "Gotta go. Frisco wants to meet tonight."

11

"Relax," Devon told Neal and hiked up the baggy jeans he'd bought at a local thrift store to look more like a gangster than a law enforcement officer.

Neal fired off a testy look. "Easy for you to say. You're not the one whose neck is on the line here."

"Actually, we're both on the line here, but if you're jittery and jumpy, you're going to spook Frisco, and I don't have a chance of getting in with them. And that means you don't have a chance at witness protection."

Neal took a long breath and hissed it out while shaking out his arms and hands.

"And remember we have backup. Couldn't ask for a better team than Blackwell Tactical having your back." Alex and Coop had taken a stance in the woods, and if Frisco made a threatening move, they were instructed to take him down. And Sam waited at the road to follow Frisco when he departed.

Headlights shone at the end of the driveway, and Devon said a quick prayer for safety for both of them. The car cruised slowly up the drive of a vacant home they were instructed to go to, and Devon's adrenaline started flowing.

Neal said he'd never met Frisco here, but they'd never met at the same place twice, so that wasn't odd.

The headlights drew closer. Closer. Now shining in Devon's eyes. He squinted to see the car, a silver sedan of some sort, come to a stop directly in front of them.

Devon prepared himself to assume his Dillan Webb identity. Thankfully, he always carried Dillan's ID in his backpack.

Neal's phone rang. "Odd. It's the burner phone."

"Answer it," Devon instructed.

"Hello," he said into the phone. "Um, yeah...sorry about that. I shoulda told you I was bringing a buddy from Portland. He has a proposition for you that I think you'll want to hear."

Devon had to give Neal props. He didn't sound nervous at all, but confident and at ease.

"'Course I can vouch for him, and yeah, I get what the consequences will be if I screw you over." He hung up and let out a whoosh of air. "He bought it."

The driver's door opened, and the headlights went off. The fog lamps remained on so it wasn't totally dark, but Devon would have a hard time making out the details of Frisco's face. Likely his plan.

Short, but muscular, he swaggered toward them. Devon could see he was packing, and Devon wished he was strapped, too, but bringing a gun to a meet like this would be a huge mistake he wouldn't make. He flexed his fingers and released them to help stave off the adrenaline rush.

"Zinzman," Frisco said, a sucker stuck in his mouth that he shifted to the side. "This guy got a name?"

"Dillan Webb," Devon said, but didn't offer a hand in greeting as that would likely earn him a gun in the face.

"You know who I am?" Frisco asked around the lollipop.

Devon wondered if he was going to keep it in his mouth

all the time. "Naw, but we got something in common. We both work for Sotos."

"Is that right?" He sounded like he wanted to laugh.

Devon ran his hand over the back of his neck, making sure that Frisco got a good look at his bandage-free tattoo. "Yeah, man. I handle product for Rickey Vargas' gang in Portland."

Frisco eyed Devon and shifted his sucker to the other side. "You expect me to believe that just because of the ink on your arm?"

Devon wanted to snap back at the guy but forced calm into his tone. "'Course not, but check with your crew to see if they know my associates."

"Why would I want to do that?"

"'Cause we're always looking for ways to branch out, and I think this certificate thing is a good fit for us."

"You don't even know what we do with them."

"Don't I?"

"Never filled Zinzman here in. No way he could tell you."

"No offense to this guy, but he doesn't have the head for business that I have. He's happy to go along. Take orders. I'm more of a dig in, figure things out kinda guy."

"That so?"

"It's a fact." Devon slowly reached for his phone. "Tell you what. Why don't I make a call and introduce you to my associate?"

"Go ahead. Make the call." Frisco's words were eager but not his tone.

Not unexpected.

Devon pushed Rickey Vargas's number on his phone. "Rickey, hey, man, I got someone you'll want to meet. Name's Frisco. Works for Sotos out of Rugged Point. Has a nice side business going on."

"And why would I want to talk to him?" Rickey's notorious suspicion lingered in his tone.

"Thought maybe we should get in on it. Make some real coin on the side."

"I don't—"

"It's just one phone conversation. What do you have to lose?"

"I don't—"

"I'll put him on the phone." Devon shoved the phone into Frisco's hand and hoped he hadn't pushed it too much with Vargas.

"Sup?" Frisco asked and pulled out his sucker while he listened.

Devon concentrated on the man's face, trying to find any distinguishing feature or other tattoos, but he turned away before Devon could catch any details.

"I don't know you, man," Frisco snapped. "Not going to tell you diddly squat."

Sounded like Devon's attempt at matchmaking failed.

"Look, I gotta skate. Will talk to the big guy and get back to your guy here if we want to talk." Frisco shoved the phone at Devon.

He saw that Rickey had ended the call so he pocketed the cell.

"I'll get back to you through Neal if we want to talk business with you." Frisco shoved the sucker back in his mouth.

Devon knew better than to press his point right now. He shrugged. "Hey, whatever you decide." He stepped back to show that he wasn't trying to be part of their transaction.

Frisco shifted his focus to Neal. "You got my merchandise?"

Neal held out a manila envelope. Frisco opened it and shone his phone's light on the paper then flipped to the second one.

The sharp light illuminated the papers, but unfortunately didn't travel to Frisco's face.

"We good?" Neal asked.

"Not quite." Frisco tucked the certs back into the envelope. "You don't bring anyone to our meets ever again, you got that?"

Neal nodded.

"And just so you remember." Frisco shook the envelope. "We'll take these for free."

"Now wait a minute," Neal said.

Frisco shot forward and grabbed Neal around the neck. "You wanted to say something?"

"No," Neal eked out.

"I didn't think so." He released Neal with such force he stumbled backward. "We'll be in touch when we need the next ones, but you should know, your rate was just cut in half." He backed to his car and got in. The headlights came on again, blinding Devon for a moment.

"Thanks for nothing, man," Neal grumbled.

"I could say the same thing to you," Devon replied.

When Frisco reached the road, Devon grabbed the Blackwell communication device he'd placed in the hollow of a nearby tree. "Suspect departing. Armed and angry. Tail with extreme caution."

"Roger that," Sam said. "But next time I volunteer to tail a subject for you, don't make him angry."

Kelsey sat at the round table across from Zoey and Isaiah and next to Whitney. A *Sorry!* game board sat in the middle of the table with brightly colored tokens scattered across the board. The children were adorable and fun to be around, and Whitney had already shown how special she was. And not just special in the looks department, though Kelsey was jealous of Whitney's beautiful chocolate-colored hair that gleamed and curled softly when Kelsey's just frizzed in the rain. But beyond her beauty, Whitney had a heart for these children, and it was clear they loved her in return. And she'd been so welcoming when Kelsey had to remain behind.

But despite Whitney's hospitality and the kids' joy in the game, Kelsey couldn't concentrate. Not with Devon and Alex out in the dark meeting with a potential member of the Sotos Cartel.

"Go, Kelsey," Isaiah said. "It's your turn."

She blinked a few times and smiled at the young boy who had dishwater blond hair, a pale complexion, and a smattering of freckles on his nose. At ten, he was slender and gangly and she wondered what Jace would look like in a few years. Would she even be in his life then?

A sob threatened to escape, and she swallowed to stop it.

He frowned at her. "Are you gonna take your turn?"

"Sorry." She smiled at the boy. "I kind of let my mind wander."

"Kinda?"

She picked up the dice and rolled a four, just what she needed to bring one of her pieces into the home space, free from attack.

"No fair," he complained and crossed his arms. "You're not even paying attention and you're winning."

"Now, Isaiah." Whitney looked at her nephew, communicating disappointment in her motherly gaze. "That wasn't very nice."

"I'm sorry, but..."

"No buts. If you can't be a good sport about this, then we'll put the game away."

"No. I wanna keep playing," four-year-old Zoey

protested. Her hair was the same blond as her brother, but in curly pigtails, and up until now she'd displayed a generous smile.

"It's okay, squirt. I can handle this. It's just a game." He sounded so mature, but Kelsey could see the hurt in his eyes.

"I'll do better," she promised. "It's only fair to all of you that I do."

The door swung open, and Devon entered followed by Alex. Kelsey jumped up to race across the room to Devon who was dressed similar to the first night they'd met. Just two days ago. Wow, only two days, and yet, it felt as if she'd known him for forever.

"Thank goodness you're back safe and sound." She didn't think but grabbed Devon in a hug. "I was so worried."

"Why worried?" Isaiah asked.

Drat. She shouldn't have said that.

"You've never seen Devon drive or you'd know why she was worried," Alex joked.

"He really *is* a bad driver," Kelsey added and didn't feel like she was lying as Devon drove far too fast for her liking.

"Hey, now." Devon grinned.

Isaiah's forehead creased. "You shouldn't ride with him, Alex."

"Yeah, I don't think I will again." Alex messed up Isaiah's hair, but Kelsey could see that the boy was still honestly worried.

She recognized that concern. She saw it on Jace's face often enough. Isaiah was worried about losing Alex like he'd lost his parents.

Oh, man, Jace was already worried. How on earth would he survive if she lost custody of him? He was just a boy who'd suffered so much loss. Could he recover from more?

A faceless man and woman taking his hand and leading

him away flashed into her brain. They were walking toward their car. Jace suddenly hung back, seeking her gaze with a pleading one of his own, but the couple dragged him forward. He tried to get free and pleaded to stay with her.

The thought stole her breath, and she felt a panic attack coming on. She couldn't lose it here in front of the kids. "I'm going outside for a minute."

She raced into the cool air, stars sparkling overhead in an unusual clear evening for this time of year. An ocean breeze drifted across the property, sending a chill over her body, but she didn't care. She needed to be out here. She gulped in the salty air. Exhaled. Gulped in more.

"Hey, hey." Devon's voice came from behind, and he was suddenly in front of her holding her by the arms and looking into her eyes. "What's wrong?"

"I saw how upset Isaiah was with the thought of Alex being in danger, and that made me think about how Jace would handle being taken away from me. I know I'll be devastated if it happens, but I don't matter. It's him. He'll be traumatized again over losing another parent."

"*If* that happens, and you don't know that it will, God will be with you both and it will all work out okay." He intensified his gaze. "I know that's easy for me to say because it doesn't impact me, but I care about you and Jace, and I have to believe God has a purpose in all of this."

She wouldn't touch the comment about caring about them. She couldn't and still keep her feelings to herself. "I wish I had your faith, but I have to admit mine disappeared at the mere thought of losing him."

He took her hands and looked her in the eye as the moon ducked behind heavy clouds. "God's working in the background, you'll see. It's just like with the gangsters I work with on my undercover work. They don't see everything going on in the background to keep me safe when I go in.

But my supervisor plans and chooses the right team to monitor me. And the tech team makes sure my equipment works. We have a code word that I simply have to utter for them to come running. Same with God. We don't see all of the things He's doing in our lives. All we have to do is utter that code word—pray—and He's there to comfort us or give us what we need."

"You're a very wise man, Devon Dunbar." A soft mist began falling, but she ignored it and kept her focus on him. "Especially for a man who looks like he just crawled out from under a rock."

"That bad, huh?" He finger-combed his scruffy hair.

"Not really. Now that I've seen Devon, I can see through Dillan to the real man."

He cleared his throat and his Adam's apple bobbed as he swallowed. "And tell me. Do you like what you see?"

She thought to ignore him, to move on, but he was being so sincere that he deserved an answer. "I do. So much."

Devon couldn't get Kelsey's comment out of his head. He didn't want to get it out. He loved the fact that she returned his attraction. Not that she was giving him any hint of it now. It disappeared the moment they headed back inside. Remained hidden through dinner at Alex's place while Riley conducted a preflight check on the helo before taking them back to Portland.

When Alex asked them to stay for dinner, at first, Devon didn't want to. He wanted to get back to Portland and keep working the investigation, but Alex seemed to really want him to get to know Whitney and his ready-made family, so Devon agreed. He now had to admit he was having a nice time.

Could be because of Kelsey. She carried a lot of the conversation, and despite the issues she was facing, seemed to be in a good mood. And of course, Devon was perfectly happy sitting back and watching her. He had to admit Alex was right. Devon was falling for her. But Alex didn't know Kelsey had sworn off men and that Devon had no chance with her even if he wanted one.

A knock sounded on the door, and Devon shot Alex a questioning look.

He shrugged and went to the door, Isaiah trailing after him. If they were anywhere other than this highly secured compound, an unexpected visitor might have Devon reaching for his sidearm, but this place was so secure it had to be a member of the team or one of their spouses at the door.

"What brings you here, Sam?" Alex asked.

Devon looked past Alex to Samantha Willis who stood in the misty night, her long blond hair pulled up in ponytail. She held an evidence bag in her hand. "Riley said Devon and Kelsey were still here, and I wanted to update them on my tail before they leave."

"You have a tail?" Isaiah asked.

Alex laughed and ruffled Isaiah's hair. "She meant she followed someone. Sometimes it's called tailing them."

"Mind if we talk outside?" Devon asked because he didn't want these kids to hear anything else about Sam's surveillance.

"No problem," she said.

Devon motioned for Kelsey to join him and then stepped out. The rain had stopped, and the clean air and the coastal breeze left the night smelling fresh.

"I know you're getting ready to leave so just a quick update." Sam tapped an evidence bag. "And I wanted to give you this to take back to Portland."

"Go ahead," Devon said.

"I tracked Frisco to a home in a nice Rugged Point neighborhood. I immediately called Eryn and had her search for the owner. Juan Gonzalez is the name on the property records."

"So not Frisco's place, then?" Kelsey asked as if thinking aloud.

"That's right. He stayed for about an hour, and then I followed him to another house." She handed a piece of paper to Devon with two addresses noted on the page. "First location is Gonzalez's place. Second one is owned by a Frisco Arroyo."

"Yes." Kelsey shot her hand up. "We have a last name for Frisco."

Sam nodded. "Looks like he's a regular family guy with a wife and two kids. No priors. Gonzalez doesn't have priors either, but he's not a family man. Twice divorced. He was accused of cheating both times, and the proceedings were pretty bitter. He has a child with each ex, and he's recently single."

Sam took a long breath and held up the evidence bag containing a sucker stick. "I got to thinking if they were dealing in forged birth certificates, they might be dealing with other forged documents and the property records could be for false identities. Arroyo tossed this stick out the window so I grabbed it for DNA."

"Great," Kelsey said enthusiastically. "I'll have Emory process it right away."

"Good work," Devon said, but actually hoped for more concrete evidence of the trafficking ring.

"I also *might* have gone back to Gonzalez's place, and when he went out, took a quick look around his house." Sam grinned.

Devon was grateful for her initiative even though she shouldn't have put herself at risk. "Find anything?"

She got out her phone, swiped the screen a few times and handed it to Devon. He took a good look at the photo of a birth certificate. "This isn't one of the certs that Neal gave to Arroyo or any that we've seen before."

"Exactly. But look at the doctor and the hospital. Eryn ran a search on the baby and parents. She found their social media account. The wife posted pictures during a pregnancy. Maybe she lost the baby or she faked the pregnancy, but either way, they claim this child was born to them."

"And you think if we look at hospital records, he won't show up."

"That's right. And if you swipe the phone, you'll see I found a bunch of certificates spanning several years."

Kelsey's eyes narrowed. "Why would Gonzalez be foolish enough to keep records of his crimes?"

"Blackmail," Sam said.

"Say what?" Kelsey blinked rapidly, her long lashes moving at hummingbird speed.

Sam pointed at her phone. "Keep swiping and you'll see photos of emails I found on his computer. He's blackmailing the families he provided with birth certificates. Threatening to expose them."

Kelsey shot Devon a shocked look. "Do you think someone was blackmailing Todd?"

He did. Without a doubt, he did.

12

Kelsey didn't like it when Devon drove so fast, but right now she wished he would speed even faster than his normal ten miles over the limit on their trip from the helipad to the Veritas Center, as she couldn't get back to Portland fast enough. Thankfully, Gage had put Sam and Alex on surveilling Arroyo and Gonzalez so Devon felt free to leave or they would still be in Cold Harbor. The Blackwell team had really stepped up for her and blessed her with their support.

God was looking out for her in so many ways. She got that, and yet, she didn't feel His presence. She felt abandoned when it came to Jace. Left alone to deal with the potential of losing Jace. Not because God wasn't there. She knew He was. At least in her brain. But her heart screamed that a loving God wouldn't want her to lose her son, and He surely wouldn't want to put Jace through the loss of another parent.

She thought about Devon's comment about not knowing what God was doing behind the scenes. She glanced at Devon where he sat sure and strong behind the wheel. She was thankful for him, too, and maybe she should listen to his advice. To accept that God was orchestrating things that she couldn't see or know. That He ultimately *did* have her best interest at heart.

Could she believe losing Jace was in her best interest? Could she trust God in such a painful thing?

She sighed.

Devon glanced at her. "You okay?"

"Sort of."

"You're thinking about Jace again." Devon was getting to know her pretty well if he knew that. Or maybe it was a guess.

"I was thinking about what you said about God doing things behind the scenes. Things I can't see."

"I was, too."

"Really?" She stiffened in wait for his reasoning in case he might be thinking things were even worse than she did.

He nodded. "I was wondering if He had a plan in bringing us together."

Not what she expected at all. "What do you mean?"

He gave her a long look before shifting his gaze back to the road. "It's no secret that there's an attraction between us. But what's the point, right? I mean you don't think you can trust a guy. I've got the whole issue with Tara."

"Exactly," she said firmly. "As you said, there's no point in putting us together for a romantic reason."

"Still, I gotta figure this attraction means something, and maybe we need to forget our past and see where it might go."

"No," she said and added a hard shake of her head as she didn't want to give him any false hope. "With this issue with Jace, I'm not even able to think about a romantic relationship, much less do something about it."

He glanced at her, and the pain in his eyes cut her to the

core. She'd hurt him, which was the last thing she wanted to do.

"This isn't personal," she said. "I would say the same thing to any guy."

He tightened his fingers around the wheel. "But it *is* personal. Very. No other guy is sitting here telling you he's developing feelings for you."

"Feelings?" She shot him a horrified look. "You didn't say anything about feelings. You just said attraction."

"Yeah, well, maybe it's more for me."

She couldn't believe this.

God, please, why this? Why now? I can't even...

"I'm sorry, Devon. I think you're a great guy. More than great. I like you and have come to respect you. But Jace...he has to come first, and that means we need to focus on the investigation. Not get sidetracked by feelings."

He gripped the wheel tighter, his fingers turning white, but he didn't speak. An urge to take his hand, to tell him she had feelings, too, hit her, but she pushed it away. Jace needed her to pay attention to the investigation and not lose focus. He had no one else to look out for him, and he was counting on her.

So she stared out the window for the remainder of the drive, watching the sparkling stars overhead and the tall trees pass on the side of the road. The cab was thick with tension and several times she almost turned to Devon to try to do a better job of explaining her stance and relieve some of the friction between them, but she couldn't open that discussion again, so she bit the inside of her mouth and kept quiet.

He parked in the Veritas lot, and she didn't linger in the tension-filled cab but charged for the door. By the time she got there, Pete had the door open and a ready smile on his face. He took a long look at her, then at Devon, and frowned.

Of course, as a former police officer, Pete wouldn't miss the strain between her and Devon.

Kelsey forced a smile to her lips and stepped into the overhead lights dimmed for the night.

"Let's get you signed in, Agent Dunbar," Pete said and led the way to the front desk.

As Devon completed the iPad form, Pete focused on her. "Young Mr. Jace was telling me you were in Cold Harbor. Working with the Blackwell team again?"

She nodded, but wouldn't divulge anything more, even if Pete had focused an interrogating stare on her that she was sure he'd once used on traffic stops. "I need to remember Jace hears everything I say and takes it in like a sponge."

"I'd forgotten about that, too, until the grandkids came along and the youngest one snitched on my cigar smoking." Pete grinned.

She *tsked*. "Since it's bad for you, I'm glad they ratted you out."

"Not you, too." He mocked affront and handed a visitor's badge to Devon.

"Yeah, me, too." She swatted a hand at him and led Devon to the elevator. "Pete's worked at the center for all five years we've been in business, and he's like family to all of us."

"Former LEO, am I right?"

"Portland Police Bureau. Retired." She stepped into the elevator and punched the number three. "Nick's had a few hours to look at Todd's computer again, so let's stop in and see if he found anything."

Devon glanced at his watch. "It's almost two. You think he's working?"

"I know he is. He's a night owl."

They fell silent, and she couldn't even look at Devon, but

she didn't have to see his face to know he was scowling at her avoidance. She could feel his discontent.

She was so thankful when they left the enclosed space of the elevator and entered Nick's domain. Star Wars music blared from his office, and he sat behind his desk. He looked up and lowered the music volume. "Glad you're back. I've got something you'll want to see."

Kelsey went around behind him, and Devon joined her, but she refused to acknowledge how good he smelled or how the heat from his body reminded her of their conversation in the truck.

Nick opened a folder on his computer. "I retrieved financial records and deleted emails from Todd's machine. He was being blackmailed, but not by Arroyo. By Kilroy. I'll print them out for you." He sent the files to the printer, and the machine whirred to life.

Devon grabbed the papers as the printer spit them out, and then handed them to Kelsey. "So we know Arroyo was engaged in blackmail. Now Kilroy? It seems like too much of a coincidence for him not to be connected to Arroyo."

"I agree," Nick said. "And I'm working on locating that connection, but I'm not finding much on a Frisco Arroyo in Rugged Point. At least not much before the purchase of his house a few years ago. I'm beginning to think Sam is right, and he created a new identity."

"Seems possible," Devon said.

Kelsey nodded her agreement. "Then hopefully DNA from the sucker stick will produce a CODIS match, and we'll find out who he really is." She didn't bother explaining that CODIS was the acronym for the FBI's Combined DNA Index System because both of them would know that.

"Were you able to review Neal or Marissa's financials?" Devon asked.

"I ran them, but they didn't deposit any of the cash from

the certificates, so there were only routine paychecks and withdrawals."

"Makes sense that they'd keep the cash separate to avoid leaving a trail." Devon frowned. "What about finding Jace's birth mother? Any progress on that?"

"Sorry, man." Nick leaned back in his chair and propped a leg on his knee. "That's not likely to pan out until we find whoever arranged to have him abducted."

"Thanks for trying," Kelsey said. "We're going to drop off the sucker with Emory now. Keep me updated on Arroyo."

Kelsey left his office, and in the hall looked at Devon. "DNA is on two. Mind if we take the stairs?"

"Glad to after sitting so much today." He pushed open the stairway door and held it for her. "I assume you asked Emory to meet us and not everyone here works twenty-four seven."

"I did, but honestly, we do work a lot. Which is why I have a live-in nanny." She started down the steps but then turned to look at him. "Do you think a judge would hold that against me? Working a lot, I mean."

"Could happen. But then again, I bet you pop in to see Jace throughout the day."

"I do. Every chance I get."

"The judge would have to understand that you have to work to support Jace. And most working parents don't have the luxury of having their child nearby like you do."

"Yeah. Yeah. Thanks for finding the positive." Glad they seemed to have found a comfortable footing again, she gave him a genuine smile.

"Keep smiling at me like that, and I'll work even harder to find positive thoughts." He met her gaze and held it.

Right. Back to that. Not on a comfortable footing at all. She should look away, but she felt drawn to him in a way she'd never experienced before. Something almost primal.

Like they were destined to be together and nothing could stop that.

Was Devon right? Did God have a purpose here beyond Devon figuring out what was going on with Jace?

Is that You, God? Is it?

Look at her. Not twenty minutes ago she told this man she would do nothing about her interest in him and here she was already questioning that decision. Stupid. Really stupid.

She broke the hold to jog down the stairs and into the hallway leading to the DNA lab. When she entered, Emory was seated at her desk, focused on her computer monitor, but stood immediately.

Emory moved to one of the lab tables and dropped her glasses from her head into place. "I've got everything ready to get started right away, but you know it's going to take a full day to process."

"I know."

"And longer if the steps are more complicated than usual."

"Steps?" Devon asked.

Emory nodded. "Several of them. I first have to extract the DNA from the stick then purify and quantify it. Then run the sample. On average, the whole process takes around twenty-four hours, but every sample is different, and I won't know what I'm up against until I get started." Emory took the evidence bag and signed Kelsey's log.

She desperately wanted to ask if Jace's test results were ready, but if she did, Devon would have to report them, so she kept her mouth shut. And after her earlier call to Emory, Kelsey knew she wouldn't offer the results until asked for. "Thanks for doing this in the middle of the night."

"No problem." Emory smiled. "Where are you off to next?"

"It's awful for me to admit this when you're working, but we're going to try to get a few hours' sleep. Normally, I wouldn't do it while you work, but we leave for El Paso first thing in the morning."

Emory waved a hand. "Don't worry about it. It's not like you can do anything here. You should sleep while you can."

Tears of gratitude formed in Kelsey's eyes, and she gave her friend a hug. "I owe you big time. Just name your price and it's yours."

Emory pulled back. "Nothing owed. Remember you came to my rescue when Cait was abducted."

Kelsey didn't think twice about helping her friend back then, and Kelsey knew Emory felt the same way. They all did. "Let me know if you get a match on this sample."

"Will do."

They left the lab and headed up to Kelsey's condo. She unlocked the deadbolt, but when she pushed on the door, the chain lock held firm.

Gun in hand, Trey took hold of the door.

"Sorry, I should have thought to call you," Kelsey said.

He unlocked the door and pulled it open. "No problem."

Kelsey smiled. "At least you proved that no one would get past you."

He nodded and holstered his gun. Once they were all inside the room with the door locked again, he introduced himself to Devon and shoved out his hand. As they shook, Kelsey gave Trey a once over. He was extremely tall and buff with a bright red head of hair, and Eryn's comment about him wanting a lot of children made her smile.

"Something funny?" he asked.

"Not funny, no, but cute. We saw Eryn in Cold Harbor. She commented on the fact that you wanted more kids, but right now she was too pregnant ever to commit to that."

He nodded. "I usually kid her about it, but she's been

really uncomfortable. Question is…how long will it take her to forget all about it and be so thrilled with our baby that I can bring up the subject again?" He grinned, his eyes lighting with humor.

Kelsey could see why Eryn fell for this handsome man. "Devon and I are going to catch a few hours of sleep before we have to leave for El Paso."

Trey arched an eyebrow.

What did he find so odd about her comment? A light-bulb went off in her head. "Oh, no. No. No way. Not together." Heat rushed over her face. "He'll get the guest room I assure you."

Trey held up his hands. "None of my business. In fact, I'm going to give you some privacy and step outside to call Eryn."

"No wait, we…" she called after him, but he continued out of the condo.

She looked at Devon and had no idea what to say. Maybe she should make light of the situation. "Kind of crazy that he thought we were a couple."

Devon didn't laugh but stepped closer. "*Is* it that crazy?"

"Well, yes, I mean—we just met."

"Trey doesn't know that. He's just going on what he sees."

"But surely he doesn't see anything that would lead him to believe…"

Heat flared in Devon's eyes, reminding her of the discussion in the truck, and she instantly knew what Trey was seeing between them. He was a very astute guy and Devon wasn't working very hard to hide his interest, but what about her? Was she transmitting the same emotions?

"It's really hard to ignore you when you look at me that way," he said.

The simple comment sent her stomach fluttering and a warm rush over her body.

"What way?" she whispered.

"Like I'm the only man you'd ever be interested in." His voice was deep and low, and she couldn't tear her gaze from his bottomless clear blue eyes as he cupped the side of her face.

"I..." She thought to deny it, but why? He was right. She'd even admitted as much to him earlier today.

He slid his hand along her cheek and around the back of her neck, her nerves firing at every spot his fingers grazed. He drew her closer. Leaned forward.

He was going to kiss her.

She should stop him, but she couldn't move a muscle or open her mouth to protest. She studied the contours of his face in the glow of the lamp, mesmerized by his unique bone structure. She had to touch him, and she did, running her finger along his solid jaw.

He paused in his descent, he gaze locking with hers for a long, intense moment. She was drawn to him like no other man, and she waited, breathless, as he slowly lowered his head and his lips touched hers. Warm, firm, insistent. His other hand went around her back, and he pulled her closer. Her skin tingled with his gentle touch.

She should argue. Do something to stop this. Instead, she went willingly and raised her arms around his neck to remove the space between them. She returned his kiss with an intensity she never knew she was capable of feeling. Her heart hammered in her chest. She lost track of time. Of place. And just was.

The sound of the door opening registered in her muddled brain.

She jerked back, and Trey, doorknob in his hand, apologized for disturbing them. Embarrassment burned a path up her neck and over her face as he backed out the door.

She didn't know what to do, but she couldn't stay here a moment longer. "I'm beat. Guest room is the last door on the left. Bedding is clean, and there are clean towels in the bathroom. Need anything else?"

Disappointment flashed on Devon's face, but he shook his head.

"Then I'll see you in the morning." She bolted from the room and could feel him watching her, but she wouldn't look back. Couldn't look back or she might find herself kissing him again, and with no future together, any additional contact could end up hurting them both.

Jace entertained them all at breakfast, joking and making Devon and the others laugh. Even Kelsey put on a good front, but when she didn't think anyone was watching her, she would glance at Devon and frown. One time he caught her touching her lips as if she was thinking about the kiss. And why wouldn't she? It was amazing. Nothing like he'd ever experienced before. But then she'd fled to her room like a killer was chasing her down, leaving him gawking after her like watching a train wreck.

Devon was out of practice in the dating world, but he didn't think he'd been too forward. Just honest about his feelings and showing her how he felt. He'd been that way with Tara, and she said she appreciated him being straightforward. But then, she was looking for a relationship when Kelsey made it clear that she was focused on the case and not on anything else. Plus, she was right—they just met. They really didn't know each other.

And still, he'd kissed her. That was dumb on so many

levels and probably disrespectful of her feelings. When he was alone with her, he would need to apologize.

"Okay, young man." Kelsey got up and pressed a kiss on Jace's forehead.

Never had Devon been jealous of a kid's forehead, but he was now.

"You listen to Ahn and Jackson," Kelsey continued. "I hope to be home for dinner, but if not, I'll FaceTime you, okay?"

He nodded and looked at Devon. "Are you coming for dinner?"

Devon didn't know how to respond and looked at Kelsey for direction.

"Devon's a busy man, and I'm sure he has something to do."

"Actually," he said when the kid's expression collapsed, "I'd like to come to dinner if we're back."

"Really?" Jace's eyes perked up.

"Really."

Kelsey gave Devon the stink eye as she picked up her laptop case, so he grabbed his plate and mug and took them to the kitchen before he did something else wrong.

She started for the door. He joined her and took her case to carry it. In the hallway, he turned to her. "Sorry. I know I shouldn't have said I'd come to dinner without checking with you first, but I couldn't say no to that cute face. I don't know how you do it."

"I didn't peg you for such a big softie."

"Never thought I was either." Surprised the heck out of him.

He trailed her down the hallway, enjoying the swing of her hips in today's purple skirt. He didn't know how she walked in those spiky black heels that he guessed to be three—maybe four—inches high. She wore a white blouse and a lighter purple sweater with the skirt, and the color really suited her.

In the elevator, she frowned at him. "I know it was just a gut reaction to Jace's request, but I can't have you leading him on. He's going to think there's something going on between us when there isn't."

Devon met her gaze and held it. "Oh there's something going on all right, you're just refusing to acknowledge it."

"Same difference."

"Is it? I don't think so."

She shook her head and stared above the door like she was counting down the floors until she could get away from him.

He hated that feeling. "I'm sorry about last night. About the kiss."

Her gaze flashed to his, her eyes wide. "You are? You didn't..."

He didn't know what she was about to say, but he wasn't going to let this go until he knew she wasn't upset with him. "You don't want a relationship, and I should have respected that."

She blinked. "It's okay. I kissed you back, in case you didn't notice."

"Oh, I noticed all right." He held her gaze. "And it was amazing."

Color rushed over her face. Was he now going to have to apologize for embarrassing her?

The elevator doors opened on the first floor, and she bolted out to the parking lot. He tried not to take her rapid escape personally. To just think it was her usual fast pace, nothing more.

They took his truck again and neither of them spoke on the drive to the airport or while boarding the small jet, but he was hyperaware of her every move.

He started up the steps to the plane, and his phone dinged. Seeing Hurst's name, Devon glanced at the text.

Cruz still not talking. Frost has agreed to let me take a run at him. Will update you when finished.

Thanks, Devon replied and stepped into the plane. He'd flown in all kinds of military aircraft, but he'd never been in a private plane before. Still, he wasn't surprised that the interior was plush with top-of-the-line furnishings. The main part of the cabin held eight comfy leather recliners in groupings with small tables. In the back, he spotted the restroom, a bedroom, and kitchen.

Kelsey stood in the small aisle, gaping at the interior. "Wow, oh, wow. This is amazing."

A blond flight attendant dressed in a blue uniform stepped from the kitchen and joined them. "If you'll go ahead and be seated, we're cleared for takeoff."

"Thank you," Devon said, offering her a smile.

"My pleasure, Mr. Dunbar." Her smile was quick and professional before she went to the exterior door and secured it.

Devon waited for Kelsey to take a seat, and instead of sitting across a table from her, he chose a seat on the other side of an aisle. The aisle was narrow, but with things kind of dicey between them right now, he didn't want to make her uncomfortable for the duration of the flight, and this arrangement gave her a buffer that he thought she might want.

He looked out the window for the uneventful takeoff. He thought the smaller plane might not ride as smoothly as a large jet, but it effortlessly cut through the sky, and he sat back to enjoy the ride. "I could get used to traveling like this."

"Who couldn't?" Kelsey looked at him wide-eyed.

He loved the childlike innocence in her expression...a

look he rarely encountered in his line of work or even when he'd been a SEAL. He tried not to become jaded, but it was difficult not to. Kelsey seemed to manage it well. He imagined being a parent would help with that struggle as it would provide a regular reminder of how the world looked through a child's eyes. He could get used to seeing that on a daily basis.

Listen to him. He'd gone from not wanting a relationship to thinking about being a dad in just a few days. Craziness. Pure craziness.

Or was it? Could God be trying to tell him something?

"Time to get to work." Kelsey took files from her computer case and placed them on the table. Devon assumed they were Todd's financial reports that she'd brought along.

She glanced at him. "Do you want to look at these, too?"

"I do, but I'm going to review information I got from my supervisor on the Sotos Cartel first. I know they have people running drugs in Rugged Point, and I hope I can make a connection to the players—be it Arroyo or Gonzalez or someone else."

She lifted an eyebrow. "When did you ask for that report?"

"I checked in with my supervisor last night after you went to bed. The email came through this morning."

"Is it something I can look at?"

"Sorry, no. It's confidential, but I'll share what I can if I find anything, okay?"

She nodded. "This has all taken me by surprise. I never even thought of drugs being a problem in cute tourist towns like Rugged Point."

"I thought that way once, too, but there really isn't anywhere these days where drugs aren't an issue." He glanced at the bandage covering his snake tattoo, glad to have it hidden as he hated to display any type of affiliation with drug runners.

"Since Portland is the biggest city in Oregon I expect it there, but on the coast?" She shrugged.

"Portland is still the biggest center for drugs in the state," he said, thinking he should explain. "Most drugs come up the I-5 corridor cutting through Portland from California. The freeway is such a busy conduit that my agency has designated it as one of the eight major drug trafficking corridors in the country."

"Oh, man. I didn't know it was that bad." She shook her head. "As a parent living in Portland, that's shocking to hear."

"I don't want to scare you, but we have a hundred street gangs with more than three thousand members who are more than glad to deal in illicit drugs."

She narrowed her eyes, and he wanted to press out the little crease between her eyebrows. "So how and why does someone like Arroyo set up shop elsewhere?"

"Law enforcement presence on I-5 has caused cartels to take other routes to avoid detection and arrest. They've also dispersed their operations to prevent supply disruptions."

"Makes sense I guess. It all sounds so organized. Not for what I thought about drug dealers at all."

"It *is* organized. Very. And the lack of law enforcement funding in a lot of these smaller cities make them unable to combat the problem. They don't have the equipment, staffing levels, or experience and specialized training for investigations lasting weeks and sometimes months like the DEA does."

"So the bad guys know it's easier to do business there."

"Exactly. And if the heat gets hot, they just pick up and move to another city. So the investigations travel from city to city and often across county and state lines. That makes it nearly impossible for an individual police force or sheriff's office to deal with."

"Sounds like a losing battle." She sounded so disillusioned.

He didn't want to leave her feeling down. "Some days it feels that way, but we *do* put away traffickers and get drugs off the streets. That's what I focus on—it's what motivates me to keep going."

"Thank you." She reached across the aisle and squeezed his hand. "You sacrifice a lot for all of us and probably never get any thanks for doing it."

"No thanks needed, but I appreciate it." He returned her smile, thrilled over her compliment, but her touch took his heart in another direction. He forgot about everything but how good it felt to be sitting with her. Too bad he'd sat across the aisle. He wanted to be closer to her. Maybe kiss her if she didn't object.

She suddenly jerked her hand free. "We should get to work."

"Work, right." He blew out his emotions in a long breath and sat staring ahead to gain control of his thoughts. What was he going to do about this thing with her? He had to admit he was infatuated with her. And not just her physical presence. Sure, she was beautiful, but his feelings went deeper. He didn't remember having these deep-seated feelings with Tara.

Was that where this was going? Was he in for a world of hurt if he didn't get his act together? Or was it God showing him that what happened with Tara didn't matter and he could move on?

If he accepted that, he was free to pursue something with this woman who wanted nothing personal to do with him. Could he really make that leap right now?

The flight attendant came down the aisle. Good. He needed a distraction.

"Can I get you something to drink?" she asked Kelsey who ordered water. The attendant turned to him. "And you, Mr. Dunbar?"

"Coke, please." If he was a drinking guy, which he wasn't, he would've asked for something much stronger.

He waited for the Coke then opened the report Hurst forwarded from the agent familiar with the Rugged Point drug scene. Neither Gonzalez or Arroyo were mentioned in the report, so maybe they were solely involved in trafficking babies. That also wasn't in the report, only their other illegal side business of prostitution. It was covered in detail, along with several legal establishments where they laundered their money.

Devon sipped his Coke and stared at the message. How had they completely missed the trafficking in Rugged Point? Only one answer came to mind. Arroyo couldn't have mixed with any of the players that Devon or other agents interacted with. Ever. Or he would have shown up on the radar.

Kelsey looked up from her report. "It looks like Todd was being blackmailed since Jace turned one."

"Interesting," he said and thought about her statement. "Seems like either they just came up with the scheme or they gave parents a year to get attached to the child so they knew they would do anything to keep it."

She cringed. "What kind of person does that? First stealing a child from their mother and then blackmailing the new parents?"

Devon opened his mouth to say the kind of lowlifes he ran into on a daily basis, but she didn't need to know that. "How much was Todd paying them?"

"It started at a thousand a month and over the years went up to three thousand a month."

"No small chunk of change." One he could never pay on his salary. "And you didn't miss that money?"

"There was always plenty of it, so I never had to ask except for major purchases, and we decided on those together."

"Was Todd secretive about money?"

"Secretive? No. He never brought it up at all. Now I know why." She took a long breath and let it out. "I won't ever be such a fool again."

Just the thought of this guy treating her so badly made Devon tense up, and here she was blaming herself for it.

He relaxed his muscles to release the anger from his body before he spoke so she didn't have to deal with that, too. "You're being too hard on yourself."

"I don't think so, but it's not worth discussing." She tapped the stack of paper on her lap. "Of course there's just the monthly cash withdrawals and blackmail emails, but nothing proving the money was actually given to Kilroy, so you can't arrest him."

"Hopefully when we talk to him, we'll find that evidence. Along with information on the parents the children were stolen from."

"Hopefully," she said, but he could tell she didn't really think they'd find the info they needed.

He didn't blame her. The more they learned, the more he knew that closing this investigation was going to be harder than he first thought. He started to look back at his information when a thought popped into his head. Todd Moore was murdered in Tucson, an easy drive from El Paso. A connection? Devon's gut said if Todd stopped paying the blackmailer, it was highly possible.

"Mind if I look at that information now?" he asked, trying to keep his tone neutral so he didn't spook her.

"Be my guest. I've seen enough." She handed the pages to him.

He quickly reviewed the payment dates. Kelsey had said Todd died about a year ago, but the last three grand cash withdrawal took place eighteen months ago.

Maybe there was something to Devon's theory. He got out his phone and created a text to Hurst to send the minute the plane touched down and he could use his phone again.

Need the homicide file for Todd Moore ASAP. Our suspects could be behind his death.

Devon stowed his phone, and an even more horrible thought hit him. Had Kilroy paid Cruz to abduct Jace as an additional act of revenge? Maybe, but why wait a year to do so? And why didn't they try to blackmail Kelsey after they killed Todd? The only reason they wouldn't was if they knew Todd kept her in the dark about Jace's birth.

He glanced at her. She was quietly looking out the window, her gaze pensive. She'd been through so much already. More than most people could hold up under. So how in the world was he going to tell her that the blackmailers might have killed Todd and tried to take Jace?

13

In the rental car heading to Kilroy's house, Kelsey glanced at Devon behind the wheel, his posture nearly perfect, and he looked so strong and competent. And yet, he continued to prove he had a generous heart. He'd been so kind to her and Jace. She could easily see him as a father—teaching and nurturing a child. But then she'd thought Todd was a good guy at first, too. It was only after they were married that she wondered if he'd married her more because he needed someone to care for Jace than that he loved her.

She resisted sighing and stared at the barren landscape.

Devon looked at her. "You look deep in thought."

"I was thinking about Todd. About what kind of dad he was." She refrained from adding that she was thinking about Devon in this capacity, too.

"I imagine after being willing to break the law to have a son, he had to be an amazing father."

"He was a good dad, but not one who lived for his son."

"So why would he take the risk of buying a child?"

Kelsey shrugged. "Maybe Margo was the one who wanted a child and couldn't have one. The cancer could have caused that."

"We could try to find her doctor and ask."

"But what would be the point of that? With her and Todd both gone, knowing why they did it really doesn't matter, right? Just figuring this out before Jace is hurt is all I care about." She glanced at her watch. "And speaking of time, we should be hearing from Emory on the DNA soon."

Devon clamped his fingers tighter on the wheel. "I'm sorry, you know. I don't want to report this. Even more so now that I've gotten to know you and Jace."

"Thank you for that." She smiled at him to ease his mind.

"Maybe Emory's running into problems."

"I doubt it."

"No." He gave her a pointed look. "I'm sure this profile is going to take longer than usual."

She watched him for a minute and then it hit her. "Oh, I get it. You don't want to know when the results come in so you don't have to report it."

"Whatever do you mean?" He grinned.

She loved how his happiness lit his face, and she also loved this sudden easiness between them. She could easily imagine dating him. Unfortunately, after Todd, she couldn't as easily imagine trusting him.

"You might want to check in with Emory to make certain she's running behind," he said.

"Right...yeah...will do that right now."

Kelsey made the call and then sat back, watching the flat and barren landscape until Devon pulled up to Simon Kilroy's house sitting on the edge of the Chihuahuan Desert. The home was part of a small neighborhood of similar houses with large lots. It was a square adobe box with flat roof with an adobe wall circling it. The property was well maintained, the house painted a stark white, but scraggly weeds grew in the xeriscape yard with drought-tolerant native plants and gravel ground covering.

"Odd," Kelsey said. "Why keep the house so immaculate and let weeds take over the yard?"

"Weeds that big didn't happen overnight." Devon parked near the arched opening in the courtyard wall.

She searched for any sign of life, but she didn't see movement or a car in the driveway. "The information Nick gave us listed this as his current address. And Kilroy owns the place, so I can't imagine him letting it get run down."

"Some people don't take care of their things. Or maybe he hit hard times and is in foreclosure."

Kelsey shook her head. "Nick would've found that in his background check. He doesn't miss a thing."

"Yeah, after working with him for only a few days, I'm beginning to think you're right." Devon took the keys from the ignition and pocketed them. "Maybe you should wait here while I check the place out."

There was no way she was going to be left behind when they finally arrived at a top suspect's home, and she pushed out of the vehicle before Devon stopped her. She knew she overcompensated for her often grisly work by dressing as feminine as she could and maybe that was leading him to think she was more vulnerable than she actually was.

She didn't like it when others misjudged her because of her attire, but she wouldn't change the way she dressed. She liked feminine clothing and having her nails done. Not in sync with her geek brain, but hey, people weren't just one thing. They were a mixture of everything. Nature and nurture. The clothing she had in common with her mom. The geek brain, her dad who was a physicist.

The heat radiated from the ground, the sun like a blow-torch. She gasped. Sure it was a dry heat, but it was still brutally hot. Portland rarely hit one hundred degrees, and the intensity of the unusual spring heat wave instantly sapped her. Thankfully, she'd already discarded her sweater and wore a sleeveless blouse.

She started up the walkway to the arched opening. A breeze kicked in, and the dry air whisked across the flat land, peppering her body with grains of sand as she stepped into a small courtyard. Adobe tile covered the ground, and the sheltered space protected them from the wind. A dry three-tier fountain and clay pots with dead plants further convinced her that Kilroy wasn't here.

She stepped up to the solid wood door holding a small window covered in wrought iron and a matching mail chute and raised her hand to knock.

Devon took her arm and urged her to move to the side. "Never know when a bullet will come flying through a door."

She hadn't even considered the possibility that Kilroy could shoot at them and was very glad Devon was with her.

With the side of his fist, he pounded on the door. The sound reverberated into the quiet neighborhood. He tapped his foot on the tile and rested his hand on his sidearm.

When no one answered, he pounded loudly. "Police. We need to speak to you, Mr. Kilroy."

"You're wasting your time," a female called from outside the wall entrance. "Haven't seen Simon in a long time. I think he moved."

A stooped woman with white hair and leathery skin stood peering into the courtyard, her hand sheltering her eyes from the harsh sun. The petite woman wore jeans, a beige T-shirt, and vivid blue athletic shoes.

Devon took a few steps in her direction and displayed his credentials. "How long has it been since you've seen Mr. Kilroy?"

"Hmm." She tapped her chin. "Guess it's been seven,

eight months. Maybe more. Did he do something wrong?"

Devon smiled, which Kelsey knew he used to disarm people. It certainly worked with her.

"We just need to talk to him about an investigation we're working on," Devon said. "What can you tell us about him?"

"He's a great guy. Friendly. Helpful." She jerked a thumb over her hunched shoulder. "I live two houses down, and he helped me keep up with my yard and house since my Earl died." She smiled, and her upper dentures dropped, but she clicked them back into place. "Our properties are over an acre, and that's just too much for me to handle."

Alarm bells rang in Kelsey's brain. She found it odd that Kilroy was compassionate enough to help take care of this woman and then left without saying anything. "Didn't he tell you he was moving?"

The woman's eyes narrowed, and she shook her head.

"Don't you find that odd?" Devon asked before Kelsey could raise the same question.

"Yes, but then young people today don't have the manners of my generation. It's all about them." She raised her chin as if she expected a challenge to her statement.

Kelsey wanted to point out that the woman was generalizing, and that in itself made her declaration false, but Kelsey didn't want to antagonize her. "Do you have any idea where he might have gone?"

"None."

"Well, thanks for your help," Devon said, his tone dismissing her.

"I...I..." She watched them for a minute, then nodded and continued down the street.

"Now what?" Kelsey asked.

"Now we try to get a look inside the house." Devon returned to the door, twisted the knob, then rattled the door, but the lock held firm. He pressed his hands on the small window and peered inside. "Furniture's still here. Piles of mail on the floor from the mail chute."

That warning in Kelsey's brain grew louder. "Not signs of someone who moved."

"Exactly." Devon lifted his head. "Let's take a look around back."

He started across the courtyard to the gravel yard. She followed him, and her heels pierced the gravel and sank into the sandy soil. Why didn't she wear more practical shoes? At least she'd chosen a skirt and that helped keep her cooler.

Devon stopped at two windows and looked inside. "More furniture. Dishes in the sink. If Kilroy moved, he left in a hurry."

"Maybe someone he worked with was out to get him."

"Could be."

They circled around back where the courtyard wall ended, giving way to a flat property that extended as far as the eye could see. Closer to the house were several outbuildings made of rusty tin. One of them was more of a lean-to and held a big motorcycle. A large white propane tank sat next to it.

Devon came to an abrupt stop. She plowed into him and flailed out her arms to try to stay upright. She nearly lost her battle when he grabbed hold of her waist. His touch lit a fire in her, but the shock barely had time to register when she looked at his worried eyes.

"What is it?" she asked, though she was afraid to hear the answer. "What did you see?"

He released her and turned to point at a small hill near the open shed. A long patch of the sandy soil had been disturbed and the soil was slightly mounded.

A heavy feeling settled in her stomach. "You think someone killed him and buried him here?"

He shrugged. "Something's buried over there, that's for

sure."

If so, that meant they couldn't question Kilroy, and this lead would be a dead end. She recalled a variety of site visits on her job that didn't turn out to be graves as police had presumed them to be. "Could be any number of things other than a grave."

"Like what?"

"A garden patch. Or an area a child dug in. A buried pet. Maybe Kilroy buried his garbage there."

Devon tilted his head. "It's possible, I suppose. We should investigate instead of speculating."

"I don't have any of my tools with me, and we can't just start digging up a potential crime scene."

"Agreed." His head bobbed. "So we go inside and also check the outbuildings to see if there are any signs of foul play."

"But the place is locked up tight."

"With a potential grave I have exigent circumstances, and I can enter."

"But we don't know if it *is* a grave."

"We also don't know that it's not." He drew his weapon and started for the door. "Stay close to me."

He twisted the doorknob and rattled the door, but the lock held. He turned and slammed his booted foot on the wood, splintering the old door in one try. A horrible smell greeted them.

"Garbage." She pinched her nose. "He didn't take out the garbage."

"Another bad sign." Devon stepped through the doorway that led directly into a small kitchen with more adobe tiles on the floor and as a backsplash. She had to concentrate on breathing through her mouth or the rancid smell would make her hurl. She was a true oddity. She could handle the smell of decomposing bodies but not garbage.

Devon paused and stared down at the floor. She moved closer and saw rusty spots leading to a large stain that had dried long ago.

"Blood," she said.

"Yeah," he replied. "Looks like we have a crime scene here."

"Hold on." She reached into her purse and pulled out booties and gloves.

He gaped at her. "Seriously—you carry those with you?"

"I'm basically on call twenty-four seven, so yeah. Never know when I might need them." She handed a pair of booties and gloves to him.

Booties wouldn't work with her spiky heels, so she shed her shoes, and for the second time today she wished she'd been more practical with her attire.

Devon gave her an intense look. "Ready?"

She nodded and they made their way through the kitchen toward a dining room. She noted blood spatter on the wall. "Spatter's in a cast-off pattern."

"So not a gunshot, but a bloody object pulled back before inflicting another blow."

"Exactly." She was impressed that he knew about spatter patterns.

They entered a hallway with an opening to a large living room with a chair and table tipped over.

"Assault started in here," he said. "Moved through the dining room to the kitchen."

"Agreed."

Devon moved down the hallway. They checked out a bathroom and three bedrooms—all without any disturbance. He holstered his weapon and looked at her. "Time to check the outbuildings."

"And get a close-up of the supposed grave."

He arched his eyebrow, likely at her use of the word

supposed, but she was simply being factual. "We haven't confirmed it's a grave."

"I know, but my gut says it is, and my gut never lets me down." He took off for the door where he shed his booties.

She slipped back into her shoes and had to hurry to catch up to his long strides as he crossed the yard toward the shed. Inside, the temps were a bit cooler due to the shade and she took her time looking around. In addition to the motorcycle, there were automobile parts, tools, and boxes of junk.

He stepped behind a few stacks and came out holding a dirty shovel in his gloved hands. "Could've been used to dig the grave and might have prints on the handle."

"If so, we can lift those. Plus, we can do soil analysis and confirm if it was used to dig in this yard…but not necessarily the grave, if it is one."

He leaned the shovel against the wall. "Why's that?"

"From my initial look at the property, I'd say the soil is the same across the property, so a sample might only prove it was used somewhere in his yard. But if we do indeed have a grave, we might find striations in the soil that we can match directly to the residual soil on this shovel."

"Interesting," he said. "Let's check the other buildings."

He broke the locks on each building, and they quickly viewed additional yard equipment, other tools, and old furniture, but didn't find Kilroy or anything suspicious.

Devon snapped off his gloves. "Time to take a look at the grave."

She turned to lead the way. Each step across the arid property she prayed that they were wrong and no one had lost their life here, but as much as she kept pointing out it was a supposed grave, in her heart she knew what they were about to find.

14

The sudden tightening of Kelsey's shoulders told Devon all he needed to know, and he didn't need to see what she'd spotted. The soil disturbance was indeed a grave. But, of course, he would look because he had to know how she figured it out by just staring at the ground.

He stepped past her, and the answer was instantly clear. One end of the mound revealed a partial human skeleton. The skull and tip of the shoulders were uncovered, most likely from the dry soil and high winds.

She squatted, and he didn't know how she stayed balanced on her high heels. She didn't touch the bones but got very close.

He believed these were human remains, but then he remembered her conversation about the bear. "Human?"

She nodded.

"Can you tell if it's a male or female?"

She bent closer to the partially buried skeleton. "From this very brief look, I suspect it's a male."

"Because of the size of the bones?"

She shook her head. "Men generally tend to have thicker, heavier skulls like this one. Plus the area where the temporal muscle attaches to the skull—the temporal line —often has a more pronounced ridge in males than females."

She pointed to the eye socket. "Also a male's orbit has a slightly blunter surface like this one. And," she moved her finger to the area above the orbits. "This slight ridging is only found in a male."

"So Kilroy, then?"

"Can't say that." She got up. "If his attacker was male, Kilroy could have overpowered and killed him, then took off."

"Could be, but I think odds are good that we're looking at what's left of Simon Kilroy."

"Why's that?" She continued to stare at the bones.

"If Kilroy murdered someone, he wouldn't likely bury the body on his own property."

"All a moot point if my cursory exam is wrong and a female is buried here."

"What are the odds of that?"

"Me being wrong? Slim to none." She grinned.

Devon loved that she could keep her sense of humor despite the situation. "Looks like we have soil erosion to thank for exposing the victim."

"A common issue when a body is buried on a hill. Not sure why this spot was chosen." Holding a hand over her eyes, she surveyed the property. "Kilroy's driver's license puts him at two hundred fifty pounds. Could be the killer wanted to place the body far away from the house but ran out of steam in dragging a heavy body and simply buried him on the spot."

Devon looked back at the house. "If he *was* dragged, those marks are long gone."

"His body didn't skeletonize overnight. It makes sense

that the wind and rain erased the marks even though rainfall is minimal here."

"Let's get law enforcement out here and maybe we can get some answers to our questions." Devon dug out his phone. "And since I'm assuming they'll be glad to have you recover the bones, we should arrange to have your equipment brought here."

She nodded woodenly. "I'll call Nick and have him contact his friend to see if we can send the plane back for Sierra and my things."

Her teammate? "Sierra?"

"She's tops in her field at trace evidence recovery. I want her to process the scene and the house. Especially the blood so she can give us an estimate of when the assault occurred."

"Seriously? She can figure that out from the blood?"

"Yes. She uses Raman spectroscopy to accurately date a blood stain. Provided said blood stain is less than two years old."

He shook his head. "You all have knowledge and skills way beyond the average lab's capabilities. Let's get her out here because I want to know if that's Kilroy's blood in the house and when he died."

He heard Kelsey make her call as he called the nonemergency phone number for the county sheriff. When the operator answered, he gave his contact information and reported finding the body. "I'd like to speak directly to the sheriff."

"Let's start with the watch commander," the woman said, not at all impressed with his credentials. "He can decide how best to handle your call. Please hold."

Devon didn't want to have to go through the watch supervisor, but he held, his gaze going to the bones. He couldn't diagram all of the bones in a human skeleton if his life depended on it, but he did know scavengers could carry away bones and the skeleton might be incomplete like the one on Kelsey's lab table.

"Sergeant Smythe," the man's deep voice boomed through the phone.

Devon quickly brought him up to speed on the discovery. "I came to El Paso to interview the homeowner for my investigation, and I'm accompanied by Dr. Kelsey Moore, a forensic anthropologist. She'd be happy to collect the remains for you."

"Good. Good. Our nearest forensic anthropologist is in Albuquerque." He fell silent for a moment. "This discovery is going to bring the news media out in force. I know Sheriff Trujillo will want to personally handle the investigation. I'll dispatch a deputy to secure the scene now, and he'll notify you of the sheriff's ETA."

"Hey, thanks, man," Devon said and gave his phone number to the sergeant.

By the time Devon pocketed his phone, Kelsey had finished her call and was once again squatting next to the skeleton.

"Any idea how long the body's been here?" Devon asked.

She shook her head. "I'll have a better idea after we excavate and do some research on the weather conditions here."

"Weather?"

"The hot arid conditions will cause more rapid changes in the body, so I need to know the span of temperatures throughout the year. Still, I can tell you that exposure of large portions of the skeleton from tissue occurs around four to six months after death. And these bones have undergone bleaching and exfoliation, which are the early stages of destruction of the skeletal elements. This typically begins at about nine months."

"So these bones could have been exposed for almost a year?" he frowned.

"That's right." She stood. "But I need to make it clear that there are many factors in decomposition, and the time frames I shared are general. Humans exposed in death to the same weather conditions will decompose differently. Some are quickly reduced to skeletons and others become mummified and retain tissue for years."

He almost forgot his role as investigator here and wanted to know more. "Why the difference?"

"It's unknown, but recent studies seem to suggest rate of decay has to do with drugs or illness. For example, scavengers and insects seem to avoid people with cancer in their bodies and this slows decomp down. The Forensic Anthropology Center at the University of Tennessee is researching this right now using their body farm."

"Interesting."

"Really?" She arched a delicate eyebrow. "Most people find all of this stuff gross. Even detectives."

Yeah, he got that. He might, too, if he didn't have feelings for her and found everything she did fascinating. "So you can't be certain of his time of death?"

"Remember I'm not sure it *is* a male," she said. "Depending on what I find in the grave, I can give you an idea of how long he's been buried, but this is why the dating of the blood in the house is important."

He shook his head in amazement. "I am so thankful for your team's expertise. And so is the sergeant I spoke to. He wants you to handle recovery of the skeleton."

She gave a firm nod. "Nick has arranged for the plane to return to Portland for my things, and Sierra is already packing up."

"I didn't tell the sergeant I spoke to that she'd be coming, but we can tell the sheriff when he arrives."

She huffed a breath. "He might not be so eager to have her step in."

"They have jurisdiction here, but I can always take over if needed." He swiped his arm over his forehead covered in perspiration. "I'd rather not do that, but I will if I have to."

"Once law enforcement gets here and takes charge of the scene, I need to find a store to get other supplies. Sierra will be bringing more practical clothing for me to wear, but you might want to find a store for yourself."

He wasn't one to wear shorts, but he'd make an exception for this heat. "How long do you think this will take?"

"Hard to say until I start digging. If it's straightforward, a day or so."

"So either way, we're not going home tonight?"

"Exactly. I need to call Ahn and Jackson." She frowned. "I hate to think I'm spending the night away from Jace when I might not have many days left with him."

He searched for something to say in comfort, but the ear-piercing sound of police sirens cut through the quiet. The craziness was about to begin, and they would soon be so wrapped up in the crime scene and recovery evidence that they would have little time to think of anything else, even someone as important as Jace.

"I'll go meet the deputy while you make your calls." Devon turned away, and as he strode toward them, he really wished he could help Kelsey find a way to keep Jace. But if they found the boy's birth mother in their investigation, and he had indeed been stolen from her, she would most likely be thrilled to have him back. If she was a fit mother, there was nothing anyone could do to stop her from claiming her child.

No person could have an impact in this situation, but God could do anything.

Devon offered a prayer on Kelsey's behalf as he walked,

and was surprised that it was the most enthusiastic prayer he'd uttered in some time.

He found a county cruiser parked at the end of the drive, and the deputy was digging supplies from his trunk. Devon quickly introduced himself and brought the deputy up to speed.

"Sarge told me to tell you Sheriff Trujillo's on the way," he said.

Devon nodded his acknowledgement, and by the time he finished updating the deputy, a white SUV, lights and siren running, raced to the curb. A dark-skinned male with shiny black hair slid out from behind the wheel. He wore a tan county uniform with wide-brimmed hat. Tall, burly, and intense with a thick black mustache, he marched up to them.

He shoved out a hand. "Sheriff Trujillo."

The man's grip was firm, and Devon shared his particulars. "It's good of you to come out."

"If you want to head back to the scene, I'll join you in a minute." He turned to his deputy. "Let's get this place cordoned off before the looky-loos descend on us."

Devon took off, turning back to see Trujillo taking metal stakes from the deputy's trunk. He would pound them in at the edge of the property and string crime scene tape between them, setting the outer perimeter. He would then do the same thing in the back, creating a smaller perimeter. And finally he would set a path of ingress and egress from the grave to keep anyone on scene from contaminating the area.

In the back yard, Devon found Kelsey sitting calmly in a lawn chair in the shade, phone in hand and her delicate ankles crossed. She'd kicked off her shoes, her pink toenails sparkling when they caught rays of sun. And her long, long legs that kept drawing Devon's attention grabbed it again.

He could keep his focus on the investigation once she put coveralls on, though with this heat, she would be roasting in them.

She looked up and held up her phone. "Just downloaded the temperature charts and I'm now checking high-resolution databases. I need to see underlying soil, geology, and vegetation so I know what to expect when I start the dig."

He was so ignorant of what her job entailed and wanted to be more informed. "Mind telling me a bit about what you'll actually be doing?"

"Not at all." She sat forward. "I'll start by measuring and diagramming the scene. Then create a grid over the site so I can further note where items and bones were found. And then, I begin the dig, removing the leaf and litter debris first. This allows me to see the parameters of the grave so I can more effectively remove the soil. This will also help me look for those shovel striations I mentioned."

"And then you finally dig?"

"Dig as in using a handheld trowel and brushes so as not to damage any bones, yes. I'll remove the soil layer by layer, taking samples of each layer first, and putting it on a tarp to be screened for evidence."

"Layer by layer?" he asked, not remembering much about his schooling on geology and feeling woefully ignorant of the ground he was standing on.

"Soil is made up of layers or horizons," she explained, no judgment over his lack of knowledge in her tone. "The first layer is top soil, which most people know about as they dig into this layer to plant flowers. Then comes subsoil, substratum, and bedrock. A grave will have distinct layers on the edges but the fill soil will likely have been mixed up by the person who dug the grave."

He scratched his chin. "Don't take offense at my question, but why does any of this even matter?"

"Soil is as unique as a fingerprint and a soil scientist can use next-generation sequencing of bacterial DNA to classify the bacterial makeup of a soil sample and provide values. So if we fail to locate sufficient evidence to convict the killer, that soil scientist can compare the soil to the shovel or any soil found on a potential suspect's shoes, in his car, his house, etcetera and place them not only on this property but specifically in the grave."

"Wow, who knew?" He shook his head. "Not me, that's for sure."

She chuckled. "I'm sure there are a million things you know about law enforcement that I have no clue about. We just have differing areas of expertise."

He was about to point out her expertise seemed far more extensive than his, but he heard footsteps approach from behind. He turned to see the sheriff march toward them and take a long, lingering look at Kelsey.

Devon bristled. He didn't like seeing the man eyeballing her. Not one bit. But what man wouldn't appreciate her good looks? Devon had never been the jealous type, but he'd never felt this way about a woman before. He'd only known her for—what?—all of five minutes, and he was practically obsessed with her.

She came effortlessly to her feet, smoothed a hand over her skirt, and then smiled. Devon hurried to her side and introduced Sheriff Trujillo. She shook his hand as he eyed her skeptically.

"Don't worry, Sheriff," she said, her tone lighthearted. "I may look young, but I have a PhD in anthropology, and I'm trained in crime scene procedures."

He scoffed. "Apparently you're a mind reader, too."

"No, but I've seen the look on your face at crime scenes so many times that I've come to recognize the doubt. But I assure you, I am skilled in forensic anthropology."

"She even interned at the Smithsonian," Devon said as he didn't like the fact that she was having to defend herself just because she looked young. "We've sent for Dr. Moore's equipment, and while we wait, we'll get more appropriate clothing and arrange for a hotel for the night."

The sheriff gave a firm nod and offered the name of a local hotel. "Not the fanciest place, but clean and reasonably priced. And there's a strip mall not more'n a few miles from here where you can get outfitted."

"Thank you." Kelsey smiled at the sheriff. "I have also asked our trace evidence expert to join me. She'll handle photography and recovery of any evidence located in the dig. I'd also like her to process the house where an obvious fight has occurred."

He smoothed his fingers over his mustache. "Sounds like you think we can't handle a crime scene."

"Not at all." Kelsey smiled again. "Sierra and I work together often, so it makes the process go faster. You seem like a sheriff who's on top of his job, so I know you'll want as much information as I can give as soon as I can give it to you."

Devon had to give Kelsey props for finding a way to flatter this man and get his buy-in when it could've turned antagonistic.

"That I am." He tensed his shoulders and set his jaw. "So bring on your associate, but just so you know, I don't have the budget to pay either one of you."

Kelsey waved a hand. "We wouldn't think of charging you. I simply want to find out why this person is buried here."

He tipped his head at the grave. "What exactly is your interest in this man?"

"First, we aren't positive it is a male," Kelsey said. "But we came to interview the property owner, a Simon Kilroy about an ongoing investigation. Obviously, if he's buried here, that won't be possible. Other than forensically."

Trujillo frowned. "I'll need more'n that."

"Sorry," Devon said, before Kelsey shared about the investigation. "We're not at liberty to disclose anything else, but we'll be glad to share any details we uncover as related to this man's death."

"You taking over this investigation? Because if you—"

"Relax," Devon said. "I'm only here to offer support."

Trujillo crossed his arms. "You sure about that?"

Devon widened his stance. "I am. But know this. If you try to freeze us out on the investigation, I *will* have to take control."

"You mean me not sharing information the way you're refusing to share with me?" Trujillo shook his head. "Talk about the pot calling the kettle black."

"Yeah," Devon said. "Sometimes life is one-sided and seems unfair, and this is one of those times. So, what do you say, Sheriff? Do you want our help here, and are you willing to play by my rules?"

He glared at Devon. "Fine. But you remember whose jurisdiction this is."

"Definitely, Sheriff. Thank you," Kelsey said. "Would you please set up the entire back yard as our inner perimeter?"

He glanced around. "Seems like an awful large area to cordon off for a grave."

"Actually, the crime scene could turn out to be a larger area."

That skeptical look returned to the sheriff's face. "How's that?"

"Erosion has exposed the body to scavengers, and it's highly likely that they carried off bones. We might have to expand the search area beyond the yard, but I don't want to waste resources on an all-out search until I know if any bones are missing."

Trujillo readjusted his hat and squinted. "And that will take how long?"

"I honestly don't know until I get started."

"Then, Dr. Moore," Devon said, looking at her. "Let's leave the sheriff in charge and gather the information we need to recover and identify this body."

15

Kelsey took one last look in the hotel mirror at her khaki shorts, blue T-shirt, and hiking boots. She'd rather Sierra would have brought a tank top as the temperature hovered at the hundred-degree mark. But she'd learned over the years that on a dig or crime scene, the less attention she drew to the fact that she was a woman in the still-predominantly-male law enforcement world, the better.

She twisted her hair up in the back with a large clip, hung the cooling towel she'd bought around her neck, and stepped outside. The heat hit her squarely in the face, and she sucked in a breath. Sierra was loading bottled water and Gatorade into a cooler with ice, and Devon hefted supplies into the vehicle.

He looked up from the rear of the SUV and ran his gaze over her. Slowly. Lingering. His careful study brought a blush racing up her neck and over her face, adding to the heat.

"Hot out here." She fanned her face, but his knowing expression said he wasn't fooled by her attempt to blame the blush on the heat.

"You look ready to work now," he said.

"Unfortunately, I'll have to put coveralls on, and in this heat, that's like climbing into an oven."

He patted a box next to him. "The canopy will help."

"Some."

"Too bad fans would disturb the scene." Sierra lifted her thick bangs off her glistening face and fanned her forehead with her other hand.

"We'll just have to make sure we take plenty of breaks and stay hydrated," Kelsey said. "I've worked on digs in hotter climates, and I know we'll be fine."

"Then let's get going." Devon closed the hatch. "And get the air conditioning running in the vehicle so we at least arrive cool on scene."

They piled into the SUV—Kelsey taking shotgun, Sierra the backseat—and Devon got them pointed in the right direction. He clicked on the AC and the mildly cool air from their trip to the store rushed into the vehicle.

"I've never been involved in a recovery like this." He glanced at Kelsey. "Can I do anything to help?"

He looked ruggedly handsome in his cargo shorts, T-shirt, and boots, and she really didn't want him nearby as a distraction, but she had to put that aside and work as efficiently as she could. Not only due to the heat, but she desperately wanted that lead that would keep Jace with her. "You can help pound in stakes for our grid. After that, only Sierra and I will work the site, but you could be our gofer when we need something."

He glanced at her. "You mentioned working in hot conditions before. Was the topography similar, too?"

She nodded sadly. "For the last few years, Sierra and I have traveled to southern Texas to do volunteer forensic work on the bodies of migrants who died after crossing the border."

His eyes widened. "How did you get involved in that?"

"I read about it in a professional journal. Once I did, I showed it to Sierra, and we couldn't turn our backs on the humanitarian crisis. You probably already know that the U.S. Border Patrol estimates there were more than six thousand deaths during illegal border crossings in a recent sixteen-year span."

"Yeah," He frowned. "That's a big number, isn't it?"

Kelsey thought the same thing when she read the article. "In the area we worked, they were mostly South Americans fleeing systematic violence. Violence we can't even imagine in our country. Although, we don't go as part of a church group, we consider it our ministry. To the families. To reunite them with missing loved ones."

"And also to the small counties on the border who continue to find bodies with no resources to identify them," Sierra said passionately.

Kelsey smiled at her friend. Many people wouldn't think of helping these agencies, but Sierra was a nurturer at heart. She tried to take care of everyone. She was a wonderful listener and a joy to be around, and she was generous with her time and talents.

Kelsey looked back at Devon. "We have very specific skill sets that can't be used for ministry most of the time, but this is a chance for us to get involved. I hate that it's happening, but on the bright side, we also bring college students to help. They not only get experience in recovering remains, but they learn about the intricacies of border policies and about people who aren't as privileged as they are when it comes to expecting freedom from personal violence."

"Sounds like a great learning experience."

"And a horrifying one as well." She shivered. "The hardest part is finding a child's body. That never leaves us."

"I get that." Devon clicked on a blinker and made the turn down Kilroy's street. "Unfortunately, children get caught up in the drug wars, too. Even more so lately. The Mexican Cartels have set up command and control centers here in Texas, especially in border towns like El Paso. They attract children with what appears to be easy money for doing simple tasks."

"That's horrible," Sierra exclaimed.

Kelsey couldn't even imagine such a thing. "What do they have them do?"

"Starts out simple like moving a vehicle from one place to another. The cartel watches the car to determine if law enforcement has it under surveillance. The kid gets fifty bucks and thinks it's easy, but then the tasks progressively get more difficult and higher paying, and soon the kid's enmeshed and can't get out." He shook his head in disgust and backed the vehicle up to the crime scene. "They call them the expendables."

"That's terrible," Kelsey declared.

"And then, of course, we have the baby trafficking." He turned off the engine. "I'm hoping while you dig and Sierra processes the scene that Trujillo will let me search Kilroy's place, and I can get a lead on that, too."

"I hope so, too, because we can't very well question him and any help he might provide will be in the way of evidence he left behind." Kelsey swallowed down her frustration so she could keep a positive attitude. "And he's our only lead with time running out before you have to report Jace."

Sierra leaned forward. "Did you get the DNA results for him yet?"

Kelsey shook her head, but didn't explain why there was a delay. "And for once I hope it takes much, much longer."

"I never expected to hear anyone at Veritas say that." Sierra chuckled.

Kelsey smiled at her friend, glad that she lightened up

the mood in the vehicle. Kelsey got out, taking a look across the street at yucca plants interspersed with cactus and grasses in the reddish sandy soil. Behind it all, red rocks rose from the desert floor like fingers from a grave, and she shivered again.

Devon eyed her for a moment. "I'll get the canopy set up and haul the cooler back to the shade."

"Be careful," she warned. "Don't trample anywhere near the grave. Use the path marked for all foot traffic."

"I *have* worked a crime scene or two, you know." He grinned.

She caught his good humor and chuckled. She loved how he had the ability to keep things light when they were anything but light. Some people might find that disrespectful, but law enforcement officers and people in her line of work, too, had to have an outlet for stress or they would burn out. Typically that outlet was humor—often what other people would consider inappropriate humor at that.

Kelsey looked down the street and spotted a county vehicle. "What in the world is a crime scene van doing here? If the sheriff touched the grave, I'll—"

Devon picked up the canopy. "I'll check with him. See what's going on."

Kelsey wanted to march along with him and demand an explanation, but he would get an answer, and she needed to ready herself for the dig. She located a Tyvek suit for herself and one for Sierra in their supplies. She tore open her package and shook out the fabric, dreading putting it on when she was already sweating.

"Seems like you and Devon are getting kind of friendly." Sierra tore open her package.

Kelsey knew what her friend was fishing for, but she wouldn't go there. "We're spending a good bit of time together, so it's only natural."

"Uh-huh. Right. *Natural.*" Sierra gave her a pointed look.

Kelsey resisted responding and slipped into the suit, groaning the moment it captured the heat under the impervious fabric.

"I know, right?" Sierra tugged the zipper up on hers and reached for booties.

Kelsey looked at her friend. "It's bad enough that I'm going to sweat off ten pounds today, but you didn't have to be here. I owe you big time for this."

"Yeah you do, and you know I *will* collect on it." Sierra laughed freely, her high cheeks rising even higher.

"Ah, but what will the price be? Can I afford it?"

"Likely not." Sierra wrinkled her nose and stuffed the booties into her pocket.

Kelsey settled a huge floppy hat on her head and grabbed her large tote holding necessary tools for the job. Most everyone could figure out that she would use trowels, whisk brooms, a tape measure, and brushes, but they might be surprised that her tools also included an ice pick, dental picks, tweezers, and root clippers.

She slung the heavy tote handle over her shoulder and grabbed the box with stakes, rubber mallet, and string. "Can you bring the tarps?"

Sierra shouldered her camera case and put on a green sun hat. "Got them."

They ran into Devon on his way back to get the cooler. "Canopy is up."

"Thanks," she said.

"And the sheriff did bring in a team to process the house, but he's glad to have Sierra look at the scene and offer her opinion."

Kelsey clenched her jaw and tried not to scowl. "Why'd he change his mind?"

"Said he felt like he was giving up too much control of evidence that he would need to investigate the murder."

"He has a point, I suppose," Sierra said. "But we would have given him a report with all the information he needed."

Devon rested his hands on his waist. "I think this decision is all about territory."

"Don't we know that," Sierra grumbled, unusual for her normally serene personality. Maybe the heat was already getting to her. "Maybe if I explain some of the things I can do that his locals can't, he'll give me access to the house."

"It's worth a try," Devon said. "If only to get a sample of the blood."

"I can be pretty convincing, so let me work on him." Sierra marched off.

Kelsey followed and saw Sierra approach the sheriff standing near the back door of the house. Kelsey continued on the designated path and unloaded her supplies. She got out her total station and mounted it on a tripod.

Devon hustled toward her and deposited the cooler nearby. "What's that thing, if you don't mind me asking?"

"I don't mind at all. In fact, I like how curious you are."

He grinned, and she felt another blush rising, so she quickly tapped the electronic device that was about a foot tall and a half foot wide. "It's called a total station, and it's used for surveying and building construction. It measures both vertical and horizontal angles and the slope distance to a particular point. It will give me the scale I need for my sketch."

"Right, it's the thing you see surveyors use."

"Exactly." She turned her attention back to her job and chose a tree for her point of measurement as it was the least likely thing to disappear in the landscape.

Sierra crossed the yard, her expression neutral.

"How did it go with the sheriff?" Devon asked.

"I have permission to process the scene along with his team. And you can search the house."

Devon shook his head. "Is there anything you all can't do?"

"Not that we know of." Sierra chuckled and handed the tarps to Devon. "You mentioned wanting to help. You can spread these out on all sides of the grave."

He started working.

"I'll get going on the initial scene shots, but I want to make sure I get a good blood sample so after I'm done I'll head inside." Sierra got out her camera.

"Go ahead, but leave the camera in case I need to record something while you're gone." Kelsey returned to the survey and took her time, making sure each point was accurate as she completed it. Measurements in hand, she made her drawing, all the while feeling Devon and the sheriff's gaze on her. She got a different vibe from each one. Curiosity and skepticism from the sheriff. Approval and respect from Devon.

She took one last look at her diagram, and satisfied she'd captured everything to scale, she put it in her bag and got out stakes, a mallet, and string.

Devon joined her and held out his hand. "I'll take the mallet."

"I'll place the stake, you pound it in." She gave him the mallet and stuck the first stake into the soft soil. He took over, hammering it in deep. The sharp reports cut through the quiet of the desert, seeming foreign and wrong. But then a skeleton buried out here was wrong, too.

They worked their way around the grave, and within an hour they had the area staked and gridded while Sierra went inside to collect blood.

"Okay," Kelsey said to Devon. "I'll take it from here."

He nodded. "Then I'll head inside, too."

Kelsey watched him go down the designated path and suddenly felt very alone. Alone with a man who was most likely murdered. A man who also could hold the key to keeping her son. Which meant she couldn't make any mistakes. A single mistake or overlooking a key piece of evidence could mean Jace would no longer be her son.

Focused now, she got lost in her work, using a sharp trowel to scrape the leaf litter into a shovel, dump it into a bucket, and then empty it onto a clean tarp. She would systematically examine the soil for fragments later. Once she'd removed that layer, she began gently loosening the soil around the bones with a wooden trowel and brushes.

Sweat trickled down her back. Her front. Her forehead. She swiped it away with the back of her hand, depositing soil on her face and matting her hair. She was a mess. A total and complete mess. She didn't care though. All that mattered was recovering these remains.

She took a few breaks for water and one to FaceTime Jace, then continued plugging along until she spotted the oddest thing she'd ever seen buried with a body.

Not knowing what to make of the discovery, she sat back and dialed Sierra. "Can you and Devon come out here? I've found something I need you to take a look at."

16

Eager to hear about Kelsey's discovery, Devon rushed after Sierra to where Kelsey sat back staring into the shallow grave. Resting on the skeleton's rib area lay a long cone made out of stiff cellophane with a ribbon tied around it and something decayed in the middle.

"What is it?" he asked.

Kelsey looked up at him. "Looks like the killer placed flowers in the grave with the victim."

"Odd," Sierra said.

"Isn't it?" Kelsey looked back at the grave. "It suggests a personal attachment between the killer and victim. Like the killer is sorry for hurting the victim."

Devon waited for her to look back up. "Or maybe the victim bought these flowers for the killer, and he or she buried them so they didn't leave them as evidence in the house."

"Maybe," Kelsey agreed. "But he could just take them with him."

"Either way." Sierra snapped on a fresh pair of gloves. "We could potentially recover fingerprints or DNA from the cellophane. And looks like there's an SKU etched in the cellophane so maybe we can track this to the store where they were purchased."

"My thoughts exactly." Kelsey smiled. "Would you photograph it then collect the evidence while I take a water break?"

"Absolutely." Sierra grabbed the camera from the tarp and began snapping pictures.

The red blotching color on Kelsey's face told Devon she needed to do more than drink water. "C'mon. Let's have that water in the SUV where the air conditioning can cool you off."

"That sounds good." She reached into the cooler for a bottle and handed it to him, then took one for herself. She rolled the bottle over her neck and moaned low in her throat.

Devon couldn't take his eyes off the bottle or her neck. Upset over his lack of control when it came to this woman, he stormed ahead to get the SUV unlocked and cooled off.

She stopped outside and stripped off her coveralls. He tried not to look, but it was like a bear to honey. He had no choice. Her skin glistened with perspiration. Dirt caked her face, and her hair was clumped in little mats, but she still looked amazing to Devon. Maybe even more so than her usual put-together appearance. This woman in front of him didn't look like a doctor and was far more approachable. The kind of woman who fit in his life. Who would be fine with the guys coming over for football or card night. Or sitting under the stars on a muggy night at a jazz concert with him.

She slipped onto the seat and leaned close to an air vent, ballooning out her T-shirt in the air. "Oh, man, this is amazing."

He averted his gaze. "I never understood how people could live in this kind of heat."

"I guess like we endure the rain for months on end to enjoy amazing summer months, they endure the summer heat for the beautiful winter months."

"Maybe." He took a long drink of the icy water, his parched throat thankful for the liquid.

"So did you find anything in the house that will help?" She sat back and crossed her legs. Long, tan, smooth legs.

Focus.

"We found traces of cocaine and—"

"So, he was into selling drugs, too? Like the men you're tracking? Or he could just have been a user."

"Or none of the above."

"But I don't understand."

Most people didn't. "Hard drugs have become an everyday part of our lives. So much so that a percentage of people who have never used cocaine test positive for trace amounts on their fingerprints."

"Oh, right. I remember Sierra talking about that. Cocaine's a very common environmental contaminant now. Likely from currency or from the occasional handshake."

"Crazy, right? I mean one or both of us could have cocaine on our hands right now."

She shook her head. "And is that what she thinks happened with Kilroy?"

"She did at first. Until we found a false wall and a kilo of coke hidden there."

Her eyes widened. "Oh, wow, do you think that's why he was killed?"

"Could be," he answered, but their finding worried him as this quantity of coke had to mean cartel involvement. "Every cartel cuts their coke with differing compounds giving them kind of a signature product. We have samples of Sotos's coke in evidence. I'm assuming Maya could compare that to what we recovered today to see if we should be looking at the Sotos Cartel for this."

"I'm sure she could and would."

"Perfect. We'll get the results so much faster that way." He was once again thankful for their team. "I just need to convince Trujillo to let Sierra take a sample."

"I could have Maya call him and explain the process so he knows it's legit."

Devon really didn't need this team to fight his battles, even if it might be easier. "Let me have a go at him first. Then if I need her, I'll let you know."

"This investigation is getting more and more complicated." She sat staring out the window. "So where do we go from here?"

"You prove that the body is Kilroy out there and give me a cause of death. Then I start hunting down the killer."

She fired him an intense look. "*We*, you mean."

"No." He shook his head to get his point across. "Just me from here on out. There's no way I'll let you near a ruthless cartel member."

She looked like she planned to argue then thought better of it. "I can still help behind the scenes."

"Exactly. Do your thing with the bones. Tell me how he died. That's the best help you can give me right now. These cartels often have signature execution styles. For example a bullet to the back of the skull can point us to a specific cartel." He stopped with that example as others were too horrific for her to hear about if she didn't need to know about them to work the investigation.

She shifted to look at him. "He didn't die from a bullet to the skull—that I already know. The skull is intact and no bullet holes. His shirt, however, has several holes, but it looks more like they were caused by a knife."

"I'm surprised the shirt didn't disintegrate with the

body."

"The portion exposed to the elements did, but the rest of it is pretty well intact because it's made of synthetic materials."

"See, that already narrows things down, and we have cause of death." He smiled at her, but he really didn't feel like smiling at all. He didn't like the fact that her son could have a potential connection to a ruthless drug cartel.

"Supposed cause of death," she said. "I've located trauma to the ribs that might be indicative of a knife blade. I need to take a closer look at it in the lab, but my preliminary guess—and it's just a guess, is that it looks like this man was stabbed in the heart."

"You're sure it's a man now?"

She nodded. "The narrow pelvic girth confirmed that for me."

"Great. That's a big step."

"If we find any unique objects like rings or other jewelry, we should check with NamUs."

He was familiar with the National Missing and Unidentified Persons System from prior investigations he worked on. "Problem with that is only a fraction of missing or unidentified remains stored in morgues get entered into the database."

She nodded. "Staffing and funding issues. I'm impressed that you're familiar with the database. Many detectives don't even know it exists."

"If they did, I know they would enter the data to potentially close out unsolved cases."

She looked out the front window. "I should get back to it. It'll be dark soon, and I'll need lights."

He stared down the street at the golden hue coloring the stark landscape. "I'll arrange with Trujillo to bring them in."

"Thanks for your help."

"Hey, you're the hero here today. I'm just your sidekick."

"Batman and Robin, but I honestly think you'd make a much better Batman than me." She chuckled and reached for the door handle but then looked back, her eyes narrowed. "Does any of this raise the danger level for Jace?"

He knew she wanted him to say no, but he couldn't. "It's not far-fetched to think that the near abduction was a cartel member trying to clean up loose ends, and it wouldn't hurt to up Jace's protection. Let me call Gage and see what he suggests."

"I'll get to work while you do that." Eyes dark and worried, she pushed out of the vehicle and put on the Tyvek suit.

He hated seeing her upset about losing her son the last few days, but now she had the added terror of potentially losing him to a vicious drug cartel.

When she trudged back toward the grave, he got out his phone and located Gage's number. Voicemail picked up, so Devon called Alex.

"Listen—this is urgent." Devon said before Alex could crack one of his jokes. He shared the recent developments. "We need to up Jace's security."

"Let me find Gage and get back to you."

"Time is of the essence here," Devon said.

"I'm on it. I'll make sure we find the right solution, and I'll personally head to Portland to implement it."

"Thanks, man. Call or text me with the details."

"You got it."

"And Alex," Devon added. "I don't yet know which cartel we're dealing with, but it honestly doesn't matter. Any one of them wouldn't hesitate to take you out to get to the kid. Bring your A game or someone could die."

Kelsey didn't like what she was seeing. Didn't like it at all. And if the person who committed this heinous act was connected to Jace's abduction, she was especially thankful for Blackwell Tactical protecting her son.

"What's wrong?" Devon asked from above. "Why'd you stop?" He must have been watching her to notice her discomfort and ask about it that quickly.

Knowing the destruction of the bone was obvious, she picked up the right radius and ulna and held them up for Devon.

He squatted by the grave. "I know the straight edge at the end of the bone isn't natural, but what am I looking at?"

She had to take a breath before saying this aloud. "Both hands were cut off just above the wrists, and so far, I haven't found the hands in the grave."

He swallowed hard and looked away.

Her worry ratcheted higher. "What is it?"

He turned back to her. "The Sotos signature. Their way of punishing people who steal from them. Cutting off their hands serves as a warning to others."

Disgusted, she shook her head. "They do this while they're alive, right?"

"Yeah. And they often post videos of it online."

She could easily visualize the scene, and her stomach did queasy somersaults, but she had to keep her cool to not only recover this body, but also to make sure her son was protected. "I'm not sure the warning aspect applies here, though, right? He died. That wouldn't serve as a warning to anyone. And there wasn't enough blood in the house for it to happen there. Maybe it was done post-mortem."

"Good point. So the killer could be trying to make it hard to identify this guy. But again, if this is Kilroy, and he was buried on his own property, then we surely could figure out his ID in many other ways."

She nodded. "So maybe this isn't Kilroy."

"Again, I ask why Kilroy would bury someone here. If it's not Kilroy, maybe he had nothing to do with this guy's death. We can speculate all we want, but what we need to do is identify this man. Can you get DNA from bones?"

"Most of the time, but his hair is probably a better source."

He pointed at the naked skull. "What hair?"

"Like teeth and bone, hair is one of the most durable parts of the body. So his hair is in the soil."

"Yeah, but how do you find it in all of this?" He waved a hand over the many tarps holding the soil she'd excavated.

"I already have. I removed and bagged the soil surrounding the skull. It contained ample hair in a mousy brown color matching Kilroy's license."

Sierra squatted next to them with her camera. "And I collected similar hair from the brush in the house to compare."

"Assuming that's Kilroy's brush, and the DNA matches the hair recovered here, we'll have an ID, but not a concrete one. We still need to try to get dental records." She looked up at Sierra. "Can you get Nick started on running down those records? And also tell Grady we're likely looking for a knife as the murder weapon, and I need his help in weighing in on potential knife blades."

"I'm on it." Pulling out her phone, she stepped away.

"Do you know how the hands were removed?" Devon asked, his expression tight.

Kelsey pointed at the end of the bone. "See the striations in the bone?"

He moved closer and squinted. "Yeah. It looks smooth from a distance, but up close there are markings."

"Exactly," she said. "Only one thing leaves that kind of mark. A saw."

"I'll search for one. Power or handsaw?"

"I don't know yet, but I will once I get a chance to get a better look at the bones. We should take all saws and sharp knives in the house or workshop into evidence."

"Will do." He stood and towered over her.

"And we'll need to get a search team looking for the hands." She couldn't believe she had to say something like this. Sure, she'd had to look for bones carried off by scavengers, but never by humans.

"I'll have the sheriff and his team take care of that, if it's okay with you."

She nodded. "I don't think we'll find them on the property. And no point in starting a search until the sun comes up."

He pointed at the grave. "Looks like you're almost finished."

She shook her head. "It might look that way, but even after I recover all of the bones, I need to continue excavating under the body until I get to the cut of the grave dug by the offender. And then I have the soil on the tarps to sift through."

A deep frown marred his handsome face. He was disappointed.

"I wish I could tell you I could do this faster, but it's a tedious and meticulous process that takes time." She rubbed her lower back. "But I'll keep going all night to move things along."

He scrubbed his forehead. "Sorry, I'm being so pushy."

She smiled. "You're far less pushy than most LEOs I deal with."

He smiled back at her, a cute, lopsided grin so at odds with his tough-guy exterior, and she was shocked that she could have a moment with him right there out in the open over a skeleton.

She pulled her gaze free. "I need to get back to work."

"I know you plan to work all night, but I want you to at least take a break. Maybe a nap at the hotel."

"I won't be able to sleep until this is done. But I can rest in the SUV for a while."

"Do that. Please." He held her gaze.

She appreciated his compassion. "I will. I promise."

She quickly bagged the bones in her hands, aware that he'd moved off, likely to go look for the saw and knives. She forced her thoughts back to the bag, labeled it, and added it to the box she'd collected. She also noted the bones on her log to record the number of and the particular bones she'd recovered, allowing her to easily tell if any bones other than the hands were missing.

She continued scraping away soil, night falling in dark purples and reds all around her, and the eerie sounds of coyotes howling in the distance. Still, she kept at it, taking breaks only for water and protein bars and one thirty-minute rest in the SUV alone with the seat fully reclined.

Now, the sun rose, upping the heat. Her back, arms, thighs, everything ached. The heat drained her even more. She needed to take another longer break. She planned to. Just as soon as she finished this layer. She removed the soil on the edge, and the soil above crumbled, revealing the actual cut from the spade.

"Sierra," she called out, suddenly rejuvenated in a way only a strong lead could bring. "I need pictures."

Her partner came running.

Kelsey pointed at the shovel mark. "Get a close-up of these striations. Then we're going to have to cast it."

Sierra got down on her stomach and eased out over the grave to snap several pictures. Her abs were made of steel to be able to hold that pose steady and not shake. Kelsey wasn't sure she could do it, but Sierra was a weight lifter, while Kelsey stuck with aerobics for exercise.

"I need to start weight training to give me abs of steel, too," Kelsey said, getting punchy from being so tired.

"Glad to work out with you anytime." Sierra smiled, her pale brown eyes lighting up. "The bones are in worse condition than what we often deal with in Oregon. A lot more like the remains we found on our mission trips."

"Exactly. The clay soil of the Pacific Northwest is pretty alkaline, but the soil here is very sandy, which usually means acidic, and it isn't kind to bones. Plus if this had happened in Oregon, I suspect we'd be looking at a body not just a skeleton."

"Why's that?"

"Clay soil reduces the circulation of air that's found in a less dense, more sandy-type of earth like this, slowing decomp."

"Oh, right, I remember you saying something about that before." Sierra scooted back. "I'll grab some plastic to protect the spade mark until you're done and I can cast it and take a soil sample to compare with the shovel we recovered. Which, by the way, had some very nice fingerprints on the handle."

"Excellent." Kelsey returned to her work, and hours later, she'd bagged every bone in the grave. She sat back to stretch and assess. She was missing both the hands and wrists which accounted for fifty-four of the two hundred six bones found in an adult. But other than that, she'd recovered everything else. A small miracle with the potential scavengers in the area.

Eager to finish, she started to remove the soil again, but quickly stopped.

"Devon! Sierra!" she called out. "You're gonna want to see this."

17

The sun was high in the cerulean blue sky, beating down and zapping Devon's energy when the excitement in Kelsey's tone brought him running. "What do you have?"

She pointed to a spot next to where she was crouched in the grave. "You're looking at the killer's shoe print. Or at least at the print of the person who dug the grave."

Devon couldn't see it, so he knelt down and spotted the telltale ridges outlining a shoe. "How can that even be?"

"Air trapped between the layers of soil preserved the print."

"I've never heard of such a thing."

"I've heard of it, but I've never seen it," Sierra said. "This is so cool."

"I need you to cast it right away," Kelsey said. "I don't want to risk damaging it."

"I'm on it." Sierra bolted away.

"We get a little excited about unique finds like this." Kelsey laughed. "Oh, and she took a cast of striations from the shovel marks, too. Grady's a tool mark expert, so he'll be able to tell us if it matches the shovel you recovered."

He sat back on his haunches and shook his head. "Who knew you would find so many leads in a grave?"

"Thankfully graves aren't covered widely on CSI shows, and it's an area where killers can still mess up." She stood and stretched. "The flowers are a great example. Why bury them when you could carry them off with you? Just another opportunity for us to catch him."

Devon got up. "Well, I'm glad he didn't take them."

"While Sierra does the casting, I'll get started on sifting through the soil." She yawned.

"Maybe you should take a break and grab something to eat."

She shook her head. "I had a protein bar a little while ago, and I want to get this done, review the findings with the sheriff, and get the evidence back to the lab for processing."

"FYI, I didn't find a saw of any kind. Which is odd when there's a fairly extensive collection of tools and a saw would be common in such a collection."

"The killer took it with him?"

"Could be, but not sure why when he left the shovel and other evidence behind." The thought bugged Devon. "Let me do another search."

He started in the outbuildings, emptying every single box and bin. He'd done it once already, but better to do it again than miss something. He searched the shelves. The trash. Looked at the earthen floor to see if it had been disturbed and the saw was buried somewhere. He came up empty again, so he went back to the house and slipped on booties.

His phone rang. Caller ID identified the caller as his supervisor. "Sir."

"Struck out with Cruz. With Vargas's lawyer sitting in, Cruz's still too afraid to talk. We might have to offer him a deal to get anything out of him. How are things going there?"

Devon updated Hurst. "Hopefully the trace evidence and bones will give us something concrete to go on."

"You keeping up your connection with Rickey Vargas? Wouldn't want the last six months to be for nothing."

"Checked in with him last night. To buy some time, I told him I had a death in the family and had to go to the funeral."

"Good," Hurst said. "Keep me in the loop, and for Pete's sake, don't get used to flying in fancy planes and helicopters or the instant forensic help. You're gonna have to come back to real life soon."

Thinking he might never want to go back to the real life of budgets and lack of funding, Devon stowed his phone. But money or not, and as much as the private sector was enticing, he was committed to the DEA for the rest of his working life. That was where he belonged, and he knew he could make a difference.

He made his way through the first floor, upstairs, and finally into a scorching attic that he had to admit he'd not searched as thoroughly as he could have. He swiped an arm over his forehead and the bandage covering the ugly tattoo fell off. He'd sweated through it a few times now, but he wasn't going to cover it again until right before they met with the sheriff.

Devon started digging. His shirt was soon drenched in sweat, but in the last corner hidden in the eves, he hit pay dirt. Not a saw, but a gun. A Sig Sauer P226, which he knew was chambered for a .357 round. The gun was designed for and commonly used in the military, but was readily available now to the general public.

He escaped the heat and hurried down to the first floor so he could breathe easier. He could see how local forensics missed the gun, but Sierra? That was odd. Maybe she hadn't finished her sweep yet.

From what Kelsey said, a gun wasn't used to kill the man buried outside. But—and this was a huge but—it could have been used to kill Todd Moore. Devon dug out his phone and checked his email for the report on Moore's murder investigation. Yes! It had come through about an hour ago from Hurst's assistant.

Devon clicked through the scanned files. And there it was. The connection. Todd Moore was killed by a .357 caliber bullet. Devon shoved his phone into his pocket and looked at the gun. What should he do with it? If it was connected to Todd's death, could Devon turn it over to Grady at Veritas and get an impartial evaluation? Yeah, Grady could be impartial. *If* Devon kept his suspicions to himself about the gun being used to kill Todd.

Meant he couldn't tell Sierra or Kelsey either about Todd's involvement. But the end result was what mattered right now. Veritas would process the gun quickly and thoroughly, where locals could botch it.

He headed out to the grave to turn the gun over to Sierra, but not telling Kelsey his theory that it was used to kill Todd left his gut churning.

They both looked up at him.

He held up the weapon. "I didn't find a saw, but did find a gun in the house."

"Where?" Sierra eyed him.

"Attic."

"I haven't been up there yet." She continued to stare at him. "I hope you didn't contaminate any evidence."

"No, but it doesn't look like there's anything up there that will help us."

She looked skeptical, and he figured she was thinking he

was trying to tell her how to do her job, when he didn't mean that at all.

"I honestly don't think this man was shot," Kelsey said. "But my exam will include checking for bullet wipe just in case."

"Bullet wipe?" he asked.

"When a bullet passes through something, it leaves behind lubricant, lead, dirt in the bore, and discharge residues. The same is true of bones. It's also called lead wipe because of the tiny metallic deposits left behind."

"So you'll know for sure if this gun was used?"

"If it passed through a bone, yes. But it could have gone through the soft tissue or organs and not hit bone. Still, the victim's shirt didn't have any bullet holes, so I think that's unlikely to begin with."

He held out the gun and nodded at the bag of gooey plaster in Sierra's hands. "Since you're busy, I'll go ahead and bag this for you."

"Thanks," she said, but sounded skeptical.

He was about to explain that he wasn't trying to do her job when his phone rang. Seeing Alex's name, Devon's gut tightened. Gage had doubled Jace's protection detail, and Alex had joined Jackson today, Riley would join Trey tonight, but maybe that had changed.

Devon quickly answered. "Everything okay there?"

"No," Alex said firmly. "Jackson and I drove Jace to school this morning, and we were tailed."

Devon's heart dropped. "You sure of the tail?"

"Absolutely."

"Jace okay?" Devon held his breath in wait for the answer.

"Yeah, I managed to lose the tail and came straight back to the condo."

Devon sucked in a breath. "You or Jackson get a look at this guy or his plate?"

"I didn't get a look at the guy and no plates on the vehicle. An older model Ford Taurus."

"The most common vehicle on the planet and without a plate."

"Exactly. But I do have Eryn working on reviewing CCTV in the area to see if she can track it. I talked to Gage, and we want to move Jace to our compound right away. No one is going to breach our security, and the boy will be safe there. Plus, we won't risk putting people at Veritas in danger."

"Let me talk to Kelsey, and I'll call you back." He disconnected the call and looked at her.

"What? What's wrong?" She clutched his arm in a death grip. "Is it Jace?"

"He's fine, but when Alex took him to school, a guy tailed them."

Her face paled beneath the layers of dirt. "You think they were going to try to abduct him again?"

"That's a good possibility."

She sighed, the breath going on and on. "Thank goodness for Alex and Jackson."

"Gage is now suggesting we move Jace to Blackwell's compound. Just to be safe."

"Yes, of course." She nodded, her head bobbing in rapid succession. "Yes. Good idea. Let Alex know, and I'll talk to Ahn and Jace to prepare them for the trip."

Devon got out his phone and so did she.

Alex answered right away.

"Kelsey agrees," Devon said. "She wants Jace at your compound. She's calling to talk to him and Ahn."

"Riley's still at the helipad, so we'll get going as soon as they're ready."

"Thanks, man." Devon let out a low breath to keep from alerting Kelsey to his anxiety.

"No worries," Alex said as if this was an everyday occurrence to him. It was, and he was very good at it. "I'll keep you updated."

"Keep your guard up and don't let anything happen to that little boy. You hear?"

Kelsey sifted and watched. Sifted and watched, but her mind was on Jace and his flight to Cold Harbor. She hoped she'd made the right decision sending him there, but her gut was twisted with worry and doubted it would settle down again before she heard the helicopter had landed safely at Blackwell's heliport.

Seeing a strand of hair on the screen, she stopped. This soil wasn't from the area where they'd recovered the skull, but near the feet. She grabbed a pair of tweezers and carefully picked up the strand to look at it in the daylight.

"What's that?" Devon asked from a lawn chair he'd pulled up earlier.

She looked over at him and noticed he'd removed the bandage covering his tattoo that was fading. She suspected he couldn't keep one on in this heat, but she sure didn't like that ugly snake.

She looked at her hand instead. "It's a hair. Black. Not the victim's color at all."

"The killer's?"

"Likely."

"Seriously, in all this soil you found a single hair?"

"Actually there are probably more than one, and finding one isn't all that uncommon."

"The odds of doing so must be low, though."

"I suppose, but this is exactly why we sift the soil and take our time in excavation. We don't want to lose even the tiniest of leads." She grabbed an evidence bag, dropped the hair inside, sealed the bag, and noted the quadrant where the soil had been recovered. "I'm nearly done here, and then we can review the findings with the sheriff and get him to sign off on taking the evidence."

"I'll cover up my tat again and then grab him." Devon stood. "He's searching with his men near the back of the property."

She nodded and resumed working. By the time Devon came back with the sheriff, she'd finished, and the soil had been returned to the empty grave. Sierra had been packing up their equipment, and Kelsey waved her over to be part of the discussion.

Kelsey quickly reviewed her findings. "We'll be taking the evidence back to our lab for processing." She grabbed her iPad. "I need you to sign off on the inventory."

As a lawman with jurisdiction here, he would know he had a choice, but he nodded just as she hoped he'd do. She handed him the iPad. He took his time reviewing the list and comparing it to the bagged samples and bones, then scribbled his name with the stylus.

Kelsey took back the tablet. "If you give me your email address, I'll send a copy of this and our findings to you."

He nodded. "We're sure lucky you happened to be here."

She smiled over the fact that he didn't seem hesitant over her skills anymore. "Everyone at the Veritas Center is glad to help. Do you have any questions before we go?"

He shook his head. "But I expect to be kept in the loop. And that means informing me of all results in a timely manner so you don't go impeding my investigation."

"Of course," she said. "But even if we waited a day or

two, which we won't, you'll still have the results far faster than if you used a local lab."

He frowned, his mustache turning down. "Wish that wasn't the truth, but it is, so no reason to argue the point."

Kelsey snapped off a glove and grabbed a business card from her tote to give to him. "My cell number is on here so you can call me directly. What number should I use for you?"

He fished a card from his shirt pocket. "Ditto on my cell."

She put the card in her tote and offered her hand. "Please let me know if you locate the missing hands."

"Doubt that's gonna happen."

Devon eyed the other lawman. "Why would you say that?"

"I've had it up to here with the cartels." He sliced a hand in front of his neck. "The brutal things they're doing these days is unbelievable. So I figure they're behind this, and if they wanted us to find the hands we would've by now. They're likely using them to send a message."

"But the guy's buried here, so how can that send a message?" Sierra asked, mimicking Kelsey's earlier question.

"They still got the hands, don't they? Seems like they can get the point across just fine that way."

Just the thought sent Kelsey's empty stomach roiling, and she was ready to move on. "Unless you have any other questions, we'll get packed up and be on our way."

"Have a safe flight."

As it turned out, they did have a safe and uneventful flight. Kelsey slept most of the trip, the others said they had as well. Still, she was dragging when they entered Veritas's back door pulling a rolling cart with all the bones and evidence collected at the site.

Kelsey sighed over being home. "I'm going to get the

evidence logged in with Blake so he can distribute it, and then I'm taking the longest shower known to man."

"I'd like to process the cellophane for prints right away," Sierra said. "So if you could sign that over to me now, I'll get to it."

Kelsey passed her the iPad holding the evidence log. Sierra signed it and took the cellophane from Devon.

"Let us know the minute you find anything," he said.

"I might not find anything."

"What? A member of the wonder team striking out?" He mocked a shocked expression. "Not possible."

They all laughed, and Sierra headed for the stairs. Blake's office was on the third floor, and there was no way Kelsey was going to climb stairs after an all-nighter, nor could she carry all this evidence, so she pressed her fingers on the print reader. "It's wonderful to have Blake coordinate all of this, otherwise I'd have to go to each person."

"Not to mention having his experience to draw from."

"Yeah, that too." She yawned and punched the number three then leaned back.

"Sorry I'm so boring." Devon grinned.

She assessed him. "Why don't you seem tired?"

"Because I took a few naps last night while you were digging."

"Really? I didn't even notice."

"I know. When you're in the zone, you're really in the zone."

"I suspect the same is true of you when you're under-cover. Maybe even more so as your life is on the line."

"Yeah." He frowned.

"What's wrong?"

"I keep thinking about why Sotos would want Jace, and I can't figure it out."

"You mentioned cleaning up loose ends. I assumed you

thought they were trying to take him back. You know, with Todd gone, they're afraid I might find out about Jace's background just like I have. And if there's no child to track back to them..." She shrugged, though the effort almost seemed like too much after the long hours digging and scraping.

He tilted his head. "I did think that at first, but now that we know about the abduction, I'm not sure it makes sense."

"They don't know that we know, though, right?"

"Not likely. But the opposite could be true, too. They could think you've known all along, and they're trying to erase the trail to them."

"So then why wait all this time to try to take him?"

"I don't know." Devon rubbed a hand over his chin now covered in a thicker beard. "Too many questions and no real motives."

She listened to the floor numbers ding, and thought about where they were in the investigation. "But who else would be behind this?"

"Maybe Jace's birth parents have tracked him to you, and they're trying to get him back."

"Could be, I suppose, but why not go to the police instead of risking going to prison for kidnapping?"

He continued to look at her, his gaze filled with questions. "They could be on the wrong side of the law, and they can't go to the police."

"That would be wonderful, right? That would mean they wouldn't get custody of him." The door opened, and she pulled the cart into the hallway.

"I suppose if I had to choose between the cartel wanting him or his parents, the parents would be the preferred choice." Devon took over the cart, and she was too tired to argue that she could manage it.

She looked at the boxes and bins. They'd really recovered a great deal of evidence but not enough. "If only we'd found something in Kilroy's house about the child trafficking."

Devon turned to look at her. "Hey, don't sound so down. We may not have found a smoking gun, but we still have all this trace evidence, and you have the bones. Plus, we can talk to the other parents with bogus birth certificates for their children. They might give us a lead."

She tried to perk up at that. "Can we do that after we clean up?"

"You sure you're up to it?"

"Are you kidding?" She smiled at him. "Talk to someone who might tell us who wants to take Jace? Of course, I'm up for that."

Poppy and Vincent Vandemere's neighborhood was located in the pricey Lake Oswego area of Portland, an area Devon knew little about, but if anyone could afford to buy a child, the people living in these big houses were likely ones who could. He parked in front of a mid-century modern single story with rich wood accents and a deep gray paint covering the front of the house.

He killed the engine and turned to Kelsey. "Ready?"

She took a hearty breath and let it out. She looked refreshed from her shower, had put on a floral dress that made her look even more perky, and had been upbeat on the way over, but she still seemed stressed.

"Having second thoughts?" He left his hand on the keys instead of pulling them out.

"No." She shook her head hard. "It's just...we're going to change these parents' lives and the child's life in a heartbeat. Tears me up inside."

Her empathy was commendable but... "They broke the law, Kelsey."

"I know, but their child didn't, and she doesn't deserve to have her life upended."

"Yeah, there's that."

She continued to shake her head but got out. He joined her and started up the long sidewalk leading to the massive home. He rang the doorbell and was thankful he'd taken time to head home to shower and change, as well as put on a fresh bandage, or whoever was home might look through the peephole and not answer.

The door opened. A petite woman with brown hair highlighted with blond streaks and wearing pressed jeans and heels answered. "Can I help you?"

Mrs. Vandemere?" Devon asked.

She nodded. "And you are?"

Devon held out his ID and introduced them. "Your name has come up in my investigation, and I wondered if you would answer a few questions for me."

"DEA?" She clutched her chest with fingers tipped in blue nail polish. "What on earth could you want to talk to me about?"

"Mind if we come in and discuss it?"

She frowned, but stood back and let them into a foyer with polished concrete tile floors and a soaring ceiling. She spun on her heel and let them into a living room with low-slung furniture in bright oranges and turquoise. "If you'll have a seat, I'll ask the nanny to keep an eye on the kids, and I'll be right back."

"Thank you," Devon said.

She remained looking at them, her hands clutched together. "Can I get you something to drink?"

Devon shook his head.

"No thanks," Kelsey said, her gaze taking in the room.

Poppy left, and Devon took a seat next to Kelsey on a leather sofa.

The leather was buttery soft, and Devon knew everything in the room cost a pretty penny. "Well, at least the child was raised in the lap of luxury."

Kelsey lifted her shoulders. "Doesn't mean that she was raised as well as her biological mother could've done even without the money."

He arched a brow.

"What?" she asked.

"It's odd that you're standing up for the birth mother, when you have more in common with this woman."

"I suppose, but in fact, the birth mothers are in the right in this situation."

"Assuming they didn't actually sell their child to Kilroy."

She bit her lip. "Yes, assuming that."

Poppy came back and perched on the edge of a matching leather chair. Her posture was perfect, but her hands were shaking. "Okay, what's this all about?"

Devon spoke gently. "Your daughter, Madison."

"Madison?" Her mouth fell open.

"Yes. Madison's birth certificate claims she was born in the Rugged Point Community Hospital and was a patient of Dr. Harriman, but the hospital doesn't have records of her having been born there or having been the doctor's patient."

Poppy paled. "Why are you looking at Madison's birth certificate in the first place?"

"As I mentioned, your name came up in conjunction with our investigation. There are several children in a similar situation."

She didn't respond but sat staring at him.

"Can you explain that, ma'am?" Devon asked.

She suddenly stood. "I'd like you to leave now."

Time to be blunt. "We know you bought your daughter

and that her certificate was falsified by a hospital employee."

"Leave. Now." She barely got the words out as she glared at him.

Devon eyed her. "This isn't going away Mrs. Vandemere."

She didn't speak but gave him a pointed look.

"I have a warrant to search your home," he said, trying to keep his calm. "You don't want me to have to use that, do you?"

"Search? But my children. They'd see that. And we don't keep any records here anyway. My husband. His office." Her gaze frantically raced around the space as if looking for a better solution.

Sometimes his job was just plain awful. He felt terrible putting her in this position, but if he remembered that she and her husband broke the law, he could continue. "My warrant includes his office and your vehicles."

"But I—"

"Please. Sit down and we can talk about this."

She remained standing, biting her lip and wringing her hands.

"I understand," Kelsey said softly. "I'm in the same position you're in."

Her gaze locked on Kelsey. "You are?"

"My son. Jace. My husband was married before me, but his wife died. We were married for two years, and I developed a deep love for Jace. I think of him as my own. My husband died a year ago, and I have legal custody of Jace. But when I looked into adopting him, I found out my husband wasn't Jace's biological father. His birth certificate was falsified." Kelsey took a long breath. "So you see, I'm likely going to lose Jace. But the mothers who lost their children so we could be mothers must wonder where their children are. That's not right."

Poppy dropped onto the sofa and collapsed as if deflating. "What do you want to know?"

"Tell us how your daughter came into your lives," Kelsey said.

Poppy clutched her hands on her lap. "We tried to have a baby for years. Doctors couldn't find a problem. Couldn't explain it. I've suffered from clinical depression since I was a teenager. Because of it, I'd done some stupid things, and we were never approved to adopt. I was already in a deep depression and that took me even lower. My husband couldn't stand to see me this way. He had a friend who knew a guy. He said he could arrange for a child with a birth certificate declaring he was ours. I didn't care where this child came from. I just knew that I wanted to be a mother. Needed to be a mother."

Devon felt bad for this woman's mental health issues, but not caring where her child came from was the height of selfishness. "And what happened then?"

"We had to get the money together, and then this man communicated with my husband through Snapchat. He said that would prevent any record of the communications."

"Didn't you worry he was just trying to scam you?" Devon asked.

"Yes, but I didn't care. I was desperate. And he didn't scam us. We paid the money, and within a month, I held our beautiful daughter in my arms."

"And your depression?" Kelsey asked.

"I still struggle with it, but it's much better."

"You said you have other children," Devon stated.

"Two. Both boys." She held up a hand. "I know you're going to ask how we got them and there's no point in lying. We got them the same way."

"When?"

"We waited two years between each child."

Devon had to work hard to hide his disgust of their repeated actions. "So you last communicated with this man when?"

"Nathan will be a year old in December. So about a year. But it wasn't the same man who brought Madison to us. We didn't even know we were talking with a different person on Snapchat until he delivered the baby."

Now they were getting somewhere. "Did he give his name?"

She shook her head.

Devon grabbed his phone, located a picture of Frisco Arroyo, and held it out. "Is this the man?"

She looked at it and nodded vigorously.

"You're sure."

"He had a sucker in his mouth the whole time, and I remember thinking how odd it was."

Devon located Kilroy's driver's license on his phone. "Do you recognize this man?"

She took a quick look. "He was the first guy we dealt with."

"Were either of these men blackmailing you?" Kelsey asked.

"Blackmailing? No. I assure you if they did, we would never have arranged additional children through them." She bit her lip. "I never asked because I didn't want to know, but I guess I should now...where did the children come from?"

"We aren't sure about that yet," Devon said. "But we believe these men helped drug-addicted mothers get cleaned up so they could produce healthy babies that they then took away and sold them to people like you."

Her mouth dropped open. "I didn't know that they were

taken from their mothers. With the amount we paid, I figured the mothers had received some of the money."

"That might be better, but it's still illegal," Devon said.

"I know, I just…" Her shoulders caved in, and she started crying.

"Are you willing to testify in court?" he asked before she completely collapsed.

"We're going to lose the children, aren't we?" She swatted at her tears.

"You most certainly will."

"Then yes. My life is over anyway." She sniffled. "I'll testify so this doesn't happen to anyone else."

18

Arroyo glared at Devon across the interview room in the Washington County Detention Center. Devon had hoped to bring the man in last night, but they didn't locate him until this morning. By the time they got him booked, it was going on noon, and then they wasted an hour of questioning while the guy refused to speak.

"Okay, fine, clam up," Devon snapped, his frustration at the tipping point. "In addition to the kidnapping and extortion charges, you give me no choice but to charge you with the murder of Simon Kilroy. You'll never see the outside of a prison wall again."

"Murder. Wait!" Arroyo shot forward in his seat. "I didn't kill no one."

Devon was glad to see he'd finally gotten the creep's attention and wiped the smug look from his face. "But see, you've claimed to be working alone this entire time, and if that's true, you're the only one with motive to murder Kilroy."

He tried to lift his arms, but the cuffs secured to the table stopped him. "I'm not taking a fall for something I didn't do."

"So you're saying you arranged the forged birth certificates and sold babies?"

"Yeah, sure, fine. I did that. But murder? No way."

Devon slowly sat back. "Tell me how the baby ring worked."

"Not really a ring. No gang like you're making out it is."

"So you're not part of the Rickey Vargas gang?" Devon asked, though after their phone call to Rickey, Devon doubted that Frisco even knew Rickey.

"Nah. It's just me and my boss, Juan Gonzalez. He took over for this Kilroy guy, but I never met Kilroy and didn't kill him."

"If you're not part of the Sotos Cartel, why tell Neal you were?"

"An extra measure to keep him in his place." Arroyo laughed.

Devon didn't know if he should believe Arroyo, but if he was affiliated with the Sotos, he would be too terrified to testify. Devon needed more details to put the puzzle pieces together. "And what exactly did you do for Gonzalez?"

"Whatever he needed done...except murder." He shook his head hard. "I ain't no killer."

"Okay, tell me about the babies."

"It was real simple. It was my job to find the mothers. Lowlifes. Hookers. Druggies. Chicks who didn't deserve to be a mom. Bring 'em in and get 'em cleaned up so they delivered a healthy kid and then give the kid a good home and collect payment. A win-win for all of us."

"And how did you find these mothers?"

"Asked around at first. Then word got out that I could help these chicks and lots of times they came to me."

"Did you pay them?"

"Yeah, sure. We didn't steal the kids. The moms turned them over for some cash."

"How much?"

"Depended on the person. A grand. Maybe more."

"And then you turned around and sold them for a hundred grand."

"They didn't know that." He grinned.

Devon had to force himself to remain seated and not deck the guy. "Did you keep records of the women and the parents you delivered their children to?"

"Yeah, sure. I had to get them to sign some form and Juan has them."

"And did you collect the blackmail money from the adoptive parents, too?"

"What? Blackmail. Nah." He shook his head hard. "We didn't blackmail anyone. Just gave 'em the kid and that was that."

"Ah, so Gonzalez played you, too, and didn't share the blackmail money with you."

Arroyo cocked his head. "You saying he blackmailed these people, for real?"

"For real. Thousands of dollars every month. So twelve times a year for how many families?"

Arroyo's eyes narrowed into venomous slits, showing Devon the first signs of the cold man who was willing to separate a woman and her child. "At least one kid a month. For three years."

"Let's see." Devon tapped his chin. "That's a minimum of thirty-six grand a month that you didn't get a cut of. Probably much more than that. That's a big chunk of change he kept from you."

"If I ever get my hands on him." He swung his head side to side.

"I'm sure we can work with the DA on your charges if you would agree to wear a wire and get Gonzalez to talk. Then testify against him."

"You know I will." He gritted his teeth.

"Great. I'll get with the DA then." Devon looked at the lowlife and took a breath before his next question. "You could also tell me why you arranged to have Jace Moore abducted."

"Who the heck is Jace Moore?"

"One of the kids Kilroy stole."

"I never had anything to do with Kilroy or his business. Juan handled all of that."

"But you knew about Kilroy."

"Yeah, sure. When I made arrangements with some of the families through Snapchat, they thought I was him. So I asked Juan about him. He said the guy moved to Texas because of his asthma and it was one of the best places to live if you had asthma. And if you were into dealing drugs, which Kilroy did, too."

Devon believed him as this was too detailed of a story to make up on the fly. "Did Kilroy find the babies the same way?"

"Yeah. He paid the mothers, too. Juan has his records."

So Jace's mother likely sold him. Now all Devon had to do was prove it, as Arroyo's word wasn't enough to allow Kelsey to keep the boy. "When you talk to Gonzalez, you're going to have to ask about Jace and Kilroy."

"Yeah, sure fine. Just give me the exact questions, and I'll ask."

"Hang tight, and I'll set things up." Devon left the room, glad to finally have a solid breakthrough in this investigation.

He wished he could rush over to the Veritas Center to tell Kelsey what he'd learned, but protocol prohibited him from sharing information on an upcoming sting with anyone. If it got back to Gonzalez, he could kill Arroyo in a heartbeat.

Devon didn't think Kelsey or anyone on her team would repeat the information, but protocol was protocol. And if she wound up hating him for it, then so be it, as Arroyo's safety had to come first now.

Kelsey put the last bone down and congratulated herself on a job well done. She'd spent a day and a half reviewing bones, first X-raying them for metal fragments and finding none, and then constructing an osteobiography—the life story of this individual from information discovered from the bones. From measuring the radius of the long bones in the arm and length of the long bones in the leg, she estimated that he'd been about five foot eleven in life—Kilroy's height as noted on his driver's license.

As humans aged, density in teeth diminished, so to estimate this individual's age, she'd measured the amount of light that passed through thin sections of the roots of his teeth. She also took X-rays of the necks of the femurs and measured that bone density. Both of these suggested he was around thirty-two, Kilroy's age.

She'd also found parry wounds on the ulna where he'd tried to fend off a knife attack. Not unusual in a stabbing. But the most intriguing thing she gleaned came from her examination of his fifth right rib. A small ridge of bone had become attached to the underside of the rib. Very unusual. She believed the vessels and nerves that ran beneath the rib had turned to bone. The most likely cause of this unusual finding would be a reaction to surgery. It looked like a surgeon had opened up his chest, most likely to treat a serious lung condition, which was consistent with asthma medicine Sierra had found in Kilroy's house.

So her study definitely pointed to Kilroy, but DNA taken

from his hairbrush and the grave that matched to a bone sample would provide a better ID, as would dental records if Nick could locate them.

She stared at the bones. Now what? She'd done her part and the osteobiography had served two purposes. It helped to ID the victim as well as to keep her mind off the other suffering parents whose children had already been taken by social services. She'd seen their pain firsthand and worried she would soon feel the same loss. Devon hadn't asked her to check with Emory on Jace's DNA, but she knew it was only a matter of time before she had to face the concrete proof that Jace wasn't Todd's biological son.

She wished Devon was here right now so she could talk to him about it. To let him hold her if he wanted to. All the signs pointed to him wanting to, and she wanted to let him. To lean on him. Draw strength from him. To love him.

Time to admit it. In the midst of this horrible, horrible time in her life, she'd fallen in love. She wanted to pursue her feelings, but how could she trust them? Especially with a man who lied for a living. He would be too good at deceiving her, and she clearly didn't have the ability to discern if he was telling the truth.

"So ignore your feelings," she warned herself. "Ignore everything about him except as related to this investigation. That's the only sane thing to do."

As if her thoughts conjured him up, her phone rang, and his number appeared on the screen. She answered.

"I'm in the lobby," he said.

Her heart leapt for a moment before crashing over the fear that he'd come to tell her it was time to get the DNA results. "I'll come get you."

She hurried from her lab and climbed the stairs. She hadn't seen him since they interviewed the second family yesterday. He was far too busy arresting and processing the parents and Arroyo. And most important to her, trying to get Arroyo to flip on the Sotos Cartel so they could find the person behind Jace's abduction.

She stepped into the lobby, her eyes taking in the sight of him as he stood tall and strong waiting for her. He started across the tile floor, his stride sure and confident. He looked handsome in tactical pants and a polo shirt. He smiled, a wide and intimate smile only for her, one that said he missed her and was glad to see her, and her heart flip-flopped.

She couldn't believe her reaction when she'd just warned herself to ignore him. She firmed her resolve and wiped any hint of attraction from her thoughts and committed to staying focused on the investigation. "I have some information to share with you on the remains."

She turned away, but not fast enough to miss the hurt in his eyes. Maybe he expected her to say something personal. Maybe tell him she'd missed him. She didn't want to hurt him, but she had to protect herself.

After signing him in, she led the way to the stairwell and jogged down the steps. She heard him keeping up with her, but they didn't speak.

In her lab, she picked up the ulna and turned. "You asked me at the crime scene about the saw the killer used."

He stood watching her, his focus pointed, and yet, reserved at the same time. Had her lack of enthusiasm at seeing him really hurt him? Seemed like it.

"And?" he finally asked.

"These marks were made by a one-millimeter saw blade with fourteen teeth per inch, and I believe we're looking for a mechanical saw."

"Believe, but not certain."

She swallowed hard and nodded.

His eyes narrowed, but his gaze never left her. "I've never

seen you uncertain like this when it comes to your work. You always seem so sure."

She really didn't want to talk about this, but she needed to explain. "I am confident. Most of the time. But one time... I was wrong. Or more accurately, I made a premature ruling. Said a man used a handsaw when it actually turned out to be a mechanical saw. My testimony was a big part in sending this man to prison when he wasn't guilty."

"But you figured it out?" he asked, no condemnation in his tone.

She greatly appreciated him not judging her error. "Yes, I did figure it out, but much later. The victim was dismembered and dumped in a creek, and as you can imagine, we didn't recover all the bones. But after a year, the second femur was located, and it was smooth and dense unlike the other bones and contained several false starts."

"Meaning?"

"I was wrong. A mechanical saw was used." She held up a hand. "Let me explain. False starts are crevices where the killer starts a cut, but the blade doesn't finish cutting through the bone. Because handsaws require greater physical effort to cut through a bone, when a killer uses one, they almost always finish the cuts they start. But with a mechanical saw, you almost always find false starts."

"So because there weren't any false starts in the first bones you located, you thought this suspect used a handsaw."

She nodded. "The police didn't recover the saw that made these cuts, but the suspect, Lucien Sparrow, owned one that could have, and it was missing. He claimed he lent the saw to a neighbor who never returned it, but the detectives never found a neighbor to corroborate his claim. Though the detectives had nothing but circumstantial evidence, Sparrow was convicted."

"When the other femur was located, was this guy released?"

She worked hard not to think of her part in putting an innocent man behind bars and stuck to the facts. "Not right away. Detectives had to find the real killer or a judge wouldn't overturn the conviction. Six months later, the detectives got a break in the investigation when the daughter of another suspect found an owner's manual for a multi-speed reciprocating saw in her dad's desk. She feared that her father killed this man, and she turned it over to the detectives. They knew from their investigations that he frequented a particular Walmart where this saw was sold. Security footage caught him buying the saw along with an extra blade, a box of trash bags, a tarp, and some goggles."

He gave a swift nod of approval. "So you had the killer."

"Yes and no. I needed to prove this make of saw would actually leave the same striations as found on the victim's bone. So I cut four pig femurs. Two with different blades and two with the reciprocating saw. It was clear even to a jury that the saw had made the same marks as found on the body. They convicted him, and Sparrow was released." She wished that brought her any measure of comfort.

"You're still frustrated about being wrong," he stated as if he'd experienced a similar thing.

She held back from answering, hoping he'd say more, but he'd been pretty reserved since entering the lab, and he didn't seem willing to offer much other than pointed questions. That was what she wanted, right? Not to put herself in a position of wanting more with him? So then why did it hurt when he obliged?

"Kelsey?" he asked.

"Yeah, of course, I'm frustrated, but it's more than that. I hate that I was part of an innocent man serving two years for a murder he didn't commit. I ruined his life. He can never get those two years back, and it's my fault."

Devon clenched his jaw and worked the muscles. "You didn't convict him. You just presented what you knew at the time, and the jury weighed that with everything else."

"I try to tell myself that, but..." She shook off the uncertainty and turned her mind back to the current case where it needed to stay. "I checked with Grady on the type of saw we might be looking for here. He said the fourteen-teeth-per-inch blade rules out a short list of saws, but the measurement is common to many saws, and that isn't going to help us find the killer. We'll need more than that."

He pointed at Kilroy's skeleton laid out on the table. "And what about cause of death?"

"As I suspected, he was stabbed in the heart." She picked up a rib and pointed at a notch in the bone. "A V-shaped wound is indicative of a knife wound. This rib would be located directly above the heart." She picked up two additional ribs with the same trauma.

"He was stabbed multiple times."

She nodded. "The blood spatter in the house corroborates that, as does his shirt. And I found parry wounds on his ulna from where he lifted his arms to try to fight off his attacker."

"How do you know these wounds occurred right before death and aren't old?"

"When our bones sustain trauma they immediately begin to replace the bone. This is called remodeling." She grabbed his femur. "You can see an example of that here. At some point, he'd broken his leg and it healed."

He studied the area she pointed to on the bone, then looked up. "But the rib injuries don't show any sign of this remodeling?"

"Exactly."

He tilted his head in thought, his expression remaining somber and closed. "So we know how he died and that his hands were removed with a mechanical saw. How about when it happened? Have you been able to pin that down more?"

She shook her head. "I'm not sure about the post mortem interval yet. I need to confer with Sierra on her aging of the blood stain. But the age and height of this body are a match to Kilroy. DNA and dental records should prove the rest."

He nodded, his expression thoughtful, and she desperately wanted to know what was making him so reserved.

But she would stick to the facts and not open a can of worms she had no business opening. "How did your interrogation of Arroyo go?"

He frowned and looked away. "It's ongoing at this point."

"What does ongoing mean?" Her phone chimed for the alarm she'd set. "Hold that question. I've scheduled a partners' update meeting. I assume since you're here that you'd like to attend."

She expected he'd be eager, but he shrugged. "Guess I might as well go."

Odd. He seemed less than enthusiastic. But why? Was he letting her rebuff keep him from wanting an update, or was there more going on here than she first suspected? "Everything okay?"

"Sure, why," he said but didn't look at her.

"I don't know. You seem different somehow."

He gestured at the door. "We should go, right?"

She didn't miss his obvious change of subject, but if he didn't want to talk about what was bugging him, she couldn't force him to speak. She stepped into the hallway. He kept up with her, but didn't start a conversation. So other than her rebuff, what could be bothering him? Maybe something happened at the station that upset him. Or maybe it was personal—there was no way to tell. Maybe the day apart made him realize his interest in her was simply because they'd been thrown together. That was only physical attraction that burned out the minute he'd left her.

Maybe. Maybe. Maybe. Sigh.

They entered the conference room where her partners were seated around the table, and Blake stood at the whiteboard. He was noting outstanding items in the investigation.

He tapped the first one. "First up. Age of the blood stains found in Kilroy's house. Sierra?"

She sat forward and looked at the others. "I won't go into details, but I put the stains at around two hundred eighty-eight days."

"So about nine months," Grady said.

"That would be consistent with the condition of the body, given the dry and arid desert conditions," Kelsey said.

"So our victim was murdered nine months or so ago." Blake wrote the information on the board.

Devon started to open his mouth, then clamped it closed. Kelsey didn't know what he was about to say, but for some reason he thought better of it. Kind of went with his behavior in the lab.

Blake moved to the next item. "And the casts for the shovel and shoe print?"

"Still curing," Sierra said. "Takes seventy-two hours before I can wash off the dirt and clean it for analysis."

Blake noted that. "And fingerprints?"

"I lifted great prints from the flowers' cellophane," Sierra said. "And the shovel handle, but no match in AFIS. However, they did match to each other."

Devon slammed a fist on the table.

"Sorry," he quickly said. "I was pinning a lot of hope on finding a match."

"A match in general, or you have a suspect in mind?" Blake asked.

"Both, I guess. I mean it would be great if it matched anyone we're looking into or a match in general could give us another lead." His vague answer didn't sit well with Kelsey.

Blake gave Devon an odd look. So it wasn't just Kelsey who thought he was acting a bit off.

"Can you email those prints to me?" Devon asked.

Sierra nodded.

"Okay, moving on." Blake tapped a marker against the next item. "Maya, do we have a match between the known Sotos cocaine and the kilo found at Kilroy's house?"

"Yes," she said with enthusiasm. "They were cut with the same laundry detergent."

"Detergent?" Kelsey fired a questioning look at Maya. "Isn't that dangerous for users?"

"Absolutely," Maya replied. "The detergent's small particles can build up in arteries causing dangerous blockages in the brain, liver, and heart."

Kelsey shook her head. "If users know this, how can they put it in their body?"

"They don't care as long as they get their fix." Maya frowned. "FYI, the detergent isn't made by the big-name manufacturers, and I'm working on finding who produces it. Maybe that will give us a lead."

Since Devon was the drug expert in the room, and he'd freely shared about the subject in the past, Kelsey waited for him to comment, but he didn't say a word.

She wasn't going to let him get away without weighing in. "What do you think about that, Devon?"

He didn't move. His expression didn't change. "Looks like Kilroy added dealing drugs to his profession."

"That's it?" She stared at him. "All you have to say?"

"Yeah, why?" He looked at her then, his expression closed and unreadable.

"This is your area of expertise. I would think you'd be upset that this pretty much confirms Kilroy was tied to the Sotos Cartel." She took a long breath before continuing. "I mean, from my perspective, even if we find the person who killed Kilroy, someone else in the cartel could take his place, and that means they could come after Jace. We may never remove the threat to him."

"I didn't think of that," he said, but shifted his gaze over her shoulder.

He had to have come to the same conclusion, and his evasive answers were starting to really worry her. Did he learn something from Arroyo, and he was withholding it from her? From them? She wanted to ask, but she wouldn't put him on the spot in front of the whole team.

"Okay, Kelsey, we're up to you," Blake said. "What did the bones tell you?"

She swallowed down her worry for Jace to answer. "I put the cause of death as a knife to the heart. I've given the measurements to Grady along with the pattern from the shirt and rib, and he's working on determining the murder weapon."

Grady nodded. "None of the knives you brought back have blood on them and they don't match the wounds. I *can* tell you the inflicted wound was made by a serrated edge. I am working on finding the actual knife, and hopefully, I can you tell what to look for soon."

Kelsey smiled her thanks. "I've also determined that a mechanical saw with a fourteen-teeth-per-inch blade was used to remove the hands. Since our only suspects in connection to Kilroy at this point are Gonzalez and Arroyo, I suggest we do a deeper dive into their personal lives to see if they may have purchased a saw with such a blade or already owned one."

Blake nodded. "Grady can you narrow down the brand of saw at all?"

"Yeah, I eliminated a bunch of them, but it's a common blade and with most tools being made by the same manufacturer, it's even harder to specify a single brand."

Blake looked at Nick. "We need to find out if either of these men traveled to El Paso near the time Sierra gave us. That should give Devon probable cause for a warrant to search their residences and maybe we can find the saw."

Nick nodded. "I'll get on it right after we break up, and I'll also see what I can find on either of them purchasing a saw."

Blake noted both items on the board. "DNA's up next."

Emory sat forward. "DNA from the sucker stick is back, but no match in CODIS. If Arroyo created a new identity, he didn't have a record under his former name."

"Maybe he's exactly who he says he is and just didn't have much of an online presence," Blake suggested.

"Could be," Nick said. "But that would be unusual in today's world."

"Any thoughts on that, Devon?" Kelsey asked.

He shook his head, but didn't speak.

Seriously, something was up with him.

"I'm running the hair and blood samples from Kilroy's place now and will have profiles soon," Emory said.

"And the dental records, Nick?" Kelsey asked. "Any luck in finding his dentist?"

"Maybe," he said. "I'm waiting on a call back. Will let you know the minute I know anything."

"Good. He has a lot of restorations, and it should be easy to ID him that way." Kelsey looked at Grady. "What about the gun? Do you have any info on it that might help us figure out the trafficking aspect of this investigation?"

Devon shot to his feet, his expression rigid and tight. "Thanks for the update, but I need to get going. I'll check in with you later."

"Going?" Kelsey asked, but it didn't stop him from marching to the door.

"You need an escort," Maya said.

"You can see the lobby entrance from here," he called over his shoulder and kept going.

Kelsey half expected Maya to race after him, but she shook her head. "What's up with him?"

Kelsey didn't know, but she did know that his sudden shift in behavior hurt. More than she could have expected. He was all secretive and closed off, like he was keeping something from her and the others. She'd expected he would be good at lying and deceiving, but maybe he wasn't as good at it as she first thought.

"About the gun," Grady said, bringing them back. "It's a Sig Sauer P226, Legion Full-Size. Not a lot else to tell you about the gun itself. Sierra lifted six clear prints. Three on the grip and three on the slide. She can tell you about that when I'm done. And the gun is a definite match to the slugs Devon dropped off an hour or so ago."

"Slugs?" Kelsey shot up in her chair.

"We didn't recover slugs at the crime scene," Sierra said before Kelsey could say the same thing.

"Hmm. My tech took them into evidence and started to compare them to slugs fired from the Sig. I just assumed they were from Kilroy's place and didn't question him."

"Go get the evidence bag now." Kelsey demanded. "I want to see what's on it."

Grady got up and started out of the room.

"Hurry!" she said, so baffled by this situation that she didn't know how to process it.

Blake frowned. "So Devon didn't get the slugs from Kilroy's house, but he obviously thinks they're a match for Kilroy's gun. I wonder what else he's been hiding from us."

The others started speculating about whether Devon played them to move his investigation forward under the guise of helping Kelsey and Jace, but Kelsey was too shocked to join in the discussion.

Devon hid something from her. He actually hid something from her. She had concrete proof of it in the form of slugs. He deceived her—just like Todd. A big fat lie of omission.

Kelsey's heart constricted, and she could barely breathe. Think. Her brain felt like it was filled with cotton, dulling her thought processes. Probably a defense mechanism to protect herself from the agony of betrayal.

She stared at the door waiting for Grady to return, and she realized Devon had never mentioned why he'd come to see her. He was here because he dropped off the slugs and what? Thought he'd come say hi, but not tell her his real reason for being there?

Grady opened the door and cast her an apologetic look. "I should've checked the bag. I'm sorry."

"About?" she asked.

"These slugs came from Tucson PD." He held up the bag. "From Todd's murder investigation."

"Todd," she said, trying to make sense of her second shock of the hour.

19

The next morning in the department's surveillance van, Devon watched his tech person wire Arroyo for the meet with Gonzalez, Devon's mind still on Kelsey as it had been all night. He prided himself in being able to put up a false front for his undercover work. He was superb at doing that. Apparently those skills didn't extend to his personal life. At least not when it came to withholding information from Kelsey.

He probably should be thankful that he couldn't lie or withhold information easily anywhere but in the drug world, but at the moment he wasn't. He'd blown it with Kelsey. Blown it big time. He knew that the minute he'd looked back yesterday and caught her gaping after him when he rushed out of the meeting. He didn't want to hurt her. Ever. But he couldn't lie to her either, and he couldn't tell her what was going on with Gonzalez. So he'd had to be evasive.

That alone would set her on edge after the number Todd had done on her, but then learning that he'd given Grady the slugs from Todd's murder to compare to the gun, which Devon was sure Grady was about to reveal before he bailed?

That would definitely put her over the edge. Devon could only hope once they knew the gun and slugs matched, that she would understand he wanted to try to save her from additional pain and not tell her about his theory until he'd proved the connection.

"All set," the electronics tech said.

"I'm not sure I can do this." Arroyo gnawed on his lower lip.

Devon took control of his wayward thoughts. He had to be on the top of his game so nothing happened to Arroyo. He looked the man straight in the eye. "Remember, your work here will guarantee a spot in witness protection for your family to keep them safe. I'm sure you'll pull it off."

"But..."

"Just pretend it's one of your usual conversations. No biggie. Just an update. You do that all the time with Gonzalez, right?"

Arroyo nodded.

"Then you'll be fine." Devon gestured at the van filled with surveillance equipment. "We're right here and our tactical team is just down the block. If you get into trouble, use the code words, and we'll be inside so fast your head will spin."

Arroyo took a long breath. "You're right. I can do this."

Devon met his gaze. "Remember, you ask about Jace Moore."

"Yeah, sure."

"And lead with the fact that you saw a news story on the murder of Simon Kilroy, we connected you to the guy, and questioned you."

"I got it."

"Then get moving."

Arroyo slipped out of the van, and Devon put on headphones to listen into the conversation. Devon heard footsteps over Arroyo's mic and then a knock on a door.

"Here we go," Arroyo whispered then raised his voice. "Hey, Juan."

Devon zoomed his binoculars in on Gonzalez's hardened glare. "Didn't know you were coming by."

"I gotta talk to you. It's important. The cops came to see me." He sounded terrified which made his plight seem more real. "They said they found my name at his place. Why would he have my name?"

"I have no idea," Gonzalez said, but his voice wavered. "I haven't seen him since we took over for him."

Arroyo clamped a hand on the back of his neck. "You think the cops know what we're doing?"

Devon could kiss Arroyo for asking a question that might get Gonzalez to admit to his actions.

"You mean the fake certificates?" Gonzalez sounded wary.

"Yeah, and you know…"

"Seriously, dude. You're such a wuss." Gonzalez snorted. "You still can't say it, can you? We buy and sell babies. No biggie. We're doing the kids a favor. They're better off with the new families."

"Yeah, but…"

Gonzalez's expression tightened. "But nothing. It's far too late in the game to be having second thoughts."

"But the cops," Arroyo whined. "They mentioned a kid's name. Said someone tried to abduct him a few days ago and think I arranged it. *Me*. You got that? Me."

Gonzalez watched Arroyo for a long moment. "One of our kids?"

"Kilroy's. Kid's name is Jace Moore."

Gonzalez tipped his head. "I'm positive I've never dealt with parents by the name of Moore."

Devon didn't want to admit it, but the guy sounded like he was telling the truth.

Arroyo took a step closer. "You have Kilroy's records, right, so we can check?"

"Yes!" Devon pumped his fist at Arroyo's great performance in asking for physical proof.

"Yeah. Got 'em from Kilroy just in case. C'mon in and we can check." Gonzalez turned back and stepped into the house.

Arroyo glanced back at the van as if asking if he should go inside. It would be a risky move, but Devon hoped Arroyo would make it. He suddenly spun and entered the house. Devon heard a jingle sounding like keys, and then what sounded like a drawer scraping open. Silence followed. Long and tense.

Concerned now, Devon looked at his fellow agents. "Be ready to go in."

"Yeah, here it is," Gonzalez finally said. "Jace Moore. Parents—Todd and Margo Moore of Portland. Birth mother —Cindy Eaton, right here in Rugged Point. Paid her a grand."

Devon wanted to pump his fist again but he jotted down the name so Kelsey and their team could begin looking for her.

"So the cops said someone tried to abduct this kid?" Gonzalez asked.

"Yeah," Arroyo replied. "And they thought I arranged for the guy to do it. But I didn't. Did you?"

"Nah, why would I? Didn't even know who he was until you asked."

"Could Kilroy have something at his place with our information on it?"

"Nah."

"How can you even know that?" Arroyo sounded skeptical, the perfect tone to get Gonzalez to keep talking.

"Let's just say Kilroy decided he needed more money than I forked over to buy him out. So I paid him a little visit a while back, and I confirmed he didn't have anything on us."

"But maybe the police arrested Kilroy for something since then, and he ratted me out." Arroyo knew Kilroy was dead so he was putting in an Oscar-worthy performance pretending he was alive to get Gonzalez to admit to killing him.

"Nah, I made sure he couldn't talk to no one." Gonzalez's snide tone grated on Devon's nerves.

"You killed him?"

Gonzalez laughed. "You should be thanking me. I silenced the one man who could rat on us, and he's no longer a threat. So unless one of the families we sold a kid to outs us, which they're never going to do as they'd be outing themselves, too, we've got nothing to worry about."

"But the cops."

"Just keep your big mouth shut, and you'll be fine."

Devon jumped up. "That's it. We've got enough. Let's move."

He grabbed his assault rifle and bolted from the van. His tactical team in an assault vehicle down the road raced up to the driveway. They piled out of the vehicle, their footfalls echoing in the quiet as they charged up to the house. A burly guy broke down the door, and the team burst into the house. Devon and his fellow agents from the surveillance van followed.

"Police," they shouted, moving through the front rooms.

Devon entered the room where Gonzalez stood gaping. Relief flooded Arroyo's face.

"On the floor now!" Devon commanded.

Both guys dropped down face-first. Devon cuffed Gonzalez and jerked him to his feet to read him his rights.

"Hey, man, I didn't do anything," Gonzalez complained.

Devon glared at the man. "You can tell that to a judge."

They had to pretend to arrest Arroyo to keep Gonzalez from being suspicious and arranging for someone to kill Arroyo before he could testify. No worries about Arroyo giving this away, though. He protested the cuffs and handling by Devon's fellow agent, giving another good performance.

Devon hauled Gonzalez out the door, Arroyo after him. The men were placed in separate vehicles that took off for the county jail where they would be booked. Devon would then interrogate Gonzalez, and hopefully by tomorrow morning, Devon would be able to tell Kelsey that he'd arrested Kilroy's killer and the man behind the baby selling ring. Only problem was, Devon still didn't know who paid Cruz to abduct Jace, and until Devon figured it out, the boy was still in danger.

Nearing dinnertime, Kelsey put the ulna under the magnifying glass for a better look at the saw cut. She'd hoped to hear from Devon so she could call him out on hiding his investigation into Todd's death from her. Since she hadn't heard a word from him, she buried herself in her lab reviewing the bones one more time, just to be sure she hadn't made a mistake.

She'd split her time thinking about Devon and about how it looked like Kilroy had killed Todd. Not some random attack, but cold-blooded murder. She'd reviewed his blackmail payments and realized she hadn't noticed in her first review that he'd stopped making the payments. Likely

Kilroy's motive for killing Todd. Could that have somehow translated into a fellow cartel member trying to take Jace?

She heard the door latch click, and Nick entered carrying a manila envelope. "Kilroy's dental X-rays."

"Excellent. I knew you could do it." She quickly opened the package, mounted the films on a light box, and turned it on. She grabbed the lower jaw to compare to the illuminated X-rays. She looked at the distance between teeth, the size of roots and teeth, and their curvatures and restorations to confirm a match and performed the same procedure with the upper jaw. "It's official. The recovered skeleton is Kilroy."

Nick leaned against the table and crossed his feet at the ankles. "Not a surprise."

"No, but let me send out a group text telling everyone it's official." She tapped the message into her phone and hit send on the text that went not only to her partners, Sheriff Trujillo, and Devon as well. Maybe he would respond.

She got a text from Maya. *FYI the blood and hair sample matched each other. The single hair had no match in CODIS. Laundry detergent a bust.*

Kelsey sent back her thanks for the update and looked at Nick. "What about the flights to El Paso? Any luck?"

"Still working on that, but I should have the manifests soon." He started for the door. "I'll text you the minute I know anything."

Her phone chimed. Devon had responded. Just one word. *Perfect.*

But it gave her an opening to tell him she needed to talk to him. He quickly replied with *In the office right now. I'll call you as soon as I can.*

Disappointed, she sat back and felt like crying. Giving in to a big old self-pity party. But that would gain nothing except a blotchy face and red eyes. Her thoughts turned to Jace. Sweet, innocent Jace. She wanted nothing more than to see her son. It was just a matter of time before they wrapped up this investigation, and Devon reported Jace to social services. She had to see him.

She grabbed her phone and dialed Gage Blackwell.

"Gage, hi, it's Kelsey Moore," she said when he answered.

"Calling to check up on Jace?"

"Actually I'm desperate to see him." Tears pricked at her eyes, and she paused to swallow them away. "I was wondering if you would send your helicopter for me and have them fly me back in the morning. I know it's a big ask but—"

"Don't even think about that," he interrupted. "If I was in your position, I'd be asking the same thing. Just head to the same heliport you've been using, and I'll get Riley or Coop in the air right away."

"Thank you, Gage."

"No thanks needed. I'm glad to help."

Kelsey stored the bones in the labeled bags and then hurried up the steps to Maya's lab. As managing partner, she kept track of schedules, and Kelsey needed to inform her of the trip. She was bent over a microscope and looked up, a question flashing on her face.

Kelsey smiled at her friend.

Maya returned it. "You look like you're in a good mood."

"I am. I'm taking off for Cold Harbor to see Jace. I'll be back first thing in the morning, but will you keep me updated on any news?"

"Of course."

"I finished a second examination of the bones and didn't find anything, so I thought I should take the time with Jace while I had it."

"I'm glad you're going. It'll do you both a world of good."

"Okay, I'll pack a quick bag, and then I'm off to the heliport."

"Did you tell Devon?"

Kelsey shook her head and made sure her frustration over the personal question didn't show. "He's busy."

Maya raised an eyebrow. "Did you two have a fight or something?"

"Fight? No."

Maya pushed back from the table and stood. "Well, something changed because he wasn't the same at the update meeting."

"So you noticed it, too," Kelsey said, as she couldn't let this go.

Maya came closer. "Would be hard to miss with the way he couldn't keep his eyes off you in the past, and at the meeting he couldn't seem to look at you."

"Likely because he brought those slugs to Grady without telling me." She gave up hiding her unease with Devon and crossed her arms. "After what Todd did, I honestly feel like a fool for trusting Devon. Trusting any guy."

"That's understandable."

Kelsey wished Maya would've disagreed with her as then Kelsey might reconsider her opinion.

"But it's not really a good way to live, is it?" Maya added.

"No, I suppose not," Kelsey said, but wouldn't put more than that out there for Maya to analyze.

"But you're not going to do anything about it."

"Like what?"

"Like maybe go see him before you leave and give him a chance to explain."

"I can't, okay? Just leave it at that. Now I have to go get ready. Call me with any news."

Before Maya tried to stop her, Kelsey rushed from the lab. She made quick work of packing her bag. She didn't need to hurry as she would easily beat Riley to the helipad, but she'd rather sit there waiting than be here where her mind kept drifting to Devon.

Or maybe she should listen to Maya and stop in to talk to Devon on the way. Could she do that? Could she confront him?

Suddenly eager to do just that, she grabbed her purse and bag and took the elevator to the parking garage. Before thinking better of her plan, she quickly merged into traffic, which was light at this time of day, and was soon driving downtown to Devon's office. She hoped he was there. She should probably text him, but she doubted he would agree to meet with her. If he wasn't still at his office, she would just head to the heliport as she didn't know his home address.

She parked in the lot and hurried to the small office where she introduced herself to the receptionist sitting behind thick bulletproof glass. "I need to speak with Agent Dunbar."

"Let me see if he's free."

Kelsey nodded and smiled, but she didn't actually know if she was happy that he was in the office or terrified that he was there. Nervous now, she tapped her foot and looked around the tiny reception area only big enough for two chairs and a small table plus a metal detector in front of the inner door.

It popped opened, and Kelsey jumped. Devon stood there big and strong as usual, but his confidence was gone, and his gaze questioning. "Kelsey?"

"I need to talk to you."

He looked at the receptionist. "Would you check her in?"

The older woman nodded and asked Kelsey questions, typing the answers in on her computer. "I'll need your phone and any electronic devices along with your driver's license."

Kelsey quickly shoved her phone and ID into the open tray at the bottom of the window. The receptionist took it and smiled. "You're good to go. Just step through the detector."

Kelsey took her time going through, glad to see she didn't set it off.

"This way." Devon turned and led her to a small conference room where he closed the door behind her. He met her gaze, worry etched in his. "What's so urgent that you couldn't have called me?"

She took a breath before snapping. She had to restrain her emotions and remain civil. "I could have called, but after the way you've been acting, I didn't think you'd answer."

He grimaced but recovered quickly and pointed at the chairs. "Go ahead and have a seat."

"Right, divert the conversation again just like you did at the meeting." She lifted her shoulders and wouldn't sit until they had this out.

"The meeting?"

"Stop it, okay?" she snapped and instantly regretted it after warning herself to keep herself together. She blew out her frustration. "We have this connection. We both know it, but suddenly you've gone cold and act like you're hiding something. Then I find out about the slugs. How could you suspect Kilroy killed Todd and not tell me?"

"I didn't want to tell you until there was proof. It would just have upset you, and you didn't need that with all you've been going through." He paused for a long breath then added in a near whisper, "I was thinking about you when I made that decision."

"Yeah, well, it's gone beyond suspicions now. The slugs are a match to the gun."

"They are?" His eyes widened. "I didn't know. I've been too busy to follow up with Grady."

"If you wouldn't have run out of the meeting, you would know."

"I had to go. I figured Grady would mention the slugs, and you would question me. I couldn't have that conversation. Not then, or I would've had to tell you..." He stopped and shook his head.

"Tell me what?"

"About Arroyo and Gonzalez."

"What about them?"

"After I arrested Arroyo, I convinced him to wear a wire and go talk to Gonzalez."

Her eyes widened. "Something else you chose not to tell me?"

"It's standard operating procedure to keep this on a need-to-know basis so word won't get back to our operation's target."

"I get that. Makes sense even, but you could've just said something was going on with these guys, and you would tell me about it as soon as you could." She crossed her arms. "Instead, you acted all evasive and suspicious like Todd did."

He cringed. "I'm not like Todd. Not at all. Did I handle this the best way by not mentioning anything to you at all? No. I could have done as you said. Could have told you about the slugs. That was something I could have shared. And as you said, I could have mentioned Gonzalez and Arroyo and given you details later. But I let my feelings for you get in the way and knew if I mentioned it at all, that I'd cave and tell you everything. I'm nothing like Todd. I don't want there to be any secrets between us."

Oh, if only she could believe that. "So you've told me everything then?"

He stood eyes fixed over her shoulder for the longest time. "I sent Gonzalez's prints to Sierra this afternoon to compare to the shovel prints."

She sucked in a breath. "And you couldn't tell me *that*, why?"

"Arroyo had nothing to do with taking Jace, and I hoped Gonzalez would admit to doing it. Once I got him to admit that, I would've told you. I was just about to interview him when you showed up."

"So he hasn't admitted it?"

"No, but he did admit to killing Kilroy because the guy was shaking him down for money. And he has Kilroy's records. Jace's birth mother's name is Cindy Eaton from Rugged Point. Kilroy paid her a grand for Jace."

And just like that she knew about Jace's beginnings in life, but it was all colored by the fact the man who'd come to mean more to her than she'd known might have withheld that from her. "How long have you known that?"

"Since Arroyo wore the wire this morning."

"So when you texted me today, you knew that?"

He nodded. "After I questioned Gonzalez, I was going to tell you."

She eyed Devon for a long time, trying to assess his honesty when he kept springing things on her. Like the name of Jace's birth mother. Devon seemed sincere, like he really was thinking about her, but she couldn't trust her judgment, and she wasn't ready to forgive him. If she kept looking into those compelling eyes, she'd have an even harder time weighing the facts, and she really needed to think about it all.

She could spend the helicopter ride doing that. She stepped back. "I have to go."

He reached out for her, then dropped his hand. "Don't run away from this. From us."

"I'm not running," she said when she was doing just that. "I have something to do."

"Don't leave mad, honey. Please." He took a step closer, his eyes pleading. "Let's talk this out."

At his use of "honey," tears came to the surface, and she didn't want him to see her cry, so she bolted from the room. He followed.

As she grabbed her phone and ID from the receptionist, she glanced back at him. His expression had changed, his face now a stony mask. She'd hurt him by walking out. She didn't like that, but he'd hurt her, too, and she couldn't stick around or she might say something she would regret later.

She raced for her car. A sob erupted from her chest, and the tears came hot and wet, streaming down her cheeks. She swiped them away and texted Nick, barely able to see her typing through blurry eyes.

Jace's birth mother's name is Cindy Eaton. Lived in Rugged Point at the time of his birth. Please find her.

On it, the reply came almost instantly.

She thanked him and gripped the steering wheel until she got her crying jag under control. She started her car and was soon out of the city on the rural two-lane road headed for the helipad, putting as much distance as possible between her and Devon. Traffic eased up even more until it was just her and a truck on the lonely road.

Her tears soon slowed and tiredness set in as the sun fell and darkness crept over the landscape. She cranked up her music and sang along to stay awake. More likely to keep from thinking about Devon. She'd done the unthinkable. She'd fallen for a man she didn't know if she could trust. She thought about Maya's words. She was right. Not being able to trust someone was no way to live, but what could Kelsey do about it when that was the way she felt?

She came to a stop at a four-way intersection and lowered her window for fresh air. She looked in the side mirror, and the person in the large pickup behind her honked the horn a few times and pointed out his window at her car.

She had no idea what he was trying to tell her, but it seemed to be serious. Was there something wrong with her vehicle?

He jumped from his truck and yelled, "Your tire's going flat."

Seriously, she didn't need that. She pulled over and started to open her door, but then realized she was out in the boonies all alone and a strange man was hurrying toward her. She reached for the button to raise the window, but the man arrived at her side and lifted a gun to point it at her face.

She gasped and met his gaze.

"Hello, Dr. Moore," he said, his tone bitter and dark. "I'll bet I'm the last person you expected to ever see again."

20

Devon ran a hand over his face and wished he could go after Kelsey. He'd totally blown things with her. She was so important to him now. He could have told her about the bullets, that her husband might have been murdered, but he wanted to keep her from suffering until he proved Todd's death was connected to this investigation.

Was that the truth, or had he let fear of being rejected again sabotage their potential relationship? He couldn't say he hadn't done so. And now she was so mad at him that she'd stormed out of his life. Just as well, he supposed. He still had a job that needed his complete focus. He had to figure out who wanted to take Jace. And Gonzalez was their best lead, so Devon needed to interview the guy again.

Feeling like the world sat on his shoulders, Devon headed to the Multnomah County Detention Center. On the way, his phone chimed and he looked at the text from Sierra.

Prints from the shovel match the suspect prints you sent over this afternoon.

Devon thanked her and tried to feel something. He should be happy. Ecstatic even. This news, along with the recording where Gonzalez confessed to killing Kilroy, meant Gonzalez would go away for murder. And with the list of babies taken from their mothers and sold to parents, Gonzalez's charges would be too substantial for him ever to be released from prison. But Devon still needed to get Gonzalez to confess to his connection to the Sotos Cartel and to hiring Cruz to abduct Jace.

Still feeling numb from the argument with Kelsey, Devon checked into the detention center and walked into the small interrogation room. His anger over Gonzalez's reckless behavior flared up, and he had to swallow it down as he faced the guy. "I've been thinking about our earlier conversation. You claim you don't have a connection to the Sotos Cartel, and yet, you removed Kilroy's hands in their signature MO."

A snide smile slid across his mouth. "Don't have to be connected to them to make it look like they killed Kilroy."

"If you're not connected to the cartel, how do you even know about them?"

"You of all people should know people in my business pay attention to players around them. Gotta protect my turf if they try to horn in."

"So you're saying you knew that the Sotos Cartel was engaged in human trafficking?"

"Such an ugly term for taking unwanted children and finding them a good home." That smile widened.

Devon curled his fists to ignore Gonzalez's comment as the man was delusional if he thought he was doing a good deed when he took children from their mothers. "Did you know about Sotos?"

"Yeah, of course."

"And you knew that Kilroy had gone into business with them?"

"I did."

"And you removed the hands to make it look like they did this?"

"Yeah. Good idea, right?" Gonzalez grinned.

"Not really. It didn't work."

Gonzalez shrugged.

Frustration had Devon wanting to pull out his hair but he couldn't let his man see how he was affecting him. "You also planted a kilo of coke in the house to further cement him to Sotos."

"Hey, man, I don't have the connections to get that much coke. And if I did, I wouldn't waste the money and leave it behind."

Devon felt like he was telling the truth, but he didn't want to admit it because that meant he didn't have a connection to Sotos, and Devon wanted him to be the man who had Jace abducted. "And what about the flowers in the grave? What was the point of that?"

"Thought maybe if someone found Kilroy's body, the flowers would throw investigators off. Make you think it was a personal thing so you'd waste time looking into that. Like the hands." He smirked.

Devon wanted to wipe the snide grin from the jerk's face. His callous disregard for life and law enforcement was too much, but Devon wouldn't give him any cause to call his arrest into question. "Tell me about Jace Moore. Why'd you hire someone to abduct him?"

"I told you before. I didn't hire anyone to take the kid. Only know his name from what Frisco said and Kilroy's records." He yawned.

The man was bored. Unbelievable. That—more than anything—set Devon's teeth on edge.

"Look," Gonzalez continued. "I copped to everything else you got on me. Why would I lie about this? I mean you got all my files from the house. With all those counts, I'm never getting out of prison, so what's one more count?"

No matter how much Devon wanted him to be guilty of this, he had a point. A valid one.

Kelsey's and Jace's faces came to mind. Their happy smiles in the condo. The love they shared. No way Devon would give up until he knew who was behind Jace's abduction. He had one last card to play. He got up and left the room to talk to his supervisor who was watching through a one-way mirror.

"Looks like it's time to bring Cruz in," Devon told his boss.

"You stay here where Cruz can't see you," Hurst said. "I'll arrange to have him brought in."

Hurst closed the door behind him, and Devon looked through the mirror at Gonzalez who was slouched in his chair, head back, eyes closed, so totally unaffected by his reprehensible behavior. And what could Devon do about it? Send in another lowlife like Cruz to see if he knew Gonzalez? Not much for Devon to pin his hopes on.

Hurst stepped back into the room, a tight smile on his face. "Showtime."

The interrogation room door opened, and Cruz stepped in, a deputy behind him.

Cruz looked at Gonzalez then at the deputy. "What's going on?"

"Thought you might want to talk to an old friend," the deputy said.

"Am I supposed to know this guy or something?" Cruz asked, looking honestly confused.

"Ditto here," Gonzalez said. "You trying to pin something else on me with this guy?"

"Just thought you'd want to talk about old times." The

deputy secured Cruz on the opposite side of the table from Gonzalez and departed.

They sat and stared at each other, but either they were incredible actors or they didn't actually know each other.

"You believe them?" Hurst asked.

Devon raked his hand through his hair. "Unfortunately, I do."

"Yeah, me, too, but I'm going to let them sit for a while. See if they talk."

"Gonzalez has to be smart enough to know we're watching, so I doubt now that the initial surprise is over, even if he does know Cruz, that Gonzalez will let on."

"Then I'll take another run at Cruz. See if I can get him to cave. You can't be present for that so you might as well head out. I'll let you know what happens."

Normally, Devon would argue and stay and watch the interrogation from the safety of this room, but he wanted to find Kelsey and talk to her, so he was thankful to go. He left the detention center and drove straight to Veritas. The lot was dark, with only one car out front. Likely Pete's vehicle as the others would park in the garage at night. Devon jogged to the front door and pounded on the glass.

Pete got up from behind the desk to open it. "Can I help you, Agent Dunbar?"

"I was hoping to talk to Kelsey."

"Sorry, she left for Cold Harbor to see Jace."

"Cold Harbor?" Devon's heart fell, and he didn't know what to do. He didn't want a night to pass with their argument lingering between them.

"Want to leave her a message?" Pete asked.

Devon shook his head. He should turn and walk out the door, but he didn't want to leave. Maybe he felt closer to her just being at her lab. He didn't know. Didn't know much of anything right now. Other than he didn't want to turn away and go home to an empty place. "Is Nick working?"

Pete glanced at his watch. "Probably."

"Could you tell him I'm here to see him?"

"Sure thing. And you can sign in while I get him on the horn." Pete strode to the desk, set the iPad on the counter, and picked up the phone. "Got Agent Dunbar here to see you."

Familiar with the form now, Devon quickly completed it.

"Roger that," Pete said into the phone and then hung up and turned to Devon. "He'll be right down."

"Thanks." Devon handed back the iPad.

Pete gave him a visitor's badge. "How's your investigation going?"

"We've made good progress, but we've still got a big question unanswered, and we're running out of leads. I'm sure you know how that goes."

Pete nodded. "Most of the time I'm glad I'm not actively involved in law enforcement anymore. But there are days when I'd be happy to be back in the thick of things."

"Gets in your blood."

"Ain't that the truth." Pete frowned. "But you can't let it consume your life. Trust me. You need something else. Looking back, I shoulda spent more time with my family."

Devon nodded, though he hadn't really thought about how he would do this job while having a family. After the argument with Kelsey, he doubted he would ever have to consider it...at least with her.

"You married?" Pete asked.

Devon shook his head.

"Got a special girl?"

"No," Devon said, but wished he could say, *Yeah, Kelsey*.

"Good-looking guy like you shouldn't have a problem finding someone. If you take the time that is."

"Yeah, time...I need to make some time." And he did. And would. Only after Jace was safe.

The elevator dinged, and Nick came to the door.

"Thanks, Pete," Devon said and headed toward Nick.

"Might start looking right here," Pete called after him. "We have some exceptional single women working here."

"Yeah, I've noticed."

"Figured a smart agent like you wouldn't miss that fact." Pete chuckled, his deep robust laugh echoing through the large foyer.

"Hey, man," Nick greeted and headed down the hall. "I'm surprised you asked for me instead of Kelsey."

"She's on her way to Cold Harbor to see Jace."

"No wonder she's not answering her phone." Nick held the elevator door that was still standing open.

Devon boarded and punched the number three. "You have something important to tell Kelsey?"

"Important?" Nick narrowed his eyes. "Yeah, I guess. It's definitely information she needs to know."

Devon's curiosity was truly piqued now. "About the investigation?"

Nick shook his head. "She worked a case a few years ago and the suspect, Lucien Sparrow, was convicted of murder. Turned out he was innocent and got out not too long ago."

Devon recognized that name. "Is that the investigation where she thought a handsaw was used but it was a mechanical saw?"

Nick arched an eyebrow. "She told you about it, huh?"

He nodded.

"Yeah, well, Sparrow spent two years behind bars, and it seems like he may be out for payback."

"Payback?" Devon's gut tightened.

The door opened, and Nick stepped out. "I don't have

anything certain yet, but the lead detective and the DA who prosecuted Sparrow are missing."

Devon grabbed Nick's arm and stopped him. "Missing? Like in foul play?"

"Like I said. Nothing concrete yet. Both of them didn't show up when expected and haven't been seen for at least twenty-four hours."

"You think Sparrow might come after Kelsey?"

Nick frowned. "Her testimony *was* a big part of putting him away."

Devon worked the muscles in his jaw. "We need to warn her."

"Yeah, that's why I tried calling her. I also texted. When she lands in Cold Harbor, she'll get the message."

"With this guy looking for payback, she couldn't have better timing than to head to Cold Harbor tonight." Devon let out a breath, and his worry along with it. "There's no safer place for her than at the Blackwell compound."

Kelsey's car took a sharp turn, and she slid across the trunk as she fought to free her wrists. For the last fifteen minutes, she'd tried to remove the wire that was cutting into her skin. Or at least it seemed like that was how long it had been since Lucien Sparrow had bound them tightly with thick wire and tossed her into the trunk without a word of explanation.

He didn't need to explain. She'd seen the venomous hatred in his eyes. He wanted payback for her testimony that took two years of his life. He'd also taken her phone and tossed it at the side of the road. She heard it crack and could only hope that it was still working and emitting a signal, so once her partners discovered she was missing, they could use GPS to locate her.

Question was, how long would that be and would she still be alive?

The car came to a sudden stop, and she rolled to the front of the trunk, her head hitting something hard. She thought to cry out, but stifled it. She didn't want Sparrow to know he was hurting her as she knew he would get a kick out of it. The very reason he used wire to bind her wrists. He said it would tear into her tender flesh and it had.

The trunk opened, and the moon shone on his shiny bald head. He glared down on her, his mouth twisted in a scowl behind his scraggly goatee that hung two inches below his chin. He was about as wide as he was tall and wore a denim shirt with the arms ripped off, revealing a black spiderweb tattoo on his bicep that she didn't think he'd had before his prison time. She remembered reading somewhere that the web was a common prison tattoo, conveying the idea of being trapped. He would feel this more than others who really were guilty and deserving of the time.

"What're you staring at?" he asked, but her gag kept her from answering.

He grabbed her arm and hauled her out of the trunk to set her on her feet. She smelled alcohol on his breath, raising her concern more.

He gripped the wire between her wrists, slicing the metal into her already-raw skin. She pressed her lips on the gag to stop from crying out. He closed the trunk. That's when she saw the house. More like a cabin. She remembered he'd lived on a wooded property and had several hand and mechanical saws for cutting wood.

He pushed her forward. "Your friends will be glad to see you. Now that everyone's here, I'm gonna hold my own trial for each of you, and I'm gonna find you all guilty. Then you'll get a fitting punishment. Yours is going to include that saw you were once so interested in."

Her heart lurched. She'd seen the damage saws did to bones. She couldn't imagine having one applied to her, and she shuddered.

"Thought that might get a rise out of you." He chuckled —deep, ugly, mean.

He might not have been guilty of murder when she testified against him, but he'd had prior arrests for violent behavior, so she knew he wouldn't have any qualms about hurting her.

He dragged her up the steps and unlocked the door. The place looked like a hunting lodge with taxidermy heads on the wall, a stone fireplace, worn braided rug, and heavy wood furniture with plaid cushions. He hauled her through the family room and down a steep set of stairs. He pulled a string hanging from the low ceiling and a single bulb blossomed into light. She blinked to clear her vision from the sudden change and saw Detective Upjohn and DA Yung bound and gagged on the floor of the unfinished basement with cold gray concrete block walls. Their arms were secured to eyebolts in the thick concrete blocks. They stared at her, terror in Yung's gaze, defiance in Upjohn's.

"You remember your playmates, don't you?" Sparrow dragged her over to the men and shoved her down between them.

The cold concrete bit into her bottom, and his rough handling brought tears to her eyes. She closed them before she started full-out crying. He jerked her arms behind her and secured them to bolts, the metal slashing into torn skin unless she remained bent in an unnatural backward position.

"Look at me," he demanded.

She slowly lifted her eyelids and took on the same defiant stare she'd seen in Upjohn's eyes.

He stood and ripped off her gag. "Thought I'd give you a chance to tell me how sorry you are for my wrongful conviction."

"I am sorry," she said honestly. "Very sorry. I wish I could give you those years back, but I can't."

"Dang right you can't. No one can." The words came out with a spray of spit.

She tried to remain calm and think logically. "But if you kill us, you'll go right back to prison."

He snorted. "I don't plan on getting caught."

"My team will figure it out," she said with confidence.

"Really?" He eyed her. "The same way they figured out I had my buddy Cruz grab your kid?"

What? She gaped at him. "It was you?"

He preened like a peacock, stroking his beard and grinning, and she hated that she'd given him a chance to feel good about what he'd done.

She leveled her voice. "Why would you want to take Jace?"

"See, your team isn't all that smart if they didn't figure that out." His grin widened.

"Then suppose you tell me." She hated asking, but she had to know.

"I didn't want the kid, but we knew you'd come running after him and Cruz would have you in the van without the chance of you getting away."

"So he was just bait for me? To get me here?" Her voice shot up, and she felt hysteria following.

"Yep."

She could hardly wrap her mind around that, but had to calm down and learn as much as she could. "Are you affiliated with the Sotos Cartel like Cruz is?"

He shook his head. "Cruz was just doing me a solid for a favor I did for him in prison."

They'd been *so* blind. Focusing only on the cartel and missing this lead totally. So blind that no one would begin to think that Sparrow had her. They would perhaps find her phone, but have no idea where to find her, and she would pay for the mistake. Pay for it with her life in some heinous act by this unstable man.

~

Hours passed. Hours and hours in the dark. Kelsey remained focused on the quick image she'd seen of the tool bench sitting across from them before the light went out and Sparrow headed up the steps. Tools hung on pegboards mounted on the wall. A large handsaw was one of them. A power saw on the bench.

The dark and her imagination fueled Kelsey's fear of what he might do with the saws. The quiet didn't help. Quiet save the skittering of feet across the space. Rats. She kept kicking her feet to keep them away. The men did the same thing. She wished they could talk to each other. Maybe then they could come up with a plan on how to get out of this mess, but Sparrow had slipped that dirty rag between her lips again and wound it tightly around her head.

But waiting here like a sitting duck? The silence. Dead silence. That was the worst.

She lifted her face in prayer.

Father, please. I know if we can't prove Jace's birth mother actually sold him, he might go to her, and he might have to adjust to a new family. A big change, but he would adapt. He couldn't handle knowing I died, too. He's seen too much death already. If not for me, please save my life for Jace. Please.

Her life. How was she going to get out of this? Was it possible that someone would come looking for her? Not Devon. Not after their argument. Was that the last conversation she would have with him? An argument?

Please, no.

She desperately wanted to see him again. To tell him she didn't care if he'd kept things from her. He hadn't lied. Wasn't like Todd. Devon had made investigative decisions that he'd had to make. And not telling her about Todd's murder? He'd done that to spare her additional agony, while Todd always did his own thing, never considering her.

Devon, on the other hand, was a fine man. She'd been so afraid to trust another man, but now?

Now what, God?

She couldn't do anything about being tied up here. Or maybe she could. Seek God and find His purpose. She could choose to believe the things Devon told her. That God was in absolute control. That He was doing things behind the scenes to help her and was always working for her good. And she chose to believe He didn't put Devon in her life for her to ignore him, and she had to let go of her trust issues. She just needed a chance to tell him that.

Please.

A sound upstairs caught her attention. Heavy footfalls thumped across the wood floors. Something was being dragged, too.

The door at the top of the steps opened. Light washed down the stairs. Footfalls followed.

Sparrow was back.

She was wrong. Way wrong.

His return was worse than the dark. Far worse.

21

Devon's phone rang, and seeing Alex's number, he grabbed it. "Alex?"

"Have you seen Kelsey?"

"No."

"She was supposed to meet Riley at the helipad hours ago. She never showed, and he's been trying to get ahold of her. She's not answering her phone, and after-hour voice-mail is turned on at Veritas."

Worry coursed like a rushing river through Devon's body. "She left here hours ago."

"What's wrong?" Nick asked.

"Kelsey never showed up at the helipad." Devon turned his attention back to the phone. "I'm going to go look for her. Give Riley my number and ask him to call me if she arrives."

"Understood," Alex said. "And hey, I'm praying for her."

Instead of comforting Devon, Alex's prayers worried him more. Alex wouldn't think she was in need of prayer if he didn't think she was in some kind of trouble.

Nick's fingers were flying over his computer keyboard.

"We have a GPS tracking program on our phones. Let me see where hers is located."

Devon went around the desk and watched the map on the screen, waiting for the program to find her phone and load. But the little circle just kept spinning, matching the thoughts in Devon's brain. "What's going on?"

Nick frowned. "Her phone must not be turned on or the battery's dead."

"She wouldn't turn it off. Unless maybe she did because she was mad at me and didn't want me to call." Devon hated that thought, but it was a possibility.

Nick studied him. "Not sure why she's mad at you, but I don't think she'd do that. She's very careful to keep it charged and on in case Jace has an emergency."

Devon met Nick's gaze. "So you think she's in trouble."

"I do."

"But who? How?" Devon's anxiety was barely controllable now, and his palms started sweating.

"We should head out," Nick said, his voice tight with emotions. "Follow the route she would've taken to the helipad."

Devon needed to take action and this was a sound idea. He bolted for the door. He didn't wait for Nick. He was a computer geek. How helpful would he be?

Devon charged down the steps and raced across the lobby. He tossed his badge to Pete. "Kelsey never showed up at the helipad, and she's not answering her phone. You have any idea the route she took?"

Pete shook his head, his eyes darkening with worry.

Nick came barreling into the lobby, fixing a holstered gun on his belt as he moved.

Seeing that, panic clawed up Devon's back. He swallowed hard to keep it under control.

"We'll have to assume she took the route I did." Devon charged outside.

"I'll drive," Nick said.

"But I'm—"

"Too shook up to drive."

"I'm good. Besides I can run with lights and siren." He clicked the remote key for his department SUV. "And other items we might need."

He had a go bag with Kevlar vests, and a rifle and other tools in the back, but he sure hoped none of it was necessary. He jumped behind the wheel and quickly got them on the road heading toward the helipad.

His phone rang and hoping it was Kelsey, he grabbed it but was disappointed to see Hurst's name. Still, he answered. "Sir."

"Cruz doesn't know Gonzalez, and he isn't part of the Sotos Cartel," Hurst blurted out.

"And Jace?" Devon asked, as he pressed his foot harder on the gas pedal. "Did Cruz come clean on why he tried to take Jace?"

"After a plea deal, but it's odd. He said some guy he owed from his prison days asked him to take the kid. But here's the weird part." Hurst paused, and Devon wanted to reach through the phone and shake him into talking. "They didn't really want the kid, but his mother. Figured she would race after him, and they'd get her in the van without a struggle. Guy's name is Lucien Sparrow."

"Sparrow?" Devon looked at Nick. "Sparrow's the one who wanted Jace abducted, but his main target was Kelsey."

"And you think he has her now?" Nick dragged his hands through his hair.

Devon nodded and turned his attention back to the call. "You have an address for Sparrow?"

"Hang on, and I'll get it for you," Hurst said.

"Hurry!" Devon hated how panicked he sounded. But he *was* in a panic. The woman he loved was missing. Oh, yeah, he loved her, and he could admit that now. He didn't know if or where it would go with her being so mad at him, but Devon did know he wanted the chance to tell her how he felt.

God, please...please.

Kelsey felt sick to her stomach, and she swallowed hard to keep from throwing up. Sparrow had turned on all the lights in the basement revealing a mock courtroom. He dragged DA Yung to the witness seat, where the man shivered under a harsh light. Sweat poured over his pale face, and he kept lifting bony shoulders to try to wipe it off as his hands were chained to the chair. His navy suit pants were torn and his white shirt stained with dirt and blood from a nasty cut on his high forehead. He kept looking between Detective Upjohn seated at the defendant's table, and her sitting in the jury box.

Sparrow took a seat behind what was supposed to be the judge's platform, his gun firmly in his hand as he plopped down with a solid thump. He picked up a gavel with his free hand and slammed it down. "We're here today to try Detective Upjohn for his part in the false prosecution of the innocent Lucien Sparrow. How do you plead, Detective?"

Upjohn was a brawny guy with a buzz cut and strong jaw. He wore jeans, scuffed boots, and a white T-shirt with the American flag on his chest. He didn't look afraid in the least and glared up at Sparrow. "Not guilty."

Sparrow grimaced and shifted his gaze to the jury box. "It's your job to evaluate the case and render a verdict. Be aware that any verdict other than guilty will add to the penalties inflicted on all the defendants."

"You have this rigged, so why even do this?" Upjohn grumbled.

Sparrow bared his teeth. "It's no different than my trial. You rigged that, too, with circumstantial evidence that proved nothing. I'm just returning the favor."

At the angry venom coming from this man, Kelsey's stomach churned, and this time she didn't know if she could keep her stomach contents down.

Devon scanned the roadside, looking for Kelsey's car. Her phone. Any indication that she'd been on this road. He came to a stop at a four-way intersection where a truck was pulled over in the ditch.

"There! On the road by the truck. A phone." He shifted into park and was out of the SUV in a flash. He picked up the device.

"I recognize the case," Nick said joining him. "It's Kelsey's."

"Sparrow ditched the phone and truck." Devon felt lightheaded with worry, but he raced over to the truck and looked for license plates. They were missing. The driver's door wasn't locked, and he jerked it open, releasing the strong scent of cigarettes. A beer can sat in the cup holder and empties laid on the floor.

Nick pulled open the passenger door and lifted papers laying on the seat. He grimaced. "Pictures of Kelsey and Jace. At his school, church. Outside Veritas."

Devon couldn't believe he failed to keep her safe and thought he might hyperventilate. Where was the guy who'd worked SEAL ops so calmly? He had to find him and get control, or he'd never figure out where Sparrow had taken Kelsey.

"So it's clear Sparrow has her." Nick tossed the pages to the seat in disgust. "I can't imagine he would be dumb enough to take her to his place."

"I've seen criminals do dumber things," Devon said. "And in this situation, he may not have a clue that we're on to him. Plus, we don't have any other idea of where he might have taken her, so we should check it out."

Devon didn't wait for Nick to agree but bolted for his vehicle. Nick jumped in beside him.

"Put the address in GPS," Devon directed, some calm returning as he at least had a game plan. "And I want to see a picture of this Sparrow guy."

"Coming right up." Nick tapped in the address and the voice gave Devon his first direction.

Nick typed on his phone then turned it to face Devon. He gaped at the image. "He's like huge."

"And mean," Nick said. "We all went to court to support Kelsey, and he glared at her the whole time. When she walked past him after testifying, he gave her a look that could kill."

"Then we better get moving." Devon floored the gas and when the vehicle fishtailed he raised his foot and drove more conservatively, but still made what should have been a thirty-minute drive in twenty minutes.

Nearing Sparrow's driveway, Devon killed the lights and pulled slowly over the gravel to park out of view. He took a look at the weathered cabin with a sharply peaked roof nestled into the side of the hill. It was surrounded by towering pines, fir trees, and trimmed shrubs. A wrap-around porch circled the cedar siding.

"Nice property and so not fitting with the dude I saw in

court," Nick said. "He seemed more like he'd be at home in a motorcycle bar than a cabin in the woods."

After seeing Sparrow's picture, Devon had been thinking the same thing. "You sure we have the right address?"

"Positive. Not that I don't trust your boss, but I double-checked."

"Okay, then we move. I've got vests in the back and an assault rifle." Devon eased out and opened the hatch. He gave his good vest to Nick and put on his backup. "You any good with that gun?"

"Absolutely." He smiled. "Courtesy of a stint in the army."

"Okay, good. Good." Devon felt better knowing Nick would be solid backup. "We go in slow. Assess the situation and then make a plan. You follow my lead, and at no time do you act without first running it past me. Got it?"

"Got it." Nick lifted his shoulders. "But you should know —if our lives are threatened, I won't ask for permission to fire or attack."

"Understood." Devon gave his eyes a moment to adjust to the dark, but only a moment, even though to be fully effective, he should wait longer. But with Kelsey likely a prisoner inside, he couldn't wait.

The moon shone above him, giving him much-needed light as he started up the gravel drive, dodging ruts and holes, moving slowly to keep his footfalls as quiet as possible. Tall pines lined both sides of the drive and opened into the clearing holding the cabin.

Nick grabbed Devon's arm. "That's Kelsey's car."

His heart soared then fell. "So Sparrow *is* seeking revenge, and he has her here."

"What do we do?" Nick sought Devon's face, looking for an answer.

He'd handled rescue op after rescue op in his career and

knew exactly what to do in a situation like this. That was, if he had a team backing him up, but tonight he only had Nick. Devon was grateful to have any backup at all, and Nick seemed confident enough to handle himself.

Devon scanned the property and registered several different details at once. The smell of smoke rising from the chimney, mixing with pine. Lights out on the main level, but shining brightly through the basement windows. Bushes near those windows that could be used for cover.

He quickly formulated a plan and checked his rifle. "I need to get an up close look of the basement. You wait here and have my back."

Nick drew his gun and planted his feet. "I can do that."

Devon nodded and crept forward, skirting the rest of the driveway for a stealthy approach to the side of the house to ease behind the shrubs. He got down on his knees by the window and risked a quick look.

The hair on the back of his neck stood up, and he pulled back, trying to make sense of what he'd seen. A man the size of Sparrow with a gleaming bald head—his back to Devon —sat in chair on an elevated platform, a gun in his hand. Another man, hands bound behind his back, sat at a table facing Sparrow. And another man was bound and sitting next to Sparrow. Kelsey sat in a folding chair to the side, bound to it with wire, her gaze frantic and terrified.

Devon swallowed down a curse and firmed his resolve. No man messed with the woman he loved and got away with it.

He looked again. The big guy facing away from Devon had a large gavel in one hand, the gun in the other. Devon pulled back. Was he holding a trial? Devon took one more look, memorizing the other men's faces and then crept back to Nick, careful to keep his head on a swivel for danger.

Devon didn't want the light from a phone to mess with

his eyes after he'd adjusted to the dark, but he needed to identify the players in the basement. "Can you pull up pictures of the DA and lead detective on Sparrow's investigation?"

Nick nodded and got out his phone. "Why?"

"I think Sparrow has them in the basement with Kelsey and is holding a mock trial."

"Creative," Nick said and tapped his phone then held it out. "District Attorney Yung."

Devon took a quick look at the photo. "Yeah, he's one of the men down there."

Nick swiped his screen a few times. "Detective Upjohn."

"Yeah. He's there, too."

Nick locked his phone and shoved it into his pocket. "So what do we do?"

Devon had to be smart and not risk Kelsey's life. "No way we can take Sparrow down in the basement. The confined space makes it too risky for the others. We have to create a diversion to draw him outside."

Nick nodded and his expression suddenly brightened. "What about Kelsey's car? I could hack the electronics and set off the horn. I can do it remotely so we can hide up by the house and set it off."

Devon liked that idea a lot. "And when Sparrow comes out, we take him down. How long will it take?"

Nick shrugged and got out his phone.

Devon couldn't just stand there and wait. Not with Kelsey under Sparrow's gun. Devon had to be close by so if Sparrow raised his weapon to her or the others, Devon could take him out. "I'll go keep an eye on things. You join me at the house when you're ready."

"Roger that," Nick said without looking up from his phone.

Devon followed the same path to the house and

dropped down by the window. The players hadn't moved. Devon risked a longer look, this time focusing only on Kelsey. Her eyes were filled with worry, her chin trembling. He pulled back and wished she would look up to catch sight of him. *No.* That wouldn't be good. If she reacted, Sparrow wouldn't miss it, and it could endanger her life.

Devon continued to take quick looks until he heard Nick coming his way. With only one exit from the front of the house, Devon led Nick to a shadowed position against the building where Sparrow would have to pass. Devon hung his rifle strap over his body and drew his handgun. He signaled for Nick to activate the horn.

The blare sounded in the quiet night, and Devon held his sidearm at the ready. He counted, hitting sixty—but no sign of Sparrow. He continued to count. Minutes passed. Long, tense minutes as sweat poured out of Devon. He wanted to look in the window to see what was happening in the basement, but such an impatient action could risk his exposure and ruin everything.

Finally, nearly five minutes after the horn first sounded, Devon heard the creak of the front door. Then heavy footsteps coming across the porch, the wood groaning under the man's weight. The solid thumps continued slowly down the stairs.

Devon held his breath. Remained hidden. Saw Sparrow take the final stair. Plant his feet on the ground. Stop. Look around. Assessing. Watching.

Devon itched to jump out, but Sparrow held a handgun, and Devon had to get behind him or risk getting himself or Nick shot.

Sparrow took a few more steps. Paused to listen. Took a few more. Stopped again, his head swiveling as he surveyed the area. Seeming satisfied, he started for the car.

Devon waited a few moments longer. Signaled for Nick

to hold his position, then bolted out, shoving his gun at the back of Sparrow's head. "Freeze, Sparrow."

The big man stopped, his hands rising.

"Get his gun, Nick," Devon instructed.

Nick came out of the shadows and reached up to take the weapon from Sparrow's beefy hand.

"On the ground, facedown, Sparrow," Devon commanded.

The big man dropped to his knees, then lunged at the ground, hitting with a solid thud and an *oomph*. "I didn't do anything wrong."

"Come on, Sparrow," Devon said. "Those are the last words of nearly every person I arrest. Can't you be more creative?"

A grumble erupted from his chest. "Who are you?"

Devon wouldn't bother to say anything else until he had this man in cuffs.

"Cover me," he told Nick.

"Roger that." Nick raised his gun and planted his feet in a solid stance.

Devon holstered his weapon to cuff the big man. Adrenaline coursed through Devon's body, and he blew it out on a long breath so he could calmly make a call to ask for backup. He got out his phone and called the local sheriff's office. He identified himself and requested transport for Sparrow from the efficient dispatcher.

"You're DEA?" Sparrow asked after Devon disconnected. "I'm not involved with drugs."

"No, you're just involved in kidnapping." Devon thought of Kelsey in the basement and he wanted to go to her, but he couldn't leave a prisoner with a civilian. He shoved his phone into his pocket and looked at Nick. "We're in luck. There's a deputy a few minutes out."

Nick let out a long breath. "I should go release Kelsey."

Devon thought about how long it took for Sparrow to come out, and he shook his head. "We wait for backup and then I go in alone."

Nick's shoulders drooped. "But why?"

"No telling if this bozo set a booby trap. I won't risk your life."

Nick's broad shoulders went back up. "I've seen my share of booby traps in Afghanistan, and I'm happy to come with you if you need me."

"Appreciate that," Devon said. "But I got it."

He stood waiting, his thoughts racing to Kelsey and how she might react to seeing him. Sure, she'd be thrilled to be rescued, but then what? Would she forgive him? Let him talk to her so he could tell her he loved her?

"You thinking about that fight with Kelsey?" Nick asked.

Devon nodded. "I blew it by keeping some things from her. Like Todd did."

Nick narrowed his gaze. "You totally hurt her in the worse way."

"I know, man. No need to rub salt in the wound."

"You should know. She's not one to hold a grudge. In fact, she's one of the most forgiving people I know. As long as you're sorry for what you did."

"I am," Devon said as lights swirled in the distance.

"Make sure she knows that, then," Nick said.

Sparrow grumbled. "Please, spare me all the sickening talk. I'm about to hurl."

Devon thought to press a knee in the guy's back, but that would just be playing into his hope of getting a rise out of Devon. Far better to ignore him.

Lights and siren running, the patrol car turned into the driveway and raced up to the clearing. Devon introduced himself to the deputy, explained the situation, and turned Sparrow over in record time.

"Wait here," he told Nick then sprinted for the house. He took his time opening the door, and moved cautiously through the rooms until he located the basement stairwell. He ran a light over the doorframe and at the floor, looking for wires. Confirming none existed, he jerked open the door.

"Kelsey," he called down the stairs. "Is it safe to come down?"

He heard her mumbling as if gagged and chains rattled, too. That was likely why Sparrow took so long. He'd gagged and secured his prisoners. But as much as Devon wanted to get to Kelsey, he didn't want to endanger his or the other's lives by rushing ahead.

He shone his cell phone at the lightbulb above to make sure there was nothing running to it, then flipped the switch. He cautiously descended the stairs, praying with each step that Sparrow didn't set a trap. Devon reached the bottom and made a quick sweep of the room. The three prisoners were lined up and chained to bolts in the concrete. He spotted the key laying on the table, grabbed it, and hurried to Kelsey.

She looked up at him, gratitude burning in her eyes.

He knelt in front of her and gently removed the gag. "I'm sorry that creep did this to you."

She cleared her throat, tears filling her eyes. "Thank you. Thank you. Thank you for coming. I prayed someone would figure this out, but how did you?"

"Cruz confessed to being buddies with Sparrow, and that's why he tried to take Jace." Devon inserted the key in the lock and freed her hands.

Wire circled her raw wrists covered with thick red welts. He had to fight not to punch the wall. "Let me get this wire off. It's probably going to hurt."

"Go ahead." She tried to smile, but her chin trembled.

He gently took her hands and untwisted the ends of the

firm wire until he had the section separated. He pulled it free, and she gasped in pain.

His heart clenched. "I'm sorry, honey. So sorry for hurting you."

"Don't worry. You had to do it." She slowly brought her arms around front and grimaced with that pain, too.

Now he wished he'd pummeled Sparrow. But in the long run it was good that he hadn't.

Kelsey glanced down at her wrists, then back up, anguish still marring those beautiful eyes. He wanted to sweep her into his arms, but two men sat watching him, expecting to be released as well.

He patted Kelsey's knee and then scooted over to Upjohn. "I'm DEA Agent Devon Dunbar. I've been working an investigation with Kelsey."

He untied the gag, and Upjohn gulped in a deep breath. "Thank God you got here when you did. That nutjob was holding a mock trial, and once he found us guilty, he was going to kill us."

He quickly freed Upjohn's hands and gave him the key. "You won't mind releasing the DA, right?"

"Got it." He offered his hand for a shake. "Thanks, man. I owe you."

Devon clasped Upjohn's hand, but released it after just one shake. He couldn't get back to Kelsey fast enough. She sat staring as if shock held her down. He offered his hands. She slipped hers into his, and he helped her gently to her feet. A sobbed rushed out of her mouth and tears started spilling from her eyes.

"Aw, honey, don't cry." He didn't care if they had an audience or if he'd fought with her, he just swept her into his arms. He held her shaking body close, her head pressed against his chest. "*Shh*, honey. It's okay. You're safe now and that man is going to go back to prison where he belongs."

Her body convulsed with the crying, and she clutched his shirt, soaking it with tears. He held her closer and stroked her back, praying that she could overcome this final setback. Her crying eventually slowed, and she slowly pushed back to look up at him.

He brushed wayward strands of hair from her face and swiped a thumb over her tears. The best thing for her now was to get her out of this basement. "Nick's outside, and he's worried about you. We should go see him."

He slipped an arm around her and started for the door, but the DA insisted on shaking his hand and clapping him on the back, and Kelsey continued on without him.

He got going as fast as he could extricate himself, but by the time he reached the outside, Nick was hugging Kelsey, and she was crying again. Devon wanted to tell her how he felt about her, but now wasn't the time. He could wait until they were alone again, and hopefully once he declared his feelings, she would find a way to forgive him.

22

It took forever at Sparrow's house for the detective to take her statement, but finally Kelsey arrived home, washed off the terrible ordeal in a long shower, and was seated on the sofa next to Devon. He tenderly bandaged her wrists, and she wanted to blurt out her love for him, but she didn't know why he'd asked to be alone with her.

She was afraid she knew why. Another reason why she showered. It was the time of reckoning, and she wanted to put it off until she felt a bit stronger. But now that everything was over and Jace wasn't in danger, Devon was going to insist that she ask Maya for his DNA profile, and then he would report Jace to social services.

She wanted to be upset with Devon about this, but as she'd told her partners so they wouldn't be mad at him, he was just doing his job. And while she sat in the basement wondering if her life was over, she'd forgiven him for the other things she'd been mad about. She'd prayed for the opportunity to talk to him again and here he was. Sitting beside her. Strong and in command as he had been when he'd swooped in to free her. Then held her so close she'd never wanted to let him go, but she also didn't want to stay in that basement for a moment longer.

She took a deep breath and looked him in the eye. "I know what you want to say."

He scratched his cheek. "You do?"

She nodded. "You want me to get Jace's DNA results from Emory, and you're going to call social services."

He opened his mouth to speak.

She quickly held her hands up. "I know I have no right to ask, but can I have one last night with Jace first, and then I'll report it myself?"

He took her hands and lowered them, but didn't let go. "That's not what I was going to say."

She blinked, her mind racing for what he might want to say, but it didn't matter. Not until she resolved this issue. "We have to talk about it, right?"

"Yes, but..."

"You probably think I'm too fragile from Sparrow's abduction, but I'm not." She freed her hands and sat up straighter. "There's no point in not dealing with it, now that everything else is resolved."

"*Shh*. Listen." He put a finger on her lips and smiled. "I wanted to tell you that I've fallen in love with you." His finger fell away.

"Oh...what? Oh." She stared at him. "That's not what I expected."

"I know. You made that clear." He grinned at her. "My timing is probably all off with you being worried about Jace and all, but when you were abducted I didn't know if I'd have another chance to tell you, and I vowed to do it as soon as I could."

"Thank you, Devon." She smiled at him.

"Um...thank you?" He pulled back. "Isn't that something you say when you don't return the feelings?"

"Oh…right…I can see how you would think that." She clutched his hands. "But I had time to think, too. I've been so afraid I couldn't trust a guy, but you know what? I was able to embrace your comment about God working behind the scenes for my good. I know that He's in absolute control. So I have to believe He brought us together for a reason, and I want to pursue my feelings for you."

"So you have feelings?" He sounded so hopeful, her heart melted.

"I fell in love with you, too. I—"

He released a throaty laugh and jerked her to his rock-solid body. His lips met hers with a sudden urgency. They were soft and warm and insistent. Every nerve in her body seemed to fire all at once, and her stomach fluttered. She lifted her arms around his neck, drawing him closer, holding on for dear life, not caring that her wrists hurt.

She'd felt this aching hole in her chest as she'd sat in the basement and now it was filled. Totally. By her love for him. By his touch. The warmth they were sharing. She matched his kiss, urgency for urgency, relieved to know that she was safe in his arms and nothing bad could happen to her there.

She was vaguely aware of someone knocking in the entryway, but she didn't care. She wasn't going to end this kiss or move out of his arms for anything.

Devon lifted his head and rested his forehead on hers. "Someone's at the door."

"I know, but I don't care."

"It could be important."

"As important as this?" She kissed him again, making sure he could feel every emotion she was feeling and would ignore the more insistent knocking now. She'd been interrupted when kissing him twice now, and that had to stop. She made it stop. Right here, right now.

He groaned and pushed free. "They're not going away."

"It's—"

"Save that thought." He pressed a kiss against her forehead, and despite her clinging to his arms, he got up and went to the door.

She took several long breaths and swiveled to see Nick and Blake standing at the door. Their serious expressions knotted her stomach. What now? Wasn't this over?

Devon stood back, and the men strode in, making a beeline for the living room, their expressions remaining terse and tight. Devon joined her on the sofa and took her hand.

If he felt a need to hold her hand, this had to be bad news. "What's wrong?"

Nick dropped into a chair. "We found Cindy Eaton."

"And?" she asked, clutching Devon's hand tighter and waiting for the bad news about Jace's birth mother.

Blake took the other chair and rested his elbows on his knees, his forehead knotted. "And, she's clearly not in a position to be a mother."

Kelsey's fear vanished, and her hopes flared, but she couldn't let them take flight. "Tell me about her."

"She still lives in Rugged Point," Blake said. "She's been arrested several times for solicitation, and has been in and out of rehab several times. She's using again and living in pretty bad conditions."

"And Jace's father?" Kelsey asked, thinking this had to be the bad news they were waiting to share.

"She never knew who he was," Blake said.

Kelsey couldn't imagine living life like that and not knowing the name of the man who fathered her child, but it was good news for her. "I need to talk to her. Get her to relinquish all rights to Jace."

"No." Blake shook his head. "Not you. A judge might see it as a conflict of interest. I'll have Trent talk to her."

"And a sheriff asking her to relinquish her rights wouldn't be seen as coercion?" Devon asked.

Blake shrugged. "It's better than Kelsey or anyone connected to her talking to Cindy."

"We need to turn this over to social services to handle," Devon said. "Anyone else will be seen as suspect."

Kelsey crossed her arms. "I have to at least see her."

Devon narrowed his eyes. "But why?"

Kelsey really couldn't explain it, but she would try. She looked into his eyes. "I have to know where Jace began his life. With who. I won't talk to her. Just go there. Stand outside her place and wait for her to come out to get a look at her."

Devon tightened his hold on her hands. "Are you sure you want to put yourself through this?"

"Yes," she said and stood. "Riley is still waiting at the helipad to take me to get Jace. We can go to Rugged Point first."

~

Squalor. Filth. Grime.

Even in the thick fog swirling around Kelsey's ankles, she could see the dismal place her stepson began his life, and for the first time, she was thankful that Kilroy took Jace and sold him to Todd.

"Have you seen enough?" Devon asked.

She shook her head, and as the door at Apartment Ten opened, Kelsey took a few steps closer to the run-down building. Syrupy, salty air from the ocean seeped into her bones, but she wouldn't move a muscle until she confirmed the woman was Cindy.

Bleached blond. Rail thin. Haggard. She paraded closer in four-inch heels, jeans, and a knit top so tight, Kelsey thought she could count the woman's ribs. Kelsey couldn't look away, and Devon took her arm to pull her back into the shadows as the *click-click-click* of the woman's worn heels came closer.

She reached them, and her cheap perfume wafted on the breeze. Kelsey got a look at her scabbed arms and her haggard face. This poor woman had lived a difficult life. One of her own making, but still difficult. Kelsey looked for any resemblance to Jace, but saw none. Still, she gave birth to Jace, and that made her special in Kelsey's eyes.

She watched Cindy disappear around a corner. Kelsey couldn't contain her disappointment for the woman any longer and sighed. "I feel so bad for her, but if I'm honest, I have to admit, I'm thankful that she's not a fit parent and doesn't want Jace."

Devon held her gaze, the love he'd expressed over and over again in the helicopter burning in his eyes. "I totally understand that."

"Will you pray for her with me?"

"Of course."

Kelsey closed her eyes and let the cool ocean air brush over her for a moment while she found the right words. She took Devon's hands and offered her heartfelt prayer then looked at Devon, but didn't release his hands. "Take me back to the compound, please. I need to take Jace home so I can meet with my lawyer in the morning and call social services."

"Let me connect you with a top-notch social worker so you can be assured your investigation is handled properly and expediently."

"Thank you." She squeezed his hands and let go.

He grabbed onto hers again. "And can we continue seeing each other? Get to know each other better and see where this thing between us goes?"

"I want that, but I don't want Jace to become attached to you only to have you disappear from our lives, so—"

"I have no plans to disappear." He locked eyes with her. "I love you, and I'm not going anywhere. Ever. But if you're worried about Jace, I won't come near him until you're comfortable with that. All I want is a chance with you. To prove I'm an honest, hardworking man who would never hurt you on purpose. Never."

Her heart melted under his sincerity, and she smiled at him. "Then let's get going so we can begin our future together."

She started to leave, but he held her back.

"Just one thing before we go." He drew her into his arms and lowered his head.

He was going to kiss her again, and despite their dismal surroundings, despite the turmoil in her life, she wanted him to and lifted up on tiptoes to meet him halfway. His lips touched hers and ignited that spark in her heart that never seemed to go out.

She couldn't get enough of him and raised her arms around his neck to draw him closer. Her heart blossomed with love, and she knew deep inside that he was the man he professed to be. A man who she could make a life with.

When he lifted his head, and they started off hand in hand, she smiled up at him. "We're going to be okay. You and me. More than okay."

EPILOGUE

Three months later

The courtroom was quiet, and Kelsey was sure everyone could hear her heart hammering in her chest. She was allowed to bring eight people to court with her, and she invited her partners, Devon, and Ahn. Kelsey really wished Devon could be seated at the table with her and Jace, but he would be—someday after they got married and he adopted Jace as well. She was sure of that and him. She was so glad he'd wrapped up his current undercover assignment, and now that he'd given up undercover work, he would be around more often. But first things first—gaining legal custody of the precious boy sitting between her and her attorney, Vern Beals.

She'd imagined this day for years, but in those dreams, Todd had been at her side. Now he was gone. She was glad that the police in Tucson officially declared Kilroy guilty of killing Todd. That gave her final closure on that part of her life, and she was now free to move on. To completely devote her heart to Jace and Devon.

She looked at her soon-to-be son dressed in an adorable little suit that he wanted to wear for the occasion. She straightened his tie and kissed him on the forehead. "Remember to stand when the judge comes in."

He looked wide-eyed at her. "Are you really going to be my official mom and no one can take me away from you?"

Tears formed in his eyes, and she wished she could erase the last few months for him. She had to tell him he wasn't Todd and Margo's natural child, of course not revealing they'd bought him from a criminal. Kelsey made sure he knew that not being born to them meant they wanted him even more. She would have to tell him at some point about his birth mother's identity and how she sold him, but Kelsey hoped to hold off on that until he was old enough to handle the news.

Thankfully, the social worker Devon connected Kelsey with was wonderful. She quickly determined Kelsey was a fit mother, and Jace was better off with her than in some foster home while they investigated. Kelsey had been blessed beyond words that the proceedings went quickly and in her favor, and that she could remain this precious little boy's mother.

She scooped him close and held him tight. "This is it, bud. I will legally be your mother in a few minutes, and we will be together forever."

He looked up at her. "I love you, Mom."

"I love you too, bud." She glanced over her shoulder at Devon who was watching them and smiling. He looked so proud and so in love and so...everything. Just everything. Her heart overflowed with love for him and Jace, and she'd never been happier.

The side door opened, and Judge Sanders entered. She quickly stood and tugged down Jace's jacket then put her arm around his shoulders.

"Be seated," Judge Sanders said.

He was an older man with kind eyes behind thick

glasses, a full head of silvery hair, and was dressed in a black suit with white shirt and red tie. She expected him to be wearing a robe, but she liked that he seemed more approachable so Jace might relax.

The judge focused on Kelsey, and her heart hammered harder. "Please introduce yourself, Mrs. Moore, and give a brief statement telling me why you want this adoption to proceed."

Kelsey stated her name and occupation. "I have been Jace's mother for three years now. One of those years I raised him alone after my husband passed away. Jace is the most amazing boy. I fell in love with him the minute I met him. I have come to think of him as my own son and wanted to adopt him from that moment on. Today, if you will allow it, I want to make a legal commitment to him and take full responsibility for his welfare and upbringing for the rest of my life."

Judge Sanders nodded and turned his attention to Jace. "Hello, young man. How are you doing?"

Jace lifted his little chin and sat up straighter. "I'd be super happy if you say yes to my mom."

Judge Sanders laughed. "So I take it this means you want Mrs. Moore to adopt you."

"Yes, please!"

The judge nodded his approval. "Just a bit of formality, and I think I can make that happen for you, young man."

"Yes!" Jace punched his hand into the air.

The judge laughed and nodded at Vern.

He stood and looked at Kelsey. "You've already stated your intentions regarding Jace, but please confirm for Judge Sanders that you agree to provide Jace with a lifelong loving home."

"I agree. I do," she said fervently. "Oh, how I do."

Judge Sanders nodded, and then quickly reviewed the

facts of the adoption. "I'd like to invite you, Mrs. Moore, and Jace to join me for an official picture."

"That means you like us," Jace announced as he hopped to his feet. "And you're going to say yes. Mr. Beals told me so."

Judge Sanders laughed. "Mr. Beals is correct."

Jace grabbed Kelsey's hand. "Come on, Mom. Let's get our picture taken."

He pulled her across the room. They stepped behind Judge Sanders' desk, and the clerk snapped pictures. The judge picked up his pen and looked at Jace. "I'm now going to sign the decree of adoption, and you will officially be Mrs. Moore's son."

Jace clapped his hands, and the judge signed the form. "Congratulations to both of you."

Jace launched himself at Kelsey's waist, holding on for dear life.

"I'm so happy, bud." She kissed his head again. "What say we go home and celebrate?"

He smiled up at her, and Kelsey knew in a heartbeat that her life was complete. Well, nearly anyway. Just one more lifetime commitment to make.

Devon couldn't quit smiling or looking at Kelsey in her condo. She wore a pale pink dress with a wispy skirt and a very fitted sleeveless top revealing toned arms. Her heels were even higher than he'd seen on her before. She'd put her hair up and little strands caressed her face. She glowed with beauty and happiness.

He'd had the hardest time not sweeping her into his arms and kissing her until they both couldn't breathe, then declaring his love again and asking her to marry him. The ring was burning a hole in his pocket, but this was all about Jace right now, and Devon had to wait until tonight to pop the question after Jace had gone to bed and Devon was alone with Kelsey.

He looked around the packed room. Her partners were smiling much like Devon. Nearly all the members of Blackwell Tactical who'd come to support Kelsey and Jace had similar smiles.

Kelsey was talking to Jackson who was holding his son, Noah. The boy was now about six weeks old, and he was kicking up a fuss. Jackson was trying everything to comfort the baby, while Maggie looked on as if she wanted to take the child, but was letting Jackson figure it out. Devon could only imagine how hard it would be to learn to care for a baby, but he could also imagine the joy of having a child of his own.

Eryn joined them and looked back at Trey where their son Lucas was asleep on his shoulder. Despite the many children running around—Devon lost count at seven—Trey was the picture of contentment as he talked with Sam and her firefighter fiancé, Griff. Once they walked down the aisle, their whole team would be married, and Devon suspected it wouldn't be long before they all had children.

After all, he'd seen it happen with enough of his friends, and he enjoyed seeing this side of the tough Blackwell warriors. They were a family. A warm and caring family, just like the Veritas partners, and Kelsey was lucky to be part of it all.

She suddenly turned and caught him watching her. He didn't look away but gave her a smile just for her—one that promised so much more in the future.

She started toward him, and he watched her skirt swish with each step. He shoved his hand into his pocket to touch the ring and remember that after tonight she would be his.

If she said yes. With their time together the last few months, he had every reason to believe she would, unless she wanted more time alone with Jace.

"You look like you have something on your mind," she said.

He didn't want to spoil Jace's day. "We can talk about it tonight."

She linked her arm in his and gazed up at him, a hint of worry in her eyes. "Is this a good thing?"

"A very good thing." He returned her smile, and the urge to kiss her had him stepping closer, but he restrained himself from actually kissing her.

Jace bolted from where he was playing with Hannah's son David. Once Jace heard that Gage had adopted David, they'd formed an instant friendship.

Jace looked up at Devon. "Are you ever going to ask Mom to marry you?"

Devon's mouth fell open, and he didn't know what to say.

"Why would you think that?" Kelsey asked, sounding completely in control of her emotions.

"'Cause you've been like staring at each other all the time, and Ahn says that means you're in love."

Kelsey bent down to Jace. "Ahn is right. Devon and I love each other very much."

Devon's heart soared to hear her admit such a thing not only in front of Jace but in front of her friends and partners.

Conversations stilled and people stared at the three of them.

"So are you going to get married?" Jace demanded.

Kelsey glanced up at Devon, her gaze begging him to help her out.

"Would you like that, Jace?" Devon asked.

"Totally." Jace grinned. "Then you can adopt me like Mr.

Blackwell adopted David. And we'll be a family." He suddenly frowned and glanced at Gage who was holding Evie. "But don't go getting a baby like they did. She cries a lot. I want a brother."

Devon couldn't stop his laughter and joined in with the others who were laughing along with them.

Jace looked confused. "Did I say something wrong?"

"Not at all," Devon assured him.

"So are you going to marry Mom?"

Kelsey's forehead furrowed. "Son, I think—"

"Well, I was going to wait until tonight so I didn't take away from your day, but..." Devon retrieved the box from his pocket and got down on his knee.

Kelsey gasped and others in the room joined in.

He gazed up at her and took her hand. "I love you, Kelsey. More than I ever thought was possible. Will you marry me and spend the rest of our lives together?"

She opened her mouth to answer but Jace stepped closer. "If she says yes, does that mean you'll be my dad?"

"If you'll let me."

Jace changed his focus to Kelsey, his gaze serious. "Then say yes, please. 'Cause I want him to be my dad. He likes robots, too."

Devon had a hard time not laughing but responded to the boy's serious statement with a nod.

Jace changed his focus to Kelsey. "Well, Mom? Will you marry him?"

This was not at all how Devon had planned the proposal, but if Jace's encouragement helped her say yes, Devon didn't care if the boy hijacked the moment.

Kelsey met his gaze and smiled at him. "Yes, I'll marry you."

"Yay!" Jace rushed Devon as he often did with Kelsey as applause broke out in the room.

Devon swept the little boy into his arms and hugged him tightly. Devon wished he was holding Kelsey at this big moment in their life, but Jace needed this reassurance, and Devon was more than happy to provide it. Kelsey would more than understand.

Jace wiggled free. "The judge is really nice so don't be afraid to get started on my adoption." And just like that he ran back to David.

Devon opened the ring box and held it out to Kelsey.

"It's beautiful," she said and offered her hand.

He slipped the ring on her finger, pocketed the box, and got up to take her hands. "I didn't want to horn in on this day and really *did* plan to wait until tonight."

"This was so much better. Now we know how Jace feels about it."

Devon nodded and drew her closer, a blip of worry in his brain. "And how do you feel about it? You didn't say yes just because Jace was pressuring you, did you?"

"No, of course not. Don't ever doubt my love for you." She cupped the side of his face, her touch as light as a feather. "I love you more than I can say, and I'm over-the-moon happy to become your wife."

His heart soared. "In that case, might I recommend a very short engagement period?"

"Absolutely," she said. "God brought us together, and I know He's going to bless this marriage."

"Hopefully not too much too soon as Jace would be very mad at us if we got a baby," he said, using Jace's words and then smiled.

Kelsey chuckled. "I'm pretty sure he'll change his mind once he realizes this is the only way to get that brother he wants."

"Do you think he'd mind if I kissed you right here in front of everyone?"

"Probably, but I'm willing to risk it if you are."

"Are you kidding?" He pulled her to him and didn't let a second pass before locking his lips on hers. She returned his kiss with a passion beyond anything she'd shown him, and he wanted to drag her out the door and marry her right now.

"Eww," he heard Jace say. "Gross, Mom."

Devon expected her to pull away, but she didn't move. When she finally did, she met Devon's gaze. "Despite grossing out my son, this is happiest day of my life. A son and soon-to-be husband in one day. What more could a woman ask for?"

"Not being a woman, I can't answer that," he said and grinned. "But from a guy's perspective, a son and the most beautiful woman in the world all mine? That's a very good day. A very good day indeed."

Dear Reader,

Thank you so much for reading DEAD SILENCE, Book Two in my Truth Seekers series. You'll be happy to hear that there will be more books in this series!

Book 1 - DEAD RINGER
Book 2 - DEAD SILENCE
Book 3 - DEAD END - September/2019
Book 4 - DEAD HEAT - March/2020
Book 5 - DEAD CENTER - April/2020
Book 6 - DEAD EVEN - May/2020

I'd like to invite you to learn more about the books in the series as they release and about my other books by signing up for my newsletter and connecting with me on social media or even sending me a message.

I hold monthly giveaways that I'd like to share with you, and I'd love to hear from you. So stop by this page and join in.

www.susansleeman.com/sign-up/

Susan Sleeman

ENJOY THIS BOOK

Reviews are the most powerful tool to draw attention to my books for new readers. I wish I had the budget of a New York publisher to take out ads and commercials but that's not a reality. I do have something much more powerful and effective than that.

A committed and loyal bunch of readers like you.

If you've enjoyed *Dead Silence*, I would be very grateful if you could leave an honest review on the bookseller's site. It can be as short as you like. Just a few words is all it takes. Thank you very much.

THE TRUTH SEEKERS
People are rarely who they seem

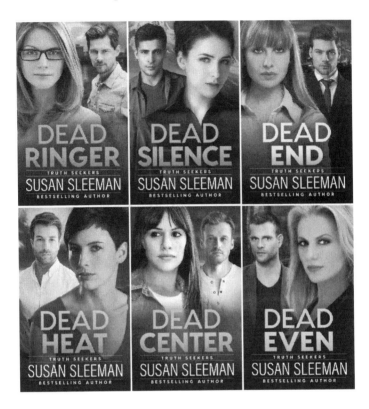

A twin who never knew her sister existed, a mother whose child is not her own, a woman whose father is anything but her father. All searching. All seeking. All needing help and hope.

Meet the unsung heroes of the Veritas Center. The Truth Seekers – a team, that includes experts in forensic anthropology, DNA, trace evidence, ballistics, cybercrimes, and toxicology. Committed to restoring hope and families by solving one mystery at a time, none of them are prepared for when the mystery comes calling close to home and threatens to destroy the only life they've known.

For More Details Visit -
www.susansleeman.com/books/truth-seekers/

BOOKS IN THE COLD HARBOR SERIES

   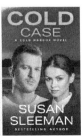

Blackwell Tactical – this law enforcement training facility and protection services agency is made up of former military and law enforcement heroes whose injuries keep them from the line of duty. When trouble strikes, there's no better team to have on your side, and they would give everything, even their lives, to protect innocents.

For More Details Visit -
www.susansleeman.com/books/cold-harbor/

ABOUT SUSAN

SUSAN SLEEMAN is a bestselling and award-winning author of more than 35 inspirational/Christian and clean read romantic suspense books. In addition to writing, Susan also hosts the website, TheSuspenseZone.com.

Susan currently lives in Oregon, but has had the pleasure of living in nine states. Her husband is a retired church music director and they have two beautiful daughters, a very special son-in-law, and an adorable grandson.

For more information visit:
www.susansleeman.com

69692910R00193

Made in the USA
Columbia, SC
16 August 2019